Books by...

Perfect Love

The Perfect Union
His Perfect Partner
Capturing Perfection
Simply Perfection
The Perfect Balance

Phantom River

The Scent of Seduction
Only a Mate's Touch
The Taste of Devotion
The Sound of Salvation

Sexy Snax

Love's Return

Totally Five Star

Turkish Delights

Anthologies

Master Me

SEALing Fate

ISBN # 978-1-78651-921-4

©Copyright Trina Lane 2016

Cover Art by Posh Gosh ©Copyright 2016

Interior text design by Claire Siemaszkiewicz

Totally Bound Publishing

This is a work of fiction. All characters, places and events are from the author's imagination and should not be confused with fact. Any resemblance to persons, living or dead, events or places is purely coincidental.

All rights reserved. No part of this publication may be reproduced in any material form, whether by printing, photocopying, scanning or otherwise without the written permission of the publisher, Totally Bound Publishing.

Applications should be addressed in the first instance, in writing, to Totally Bound Publishing. Unauthorised or restricted acts in relation to this publication may result in civil proceedings and/or criminal prosecution.

The author and illustrator have asserted their respective rights under the Copyright Designs and Patents Acts 1988 (as amended) to be identified as the author of this book and illustrator of the artwork.

Published in 2016 by Totally Bound Publishing, Newland House, The Point, Weaver Road, Lincoln, LN6 3QN, United Kingdom.

No part of this book may be reproduced, scanned, or distributed in any printed or electronic form without permission. Please do not participate in or encourage piracy of copyrighted materials in violation of the authors' rights. Purchase only authorised copies.

Totally Bound Publishing is a subsidiary of Totally Entwined Group Limited.

If you purchased this book without a cover you should be aware that this book is stolen property. It was reported as "unsold and destroyed" to the publisher and neither the author nor the publisher has received any payment for this "stripped book".

Printed and bound in Great Britain by Clays Ltd, St Ives plc

SEALING FATE

TRINA LANE

Dedication

I would like to take this opportunity to thank the men and women who serve in all branches of the armed services, as well as their families. I have the utmost respect for your dedication and sacrifice to protect our country and allies. I've made every attempt to make the military aspects of this book as accurate as possible, but take full responsibility for any misinformation regarding procedures and/or protocols.

Chapter One

The scent of the flowers climbing the trellis behind her back wafted in the warm air, and occasionally a light breeze cooled and caressed Kat's hot skin. There was nothing like a summer night in St. Louis. Oh sure, there were times when the humidity could make her feel like she was breathing soup, but tonight was actually quite pleasant. It was mid-September and an oppressive heat wave had sent temperatures skyrocketing above one hundred degrees for the last two weeks. When she woke up this morning, the air coming through her open bedroom window felt clean and fresh, not stale and stagnant as it had been. The change was being celebrated all over the city.

She listened to the music blaring from the speakers on the dance floor, a slow hypnotic rhythm calling to the soul. Her eyes were having trouble tracking people in the colored and strobe lights winking on and off, the effect causing people to catch only glimpses of their dance partners and making the atmosphere seductive and anonymous. The dancers tangling on the patio made Kat wonder how it would feel to move so freely, so seductively. Fantasies of a man holding her close and moving to the hypnotic music flitted through her mind. Too bad said man did not exist.

Looking up, she spied her best friend Amy with her fiancé and smiled. Seeing their happiness warmed a place in her heart, but it could not fulfill the longing to feel that closeness with another person. Kat didn't see that happening for her very soon, if at all. Allowing someone that close left a person defenseless. Kat had known vulnerability and complacency from a very young age and refused to allow those weaknesses to control her again. She deemed the occasional twinge of loneliness an acceptable after effect for securing herself from susceptibility.

Kat saw a couple on the dance floor so wrapped up in each other that it looked as if they had created their own little world. They were an attractive couple. The solid-built man stood tall behind his dance partner, whose height complemented his. She leaned into the man's chest with her head resting on his shoulder as he circled her stomach with his arms and leaned down to kiss her nape and shoulder where perspiration glistened. Although they were barely moving, the dance—a gentle sway back and forth and a grind of the hips—made it easy to envision them standing just like that and slowly making love.

Kat became lost in the fantasy for several minutes until a man's deep, husky voice whispered into her ear, "Enjoying the show?"

She turned to examine the owner of the sexy voice. In the darkness all that was visible were a strong face and sensual lips. She coyly smiled at him. "I always enjoy a good performance."

A playful smile shaped his lips. Kat couldn't help but stare.

I wonder what they feel like? Are they soft, and does the touch linger or do they command surrender? Do they bring pleasure or spew venomous pain?

Returning her attention to the conversation, she heard him say, "Ahh, so you're a voyeur?"

Kat considered her response before answering. She didn't want to encourage some deranged stalker by answering with a suggestive remark.

"Isn't everyone to a certain extent? How else do you explain the obsession with physical appearance or rubbernecking motorists trying to catch a glimpse of fatalities on the freeway?"

"I never thought about voyeurism in those contexts, but it certainly makes sense. It is the human response to innate curiosity. I'm Jace Hudson." He offered his hand to shake, and when she hesitantly answered, his hand enclosed hers in a warm, strong grip.

"Kat Martin." She felt rough calluses as their hands separated, giving a clue to his rugged nature. Whatever this man did, it was not behind a pampered desk. That realization only enhanced Kat's interest.

Jace looked at the woman sitting in front of him. In the darkness, he could barely identify any distinguishing features but he felt drawn to her in a way he could not explain. Jace watched as the lights from the dance floor flashed across her face and caught the aloofness in her eyes. The detached demeanor was one he knew well, one he often saw in himself.

The nature of his work required a degree of separation from others. One could not serve in his capacity and maintain close relationships. He wondered what had caused the isolation in this beautiful woman's eyes as she sat watching the exhibitionist couple. She managed to portray a heady combination of both loneliness and arousal.

The dim lighting made it difficult to tell the exact shade of her long, dark hair, which could have been anywhere from rich sable brown to inky black silk. Soft curves on her petite frame made him want to cup his hands around them. Jace had caught her scent as he walked up behind her—an enticing blend of vanilla and peaches, with a darker hint of womanly musk that instantly made his blood heat. Her voice hit him like warm Kentucky bourbon, soft and seductive.

Her face wasn't what would be called classically beautiful, but very intriguing with deep-set eyes, a small nose with a little turn at the tip, and full lips designed to be kissed. When she'd turned around to look at him, a flash of the lights left him momentarily stunned by a glimpse of the most incredible green eyes he'd ever seen. They were somewhere between emerald and sea green, with brown flecks at the center, just like a cat's.

That thought presented out loud. "Is your name because of your green eyes?"

Kat chuckled. "No, actually my name is Kathleen, but nobody except my mother called me that."

Noticing that her reference to her mother was past tense, he wondered if that had something to do with the look in her eyes earlier. He watched as she closed her eyes and began to sway to the music thumping through the speakers surrounding the dance floor. Jace felt an overwhelming desire to see how she would feel moving in his arms.

"Kat, would you like to dance?"

Gasping, she responded with, "Oh, gosh, no... I...don't dance."

Jace gave a puzzled look, considering their location and her apparently unconscious movements just moments ago. "You don't like to dance?"

"Oh, I love to dance, but only in my socks, in the kitchen late at night."

He smiled. "Why is that?"

Kat looked straight into his smoky-gray eyes. "Let's just say I don't like being judged based upon my lack of dancing skills."

"And who do you think would be judging you?"

Kat looked at him like he was a simpleton. "Everyone."

"So, why come to a dance club?"

"Well, I let my friends think they were dragging me out, but actually I love to come and listen to the music. I love letting the beat move through my body. There's something about feeling the rhythms as they blast through the air that can never be matched with any personal listening device. It's very stimulating."

Jace wasn't sure if she had meant that to sound seductive, but it definitely gave him stimulating images. "Okay, I have a solution for you. Come dance with me in the corner over there. We can feel the music together, but nobody will be able to see you."

Kat nibbled on her lower lip and glanced around the crowded club for several seconds. She wrong her hands and shifted on her heels. Jace watched as resolve filled her eyes and she squared her shoulders.

"Okay."

Jace took Kat's hand and led her to the dark corner of the tented patio. Out of the corner of his eye, he saw her give a little wave to some girl with a huge smile on her face and two thumbs sticking up as a sign of approval. *Probably the friend who dragged Kat to the club.*

Kat moved into his arms as a deeply rhythmic song began to make the air pulse. Heat radiated from her, and he didn't think it was all owing to the warm summer temperatures trapped under the tent. Her soft chest pressed against his hard one. Jace instantly recognized the potency of her body.

She wore a short leather skirt, silk V neck sleeveless top, and the kind of heels that make a man think about a woman wearing nothing but the shoes. Her head came just above his shoulders. Putting his arms around her waist, he pulled her close. Kat's hands held onto his hips, and he felt her grip tighten when he pressed one of his legs between hers.

The slow heavy beat, hypnotic melodies, and trancelike vocals worked perfectly for keeping her close to his body — his primary objective.

"Okay, Kat, close your eyes, feel the music, and just dance like you would at home in the dark."

Kat began to move to the music and Jace had to stifle a groan.

Oh, man, the way she's moving her body should be illegal.

Her movement was sensual, rather than blatantly sexual like the couple Kat had been watching before, but Jace's blood grew hotter by the second. He turned her around so her back was to him. Unable to resist touching her just a little, he slowly slid his hand just under the hem of her top to feel her warm, soft skin. Not wanting her to get anxious, he turned her around again and rotated their bodies so his back was to the room.

Jace turned out to be a perfect dance partner. For some reason, he didn't make Kat feel pressured to perform at all. Able to close her eyes and just let the music guide her body, she slipped into that elusive fantasy she'd dreamed of earlier. His hand on her stomach burned and instantly stoked the fire in her blood from warm to a raging inferno she knew wasn't owing solely to the summer night.

When he rotated their bodies again, she looked over his shoulder and could not believe her eyes.

He must have felt her tense because when Kat looked back at him, he asked, "What's wrong?"

"Nothing. I just saw some people I know."

Jace pulled her even closer. "Do you want to stop dancing?"

Kat thought about it for a brief moment and realized that was the last thing she wanted at the moment. The feel of his arms surrounding her brought all kinds of fantasies to mind. His touch was strong, not forceful. Kat could sense a latent dominancy in him, but he let her control the situation.

Not wanting him to get the wrong idea about her silence, Kat said, "No, I'll just ignore them."

"Are they friends?"

"Hardly. In fact, for many years, they were my staunchest adversaries."

He looked down at her, frowning. "Why were they your enemies?"

Kat saw what she thought might be concern and a hint of protectiveness in his expression. She considered blowing off the sticky emotions and downplaying the situation, but felt that would be dishonest and cowardly. She took a deep breath. "I wasn't exactly popular in school, and to put it bluntly, they made my life a living hell for twelve years." Figuring this comment was going to call a halt to their time together, Kat expected him to look at her like she was crazy and find some lame excuse to take her back to the table.

Instead, Jace turned them in a circle and looked over her shoulder. When his body tensed, she peeked over his shoulder again to see the two men standing behind them with shocked expressions.

They mouthed what looked like, "What are you doing?"

Before she could figure out what was going on, Jace turned back to her.

"Want to have a little fun with them?" he whispered to her.

She thought about asking him to take her back to the table, not wanting to disturb waters better left still. Instead she heard herself answer softly, "Sure, a little revenge might be fun."

What little demon inside her came up with that response? She wasn't a vengeful type of person. She avoided confrontation when at all possible. Another song came over the speakers, this one faster, edgier, and definitely sexual. Jace started to caress her body, pulling her tight into him.

Her neurons skipped a couple of pulses before she caught on to his intent and started rotating her hips. Making her movements much more overt, she moved her arms up his hard chest to circle his neck. His dark hair, crisply trimmed, gave the impression of discipline. However, the look in his eyes at the moment gave the impression of the exact opposite. In the chaos of the thumping music, writhing bodies, and pure vitality being in Jace's arms caused, she tilted her head back and molded herself as close as possible to his body, giving herself over to the night and the music.

Jace took her hand and whipped her into a spin, turning their bodies so she was facing the crowd again. Kat wasn't quite ready to face the audience yet, so she closed her eyes.

I wonder what they are thinking now.

She hoped it was sheer jealously that they couldn't touch her the way Jace was—so tenderly and seductively. His touch made her feel desirable for the first time in her life. Ever so slightly, she raised her eyelids to see if they were still standing there.

Jace's hands moved up and down her torso, then he grabbed her hips in the erotic dance. The feel of his soft lips and hot breath on her sensitive skin nearly made her legs collapse. In fact, she probably would have ended up at his feet if Jace wasn't holding her so tightly.

As the song came to a grinding end, he turned them back around and dipped Kat in a slow arc. He reached a hand under her hair and caressed a trail leading from her neck to between her breasts. Kat opened her eyes, and, looking right in the eyes of the men standing across from them, gave a slow wink.

Their eyes widened when they caught that.

Mmm, revenge is sweet!

Chapter Two

The woman was a closet vixen. After their little show for the boys, she excused herself to use the restroom. As she walked away, Jace couldn't help watching her movements. They were natural, not overtly sexual or hurried. He turned to search out his teammates. He couldn't believe his eyes when he'd turned to see who Kat was talking about earlier. The squad had come to the club to celebrate the bachelor party of one of their members.

He guessed he had been gone a while because he heard the raspy quality of his language guru Collin's voice behind him. "We were wondering where the hell you went. Apparently, you found better things to do than hang out with your buddies. Do you know who she is?"

"I know her name is Kat... And she does *not* like the two of you," he said.

With a pinched look on his face, Peter, his demo expert, asked, "She told you that?"

"In a few more multi-syllable words."

Collin actually looked slightly chagrined, but Peter just laughed. "So why the show? I mean, you saw us and she saw us. What was the point?"

"I just thought it'd be gentlemanly of me to assist the lady in extracting a little revenge. Plus, I couldn't resist the astounded looks on your faces." Being senior man of the team, Jace looked upon it as part of his sworn duty to rib the two subordinates on a regular basis. All in good fun, of course.

Looking at Collin, he asked, "What's with the bad blood?"

Collin answered, "You know all those cliché stories about

popular kids who loved to torment unpopular kids for reasons that only make sense when you're young idiots? That was us. I actually haven't seen Kat in twelve years."

Peter took the opportunity to chime in. "Her looks were always frazzled. She had frizzy hair, big glasses, and was never into sports or fashion like the other girls. We just teased her a little bit. But it is quite apparent that the years have been good to her. That is a smokin' little package she has now."

Hearing Peter say that about Kat rankled Jace's nerves a little bit.

What is it about this woman?

* * * *

While she left Jace to get them some drinks, Kat went to the bathroom to cool her blood and quiet her nerves for a second. She caught a glimpse of Amy running to catch up out of the corner of her eye.

The bathroom was nothing special and offered little in the way of privacy, but Kat had a hunch that Amy was going to demand the scoop.

"Who is that gorgeous man you just snagged?" Amy asked, wide-eyed.

"His name is Jace. And I didn't snag him. We were just talking and he asked me to dance."

"Girl, that was not just a dance. You two could have melted the floor. I have never seen you act like that before."

Kat wanted to make sure that Amy didn't have the wrong idea about her dance with Jace. "Well, the second dance was sort of a ploy to extract some revenge on two guys I recognized from school."

"Ahh. Well, that makes a little bit more sense, but I still say the two of you have incredible chemistry."

Chemistry was putting it mildly, in Kat's opinion. In fact, chemistry just made her think about periodic tables and organic compounds. The second Jace's arms had enclosed her she had felt a fire race through her. A burning hunger that made her want to just absorb all the heat she had felt emanating from his body. But it couldn't last.

"I barely know him, and I'm sure I won't see him again after tonight. Guys like him do not stick around girls like me."

"Oh, shut up! You're intelligent, beautiful, and you have a quick sense of humor. What isn't to like?"

Kat was surprised when Amy flipped from gossipy to complimentary. Although given the fact that this was Amy, Kat really shouldn't have been surprised. It was impossible to keep up with the woman's pinball thought processes on a normal day, let alone after she'd had more than a few drinks.

"Amy, I may have lost the extra weight I've carried around in my life up to this point, but I am *not* beautiful. I have a few fancy degrees but I'm not very street-smart, and my sense of humor is basically sarcasm."

Exasperation crossed Amy's face as she rolled her eyes. "Whatever. You need to get his number. Eric and I are going to head out. You cool by yourself?"

Since she didn't plan on staying too much longer and they had driven separately, Kat indicated that was fine. "I'll see you later this week, okay?"

"Sure, have a good night and tell me everything."

Kat just smiled.

Coming out of the restroom, Kat heard her name being called and turned to see Jace standing next to the two people she had really hoped to never see again.

Oh, well. Might as well get this over with.

Just then four other rather large men joined their group. Jace smiled. "Kat, I'd like to introduce you to my teammates. This is Kurt, Eric, Justin and Cory, and I think you already know Collin and Peter."

Looking at the first four, Kat responded, "Nice to meet you." Then she glanced over at Collin and Peter. "Hi, it's been a while... How are you?"

She was a little surprised that Collin's and Peter's expressions looked more like avid curiosity than disdain.

"We're good," they said in unison.

Kat looked at Jace and asked, "So... Do I have to guess or are you going to tell me why you cart around teammates?"

Jace threaded his hand into her hair, leaned down, and whispered in her ear, "I'm a Navy SEAL." Then he straightened and gave a little gentlemanly bow. "Lieutenant Commander Hudson, at your service." He stepped over to drape his elbow over the shoulder of one of the other men. "We are here tonight to celebrate Cory's bachelor party."

Jace's fingers running through her hair sent a shiver of arousal skimming down her spine. The touch had seemed instinctual. Almost as if he were unable to resist touching her again. She snorted internally at the fanciful notion. She'd been spending too much time reading romance novels.

An officer of a naval special ops team certainly explained the physique and mental strength Kat had noticed earlier. Although she expected a negative answer, she was still compelled to ask, "So do you live in St. Louis?"

"No, we're all stationed out of Virginia Beach, Virginia. Cory's soon-to-be wife is from here, so that's why we came to St. Louis."

That was the cue she needed. As much fun as she'd had, she definitely did not want to get attached to this guy. It was time to make her excuses and leave. It was late anyway, closing in on one in the morning.

Taking what she intended to be one last look at Jace, she said, "I really enjoyed our dance. Thank you for making tonight fun, but I need to leave."

"Let me walk you to your car. It's late, and I want to make sure you're safe."

"That's very nice, but not necessary." She took a few steps before he caught up to her.

"Hey, I am trained to protect and serve."

Kat glanced back over her shoulder. "I thought that was the police motto."

"Well, the SEAL motto didn't seem to fit here, so I borrowed theirs. Seriously, I would feel better if you let me walk you out."

What harm could a little walk do? It's not like I'm going to declare my undying love and offer to bear his children.

"Okay. Thank you."

Jace and Kat walked toward the entrance of the patio, his hand casually resting on her back. Jace took her hand and gently pulled her to a stop. "Can I see you again?"

Kat looked down at their hands. Despite how his engulfed hers, she felt their strengths combine. "You're leaving soon. Doesn't that seem counterproductive?"

"I'll be in town for the next two weeks. We catch a flight back after Cory returns from his honeymoon. Our team has been placed on standby, so the other guys and I are sort of on leave till then. I've never been to St. Louis and I wanted to see some of the sights."

He seemed genuinely interested in spending more time with her, but Kat wasn't ready to trust this complete stranger. "I really had fun tonight, Jace, but I'm a simple girl, and frankly, you would probably be bored spending your vacation with me."

Jace knew deep in his gut that was impossible. Everything about this girl was turning him on, from the way her eyes lit up when she smiled to the way she felt in his arms. She had an unassuming quality about her that he sensed was a covering for a core of determination and strength.

"Well, if I'm to never see you again"—*I am going to do everything in my power to track her down*—"can I have a kiss to remember you by?"

Kat didn't respond at first, and he waited as she searched his eyes for whatever answers she sought.

"I guess a simple kiss is harmless enough."

Jace leaned them back into a dark corner of the building they were walking by to escape the late-night crowd that filled the streets of this recently rehabbed section of downtown. Partiers were walking past, and he could still hear the music in the background.

When Jace started to lower his head, he heard Kat's breath stutter for a second. Her hands slid up his chest as his lips met hers, barely a whisper against his own. With a little more pressure, he molded himself to her. Kat opened her mouth just a little, and his tongue slipped inside, slowly stroking the roof of her mouth, rubbing against her tongue. Her taste was intoxicating — a blend of warmth, spearmint and rum.

Jace had intended to keep the kiss light and teasing, but quickly lost the battle against the deeper imperative to devour her, to melt into her as much as humanly possible. With a groan, he cupped either side of her face as he drove the kiss harder. Angling his head, he slanted his mouth against hers. He knew he should attempt to restrain his response, but the control seemed to elude him.

At first, Jace thought Kat would resist when he turned the kiss aggressive, but she just held on and kissed him right back with all the passion he'd sensed in her earlier.

It seemed as if they stood there for hours, completely oblivious to anyone around, lips caressing, tongues mating, teeth gently nipping. Kat burrowed against him, almost as if she sought to wear his strength and heat like a cloak. The kiss turned gentle again. He backed away with just the slightest touch.

Eventually, they had to break apart or be arrested for public lewdness, but he did not want to stop. Even so, with reluctance, Jace nibbled on her lower lip one last time. He knew she had to feel his erection against her stomach, but did nothing to hide it. *I want her to know exactly what she does to me.*

Her eyes were cloudy with desire as she murmured, "That hardly seemed like a simple kiss."

"I know... Are you sorry?"

"Not at all. In fact, if I didn't know you were leaving in two weeks, I'd want to try that again. But I think for my sanity, I'd better get to my car now."

As they walked down the street, she stopped at a silver sporty-looking car. Jace raised his eyebrow a little and smiled. Not in a million years would he have imagined she would drive a car that had the power he knew this had. "You drive an SRT-4?"

Kat looked up at him slightly surprised. "You know it? What can I say? I like the adrenaline rush of high speeds and feeling the power of the road. There's nothing like driving on a summer night with the windows down, music pumping its way through the sound system, and the wind whipping through my hair. It's my favorite time to think."

He smiled. *It's always the quiet ones you have to look out for.*

Kat chuckled. "You're in shock, aren't you? I usually find myself faced with two types of men. Ones who are either really intrigued and engage in intelligent discussions, or ones who sarcastically ask if my boyfriend knows I have his car out."

Jace crossed his arms. "And you assume I fall into the latter category? Shame on you, Kat. But I'll let you get away with your misconception because we really don't know each other very well... yet."

She frowned then turned around, reaching for the handle.

He leaned into her body, caging her in the circle of his arms. "Sorry. Please let me see you again. I know I'm here only for a short while, but I *really* would like to get to know you. I need a good tour guide, and who better than a native?"

Kat paused. "I have a feeling this decision is going to come back and bite me in the ass, but I'll make you a deal. If you can find me, I'll go out with you."

Triumphed soared through him, but was replaced with confusion. "And just how do I find you?"

Kat gave an enigmatic smile that made Jace think of the Mona Lisa. "You're a SEAL. I'm sure you have ways of tracking people down. Besides, if you look in the right

19

spots, I'm right in front of your eyes."

With that cryptic remark, she got in the car and started the engine. Jace watched her tail lights recede. *That is a seriously sexy machine.*

Whether he meant the car, or the woman driving it, he wasn't certain.

Jace walked back toward the club, his mind still on his explosive reaction to Kat's kiss. He had not exactly been a recluse when it came to women, but he couldn't recall a time when he ever felt that kind of searing heat from just a 'simple kiss'.

He had to figure out how to find her. Well, he didn't mind pulling a few strings with his contacts to get that information. After all, he had her name and the city where she lived. That should give him a place to start. Confident that he would have the mystery solved by Tuesday at the latest, he joined his buddies at the bar.

Sitting down next to Collin, Jace ordered a Bushmills single malt Irish whiskey, neat.

"Hey. Did you see Kat to her car?"

"Yeah."

"So... Did you get her number?"

"No, she wouldn't give it to me. Some BS about how bored I would be hanging around her on my vacation. She didn't want to give me her number then have me call only because I feel obligated to."

"Man, that sucks. Oh, well. You gave it your best shot. So what do you want to do tomorrow?"

"She gave me a challenge. If I could find her, she would agree to see me again. So tomorrow I'm going to find her."

"You really like her, don't you? I don't think I've ever seen you this twisted over a woman you just met before. Did you try to kiss her? I mean just to see if there is really chemistry there?"

"Yeah, I kissed her..."

"Oh, come on! You're making me feel like a goddamn teenybopper at a fucking slumber party. Don't make me beat it out of you... How was it?"

Looking directly at him, probably slightly scary with the intensity he suspected shined in his eyes, Jace said, "Incendiary."

He knew Collin had never seen that particular look in the eyes of his commanding officer in the most volatile of situations, let alone in response to a woman.

"Damn... Okay, then... Well... I know where she grew up. I guess we could start there."

Jace looked over at him, surprised he was willing to help him find this woman, especially considering their apparent past.

Collin looked back with a negligent shrug. "What? I can't turn you loose in a foreign city all by yourself."

Thinking about all the missions they had been on in foreign cities where they'd had to watch every corner for assassins, the thought of getting lost in the streets of suburban Midwest America was comical. Rolling his eyes, Jace let Collin know exactly that.

As he reached into his back pocket to grab his wallet to pay for the drink, he felt something that had not been there before. Taking it out, he looked down at a little white card with a number scribbled on the back. Turning it over, he laughed out loud — loud enough to startle Collin.

"What's wrong with you?"

Jace showed him the card. "I have no idea how she did it, but this was in my back pocket. I guess she must have slipped it in while I was... Never mind." How she did so without him even noticing attested to how utterly focused he had been on her and not the surroundings. That could be very dangerous in his profession, and something he would definitely have to watch out for.

Collin was looking at the card. "I'll be damned. She's a doctor. It says here 'Kathleen Martin, Doctor of Anthropology'. She works out of Washington University. You know, for some reason it does not surprise me that she made something of herself."

Jace sat looking at the card with a smile on his face.

If you look in the right spots, I'm right in front of your eyes.

The sneaky little minx. Jace started to ponder. *Should I call her tonight, or wait a couple days? Oh, to hell with it! I want whatever time I can have with her.*

Having decided that, he looked around. The boys seemed to be growing a little annoyed that he wasn't all there, so he slugged back a few more drinks and joined in the frivolities.

Chapter Three

It was Sunday afternoon, and the most thrilling thing in Kat's life was folding laundry. The ring of the phone almost didn't penetrate the blare of the stereo. Anticipating the sound of Amy's voice she answered with a breezy, "Hellooo?"

Instead, she heard a deep voice reverberate through the handset. "I guess I found you."

Oh, my God!

That voice was most definitely not Amy's. Kat closed her eyes to savor the feel of the rich sound that would never be erased from her memory. "How did you get my home number? I gave you my cell, and I'm not listed."

"Remember what you said about tracking people down? I pulled a few favors."

Kat couldn't help but smile that he'd gone to such measures to reach her again. "Well, aren't you resourceful."

"I have my moments. So... Since I tracked you down, does this mean you'll hold up your end of the bargain?"

Kat let out a soft laugh. "I guess I have to. If not, that would be very unsportsmanlike. What did you have in mind?"

"How does a quiet, casual dinner tonight sound? You pick the place."

Contemplating the excitement of seeing him again, Kat quickly agreed. "Okay. Where are you staying so I can pick you up?"

"I picked up a rental, so if you give me directions to your house, I'll meet you there. How does dinner at 2000 hours sound?"

"What time is that for normal people?"

Jace chuckled. "Sorry. Habit. That's eight o'clock."

She knew that, but it was fun to tease Jace. After giving him directions and ending the call, Kat had to sit on the edge of the bed and take a few deep breaths.

He found my number and he called! Oh, boy. Now how do I handle this? First things first—I need a plan. Keep this casual, light. He's leaving in two weeks and just wants a tour guide, not a hot affair.

Trying to think of a good place for dinner, Kat remembered a quiet little restaurant in the heart of downtown Webster only minutes from her place. Calling ahead, she made reservations for eight o'clock. After hanging up the phone, she looked at the clock.

Oh, crap! It's four o'clock now. I only have three and a half hours till he arrives.

Trying to find something in her closet that said casual but attractive was more difficult than she'd thought. She definitely had casual, but attractive was a whole other ball game. Most of her attire leaned toward business dress or super comfy. Very little fit into the categories of formal, dressy, or chic. Finally finding a pair of silk capri pants and a strapless top with matching jacket she'd purchased but never worn, she was set.

Kat's mind buzzed with questions—two in particular.

Will he kiss me again tonight? And do I want him to?

Hell, yes! God, can he kiss.

She wouldn't volunteer this information to anyone, but she hadn't racked up any impressive statistics in the sexual partner game. Still, she knew enough to know that their kiss last night had been cataclysmic.

I wonder if he felt anything.

Now, whether kissing again was a smart idea was another matter entirely.

* * * *

His watch read exactly seven thirty as he pressed the doorbell to Kat's house. When he'd driven up, he immediately saw the charm and appeal of the home. It was even something he might like to own one day. He really liked the wide, deep porch with square wood-and-stone columns and wooden railings of the Craftsman-style. The door opened, and Jace was momentarily stunned by the sight in front of him. Kat stood in the doorway with the orange glow of the setting sun highlighting her features. She looked amazing. Her hair fell softly around her shoulders, and he saw now that it was a rich, dark brown with red highlights.

"Please come in and make yourself at home."

"Thank you." As he walked into her home, he caught the light scent of her perfume. It smelled of peaches.

"I have just a few things to take care of, if you'll give me a minute."

"Sure, no problem."

Jace glanced around the living room and took the opportunity to study Kat's home environment to pick up more clues about the woman who had intrigued him from the moment he caught sight of her.

After he'd gotten off the phone with her earlier his first thought had been, *Hot damn, she said yes!*

His next thoughts centered on figuring out a way to get her relaxed enough in his company to share the real information he wanted. What was it that made Kat tick, what was it that made Kat so hot, and, of course, what could he do to get another one of those kisses?

He'd put in the duty call to Collin and let him know that he wouldn't be joining the guys tonight, taking the licks from his cohorts, as was his due, for ditching them over a girl. But the whole time he wore a smile on his face imagining exactly what might happen in the next several hours.

Kat walked down the hall, and when Jace managed to tear his gaze away from the slight sway of her hips, he went to studying the room. There were small architectural details built in that added character. He stood in a medium-sized living room, which contained a slate-tiled fireplace centered on the exterior wall. The one with the fireplace was painted a dark, rich red but all the others had a vanilla-cream tone. All the woodwork was stained a dark color that balanced out the warm jewel tones it seemed Kat preferred to use for her furniture. The atmosphere was one of warmth and coziness. Very appealing to someone who was used to generic base housing. He glanced up the staircase, but from this angle he couldn't get a good idea of the layout of the upper level. He noticed all the photographs. Several in varying sizes were displayed on nearly every wall. It looked as though they'd been taken in a variety of settings.

"You enjoy photography?"

She called from the back of the house, "Yes, very much."

"Can I ask why?"

Her sandals clicked on the hardwood floors as she came back into the room.

"If I said that I merely like pretty things, would you think me vapid?"

Interesting. She turned the question on me. That was a technique he used when interrogating targets, but one he also remembered being widely used during his time at the Naval Academy by his professors. *So she's either interrogating me to see if my response meets her expectations, or she seeks approval from others regardless of her personal feelings. By her use of vocabulary she's obviously not afraid to let people know she's intelligent.*

"No. Of course, based on what I've learned about you so far, I believe you're a sensualist. Take for instance the way you responded to the music the other night. It took life inside your body while we danced. And the way you described driving. So you may enjoy pretty things, but I think there's a deeper meaning. One much closer to your soul."

Kat swallowed and turned to look at one of the prints on the wall in the living room. "It's not all that dramatic. When

I look at a well-composed photograph, no matter what is happening in my life, I feel inner peace." She looked back at Jace, smiling weakly. "Silly, I know."

"Not at all. We all need a little peace in our lives at times. Do you have a favorite photographer?"

Jace understood the need for peace in one's life, something that could center you in the midst of chaos. He'd often been in situations when all hell was breaking loose around him and he'd searched deep inside himself for strength to get him, and his men, home safe.

"I guess it depends on what subject is being photographed. For landscapes, the classic artist is, of course, Ansel Adams, but if you're looking at photojournalism, the genre was really fathered by Henri Cartier-Bresson. I'm not picky, though. Like you said, I pretty much like anything that calls to my soul. Guess you've got me pegged."

"Not nearly, but thank you for sharing."

One print really caught Jace's attention. It showed a gently flowing river against the backdrop of a snowy mountain peak. The water looked like a bed of cotton, soft and wispy.

"Who took this one? I can almost sense the water and feel the sun on the bank."

Jace didn't hear any response, so he turned around and caught her proud smile.

"I did... On vacation last year. Actually, most of the prints in the house are mine. When I look at them, I remember that particular day. I remember the beauty of the land surrounding me, what the air felt like as it blew through my hair, what scents and sounds filled the air. I remember just how I felt at that one moment in time."

He looked around with renewed interest. This was exactly what he was hoping to learn about her. The images adorning her walls were very impressive. "You're very talented. Have you ever sold your pictures?"

"Oh...no... I'm not that good. It's just a hobby. Are you ready to go? I made reservations for eight o'clock."

"Sure, but first we need to get something out of the way."

Jace walked toward her, capturing her by the waist, and pulled her to him. They paused for a second with their lips barely a breath apart, then he kissed her. His mouth was hot, his tongue soft, but firm. His lips molded and caressed, shaping hers and seeking entry. Kat slid her hands up his hard chest, reaching around his neck for an anchor and held on for dear life as he took them higher. He groaned into her mouth and pressed her against the wall behind her.

Kat felt intoxicated. She felt his hard body press into hers, and she throbbed with arousal. Feeling a trickle of moisture escape between her folds, she tilted her hips, desperate to get closer. His spicy male scent made her dizzy. When she'd opened the door, all she'd been able to think was how the lines of Jace's body held an animal-like quality. He looked like a tiger — deceptively calm but having a body covered in sinewy muscle that could only be described as graceful.

He changed the angle of his kiss. In a never-ending exploration, one kiss turned into three, then four. She met his tongue with her own, whimpering in the back of her throat. She was shaking when he finally broke off, breathing a little heavily.

He leaned his forehead against hers. "God, Kat, you taste as good as I remember. I couldn't wait another second. I had to sample that sweet mouth of yours again, but we'd better leave before dinner is forgotten."

* * * *

The restaurant was quiet as the hostess seated them at a corner table. The soft lighting created shadows and highlights on the walls, and the smells of fresh bread and enticing spices filled the atmosphere.

Slowly spinning his water glass in his fingers, Jace said, "Tell me about your family."

"Well, I have two younger brothers. Both live on the West Coast. Jack is a public health lawyer and Christian is an advertising executive."

"What about your parents? You referred to your mother in the past tense the night we met, but I didn't hear you say anything about your father. Is he still living?"

Kat glanced down at the crisp white tablecloth and swallowed before looking back into Jace's eyes. "Actually, we lost both our parents a few years ago in a car accident. The boys were in college and I had just finished my master's degree."

He noticed her eyes glisten with moisture and reached out to gently hold her hand. "I'm sorry. Do you want to tell me what happened?"

She took a drink of her water and smiled. "It's okay. I don't mind talking about it. They were driving during an ice storm and their car skidded, hitting the side rail of the highway and flipping down an embankment. I'll always miss them, but I'm constantly grateful they were around to raise all three of us into adulthood."

Jace listened to her story of losing her parents, and despite the tragic occurrence, didn't feel that was the source of emotions he'd sensed the night they met.

He didn't want her to feel like the dinner was a grand inquisition, so he said, "I can relate somewhat. I lost my parents as well, but I was very young at the time, only ten years old. They also died in a car accident. After that, I was raised by my uncle until I joined the Navy when I turned eighteen."

Talking together felt natural and easy. Not once did they have an awkward silence of the kind so common on first dates.

Halfway through the dinner, Kat shrugged off her jacket. From that point on, it took everything in Jace's control to stay focused on the conversation. The sight of her soft skin with just a glow of tan made it very difficult to concentrate. Jace thought it was very interesting that she had chosen the profession that she had. It wasn't very often that someone came across an anthropologist, so he wanted to appease some of his curiosity.

"Why anthropology? It's kind of an obscure profession."

Kat's eyes lit up with excitement. "They always say a person's journey is like a giant puzzle. You have to find a way to make all the pieces of your life fit together. When you find the partial or, in rare cases, complete remains of an individual or a civilization that lived hundreds, maybe even thousands, of years ago, it's my job to figure out their puzzle."

Jace pondered this for a moment. "Do you ever do forensic work?"

"I've occasionally been called in on a case. Most often, it's when older remains are unearthed, either at a construction site or come upon accidentally."

Desperately wanting to keep the connection he felt between them, Jace took a leap of faith "So, Kat, tell me something... What will it take to have you spend the week with me?"

"Wow, you don't beat around the bush, do you?"

"I know that wasn't the most tactful way of asking, but I want to spend more time with you."

"You know, all afternoon I thought how I should respond to a question like that."

Jace didn't dare to hold his breath. "Did you come up with an answer?"

Kat smiled. "Yes. The way I look at it is that I've led a fairly introverted lifestyle. Last night you showed me how it feels to let go. I liked it. So this doctor is recommending the addition of a little spontaneity and adventure. I have to work during the day but I'll be happy to spend my evenings with you. I don't have any classes scheduled on Wednesday, so we could spend the whole day together then."

Jace tilted her chin up so his eyes were locked on hers. "That would be perfect. I have commitments for the wedding on Thursday and Friday, and the ceremony is Saturday."

Kat smiled as she broke eye contact. "So, what places do

you want to see in St. Louis? There are the obvious tourist attractions, or some not so publicized places we could go to."

"I'm not picky. I pretty much just wanted to get a flavor of the city."

"Well, how about tomorrow you meet me at my office and I'll take you to Forest Park. The zoo's there, and I've wanted to see the baby animals born this spring. That is, if you like zoos?"

"Sounds great. What time should I pick you up?"

"I finish classes at five o'clock."

Jace grinned. "It's a date."

Chapter Four

When Jace arrived at the campus to meet Kat, he had no trouble picturing her in a lecture hall surround by eager young co-eds thirsty for knowledge. Or maybe more accurately trying to instill excitement in young co-eds who were hungover and secretly updating their social media profiles during her lecture on the subjects she loved. After he'd found Kat's business card, he had done some reconnaissance on both her and the institution where she worked. He'd discovered that Dr Kat Martin was highly respected in her area of expertise, having published several papers, and was regularly sought after for research projects around the world. He'd also discovered that Washington University was a top-ranking institution in the country. He was very glad that Kat had access to resources that would continue to support the growth of her chosen profession.

Now, approaching the campus, he saw that the ivy-covered stone buildings, arched walkways, and green grass reminded him of the touted halls of the East Coast universities he was familiar with.

He heard the click of a high heel on the stone walkway and turned to his left. Kat walked toward him with a bright smile on her face, and a little flutter vibrated in his chest.

She was dressed in a navy pinstripe suit with a short skirt, tailored jacket, and sharp little heels with straps crossing around her ankles that added an inch to her petite height.

Funny, I've never thought of pinstripes as sexy before.

Jace let Kat come to him. When she stopped, leaving a couple of feet between them, Jace closed the remaining distance by sliding his arm around her back and taking the final step forward. He greeted her with a soft hug and a chaste kiss. "Are you going to be able to walk around the zoo in those shoes?"

"Oh, sure. I can wear these all day."

"Okay, then, let's go."

It was a good day to walk around the exhibits. The sun was out, but the air held a trace of fall. Since it was after the Labor Day crush, and kids were back in school, he and Kat only encountered other visitors occasionally. Jace took every chance he could to touch Kat — a hand on the small of her back, a soft caress of the shoulder. They came to a halt at the big cat enclosures. Inside was a pair of tiger cubs running around and playfully fighting under the watchful eye of their momma. Kat leaned against the railing laughing, and he smiled at the carefree sound. He moved behind her and wrapped his arms around her waist, leaning his chin on her shoulder.

"They look like they're having fun," he said.

Kat tilted her head back and smiled. "Yeah, I guess some things transcend species. Kids will be kids."

He placed a soft kiss on her neck. "Hard to believe that one day they will be powerful predators."

He looked around to see if there was anyone nearby. With confirmation that they had the area to themselves, he slipped open the button of her jacket. Beneath his palm he felt the delicate fabric of a silky camisole. He kept one hand visible on the outside of her jacket, but slipped the other between the gap to caress her stomach through the material. He worked upward at a lazy pace until he was cupping her breast.

"Jace... What if someone...?"

"Nobody's anywhere near us, sweetheart. Just forget where we are and concentrate on my touch. What does it feel like to have my hand caressing you?"

Kat closed her eyes and relaxed back against his shoulder. "Warm... And it makes me feel like my skin is tingling."

"You feel wonderful in my hand, soft and full. I can feel

your nipple hardening against my palm. Makes me wish I could lick and suckle it between my lips."

Kat moaned in the back of her throat. With her head tilted back, he kissed her as he continued to caress her breast. The kiss started out soft, but quickly escalated, his tongue thrusting deeply into her hot, sweet mouth. He couldn't seem to stop kissing her. She was like a drug racing through his system. The mama tiger let out a loud roar, and they broke apart.

Kat laughed. "I guess she didn't like us corrupting her children."

* * * *

On Tuesday, they decided to stay in and watch a movie. Kat let Jace pick, and wasn't surprised when his choice turned out to be an action flick with lots of explosions.

Sitting on the sofa of her living room, he casually rubbed his hand up and down her arm while she leaned back against his chest and watched the movie. Occasionally Jace's lips would nuzzle her temple, and Kat found it harder and harder to concentrate on the plot of the movie. After one such kiss she angled her head up to look at him. His strong jaw was highlighted by the light flickering from the television set, and directly beneath, a shadow ran down the column of his throat. She wanted to lift up and kiss the firm skin, inhale the scent from his aftershave. As if he heard her thought, Jace looked down and their eyes met.

Kat's heart beat frantically in her chest when Jace adjusted their positions.

He guided her into a reclining position against the arm of the sofa. Jace moved to kneel on the floor. The look in his eyes conveyed that the movie had been completely forgotten.

Softly, he ran his fingers from her neck down her arms and back up, softly blowing into her ear. He whispered, "You are the most honest and passionate woman I've ever met. Tell me what you like."

Kat swallowed and took a leap of faith that her response would not be met with ridicule or laughter.

"I know that I love it when you take control. It makes me feel very soft, and feminine, and desirable."

"Have you ever played Dominant/submissive games before?"

Her insides heated with desire.

"No... But the idea has always appealed to me. I like the idea of not having to tell you what to do, how to touch me. My job requires a lot of responsibility and decision-making. It'd be nice not to have to do that for pleasure. Do... Do you? Play those kinds of games?"

"I'm not into hardcore BDSM, and don't really play in the scene, but light bondage and asserting control turns me on."

"Okay then..."

He maneuvered her into a new position—her legs stretched out on the sofa, her back gently arching. Jace ran his hands back down her arms, imprisoned her wrists in his grip then raised them above her head.

"Don't move your hands. Pretend they're tied in that position." Leaning down, he kissed her softly at first, then harder, more insistently, demanding that she give him what he wanted.

He caressed her stomach beneath her T-shirt, slowly raising the material until she felt cool air from the open window gently brush the underside of her breasts. She kept her eyes closed, and her breathing was shallow and fast.

"Kat... Look at me."

Slowly she opened her eyes.

"I will not make love to you tonight, but I can give you pleasure. Do you understand?"

A flash of disappointment arced through her body. But she thought maybe this was part of the game. She had to do what Jace commanded. "Yes."

35

Jace raised her T-shirt above her head, and keeping with the fantasy, only moved it as high as her wrists so she became slightly entangled in the soft material. At this moment she was so glad she'd dug out her lacy bra instead of one of the more serviceable cotton bras that filled her drawer. He unsnapped the front closure, spread his hands around her ribcage and used his thumbs to slowly reveal her breasts. They weren't very big, and generally Kat wasn't self-conscious about their size but at the same time she wanted Jace to find pleasure in her body.

Jace sucked in his breath. "I always have had a thing for large nipples and dark areolas."

He cupped her right breast in the palm of his hand, and Kat moaned. It was a perfect fit. He leaned down and slowly began to lick around the breast in his hand, his fingers softly drawing circles around the left. When he got to the center, he took her nipple into his mouth just as he lightly pinched her left one between his thumb and finger.

Kat gasped and moaned. *Oh, my God, the heat!*

She couldn't believe how hot his mouth was on her. The combination of the suction of his lips and the tug of his fingers just about had her leaping off the sofa. Kat had been in this spot before with other guys, but had never felt this gut-clenching ache for completion.

He moved from one side to the other, giving the left just as much attention as the right. Pressure slowly mounted in her blood and dampness gathered between her legs. His hand started moving down her stomach again as he continued to suckle. When he reached the button of her shorts, she felt him undo it and slowly slide the zipper down, his fingers skimming over the top of her panties.

Yes! Please, ease this burning ache!

He leaned up and kissed her again. She desperately wanted to hold him, but didn't want to ruin the fantasy of shackles, so she put everything she had into the kiss.

Had Jace noticed yet she was completely shaved down there? Would he like it? Her answer came in the form of a groan when he slowly dragged his fingers under the edge of her scant, silky panties. She knew that her heat and moisture now covered his fingertips and she cried out when he found her clitoris.

Oh, Lord, I can't believe how soft she is.

The scent of her arousal was like ambrosia. He had to taste her, couldn't wait another second. He slipped her shorts down her legs and gave a gentle lick right up her slit through her panties. She shuddered, and he drew her panties down her legs and set them aside. At first, he just kissed the tops of her legs and her lower stomach, making Kat squirm. Finally, not being able to resist any longer, he slowly licked her.

Much to his pleasure, the sensation of his tongue on her sensitive labia made Kat jump about two inches in the air. Holding her down so he could get to her, he ran his tongue through her lips again. Vanilla, peaches and her natural musky scent exploded on his taste buds. He moaned his approval. Never had he tasted anything like Kat aroused.

He began to slowly slide his tongue inside, while he lightly scraped her with his teeth. She moaned, pressing herself into his mouth as he suckled greedily. Alternately stroking her with deep glides and quick stabs, he teased her.

Then, slipping his fingers through her vulva, he slowly pushed one inside her.

God, she's tight!

His fingers hit a barrier, one that was only present in the innocent, that left him stunned. There was no mistaking the implications of that discovery.

Kat's a virgin! How did a woman as sensual as she is remain untouched for so long? She's thirty years old.

Putting aside these questions for the moment, Jace refocused on his pleasurable task. He wanted this experience for her to be memorable. He took a deep breath and began easing his finger in and out while he licked. Gently adding a second finger and circling her clit with his tongue, he felt her body tighten.

Kat's moans were growing louder, her breathing more rapid. Pools of moisture were spilling onto Jace's hand. Noticing that she was beginning to contract around his fingers, he pushed up behind her pubic bone, then finding that one spot, and enclosing her clit in his mouth, gently suckled. Her body tensed again, then she screamed and contracted tightly around his hand.

Kat sighed and her face softened. Before he knew it, she fell into a lax sleep, her body languid and replete from the pleasure he'd given her, while his remained tense and aching. He didn't want to disturb her, though. Jace lifted her in his arms and carried her upstairs to her bedroom. Pulling back the blankets, he slid her into bed. He looked down at her for a moment, remembering how soft and sweet-smelling her skin had been beneath his hands and lips.

Tomorrow they'd planned to go to the baseball game. Cory's almost father-in-law had purchased all the groomsmen tickets, and since they were using his company's box seats, there was an extra for Kat.

They needed to leave for the stadium at 1000 hours, so he set her alarm for 0900.

He kissed her softly on the lips. "Goodnight," he whispered then walked out of her bedroom door, pulling it shut.

Jace made sure to close all her windows, and locked the door as he left. He really wanted nothing more than to slide into that bed with her and hold her all night long, but thought that might lead to more than holding, and he wanted to make sure she was ready for that next step. She obviously had held onto her innocence this long for a reason, and he was going to find out why.

* * * *

The alarm buzzing dragged Kat from a deep sleep. She slapped at the offending sound and snuggled deeper into her pillows. When the buzzing started again, she groaned and opened her eyes, blinking the sleep out in order to read the blue numbers. She still had an hour before Jace picked her up for the trip to the ballpark.

Kat bolted up in bed. "Oh, my God!"

Last night. Oh, holy hell. Memories of last night flashed through her mind. Jace's lips on her nipples, his fingers inside her. She'd never experienced anything like the incredible climax Jace had brought her to. Then what did she do? She passed out on him, left the man hanging after he'd given her the best pleasure of her life. She vaguely remembered him putting her in bed and saying goodnight, but after that she was dead to the world.

"Real smooth, genius," she scoffed.

She turned to look out of her bedroom window and saw that the sky was bright blue. It had been forecasted to be a good day for the baseball game, and it seemed that Mother Nature was cooperating. So far anyway.

What could she do to make things up to Jace? How could she show him that she wouldn't be a selfish lover if given the chance? Now that they'd crossed into a new dimension of their relationship, Kat planned on making sure he received as well as he gave.

Tonight, if the opportunity presented itself.

She scrambled out of bed, noticing instantly that she was naked. A groan of mortification escaped. Jace had seen all of her, but she'd seen nothing of him.

Well, tonight that's going to change.

Kat walked into her en suite bathroom. Opening the glass door of the shower, she turned on the spigot. There was nothing like the pounding spray of hot water to wake her up. She took care of her morning rituals then stepped into the cubicle and sighed as the water hit her skin. She had wasted too much time since her alarm went off — the alarm that Jace had so thoughtfully set for her — to luxuriate in the shower. A quick wash of her hair and body, followed by the fastest shave in history, and she was done.

Kat wrapped a bath sheet around her torso and stepped back into the bedroom. As she passed the nightstand, the phone rang.

She picked up the receiver. "Hello?"

"Morning, sweetheart. I wanted to make sure you'd got up and are ready for me. The boys and I are leaving in a few minutes. Hope you don't mind sitting on my lap. The car is pretty full."

She heard several deep chuckles in the background. Obviously Jace had an audience, and was playing to the crowd. Was it time to test out her flirting skills?

"I'm definitely ready for you. My body's all warm and wet. Tell me, Jace, how do you feel about morning sex? Because right now I'm thinking a good hot tussle between the sheets sounds like the perfect way to greet the day. Too bad you didn't stick around last night."

There was a low groan then the sound of a door being slammed. Had she gone too far?

"You little temptress, I may have acted the gentleman last night, but talk like that is going to get you tossed up against a wall and fucked to within an inch of your life. If there wasn't going to be a car full of my teammates waiting outside your house, I'd show you exactly how much I like a good workout in the morning," Jace said with a low growl.

Kat fanned her face. Her SEAL definitely had the dirty talk down to a science. Way beyond her skills.

"Kat? You there?"

She nodded then realized that Jace couldn't see her. "Yeah, I'm here. You just... Oh, wow."

Jace's low chuckle vibrated into her ear through the receiver of the phone. His description and her imagination turned her teasing about being hot and wet into reality.

"Don't do anything to ease your ache. You brought this on yourself, and it's going to be my pleasure to tease you until you're ready to scream later. Much later. I want you to be ready for me all day. I'm looking forward to sitting next to you and breathing in your aroused scent. Nobody but the two of us will know how turned on you are, how eager you are for my touch. Nobody will know just how badly I want to slide my cock deep inside you and soak up all the damp heat that surrounded my fingers last night."

Kat let out a soft whimper and clenched her legs together. "I give! I give. No more!"

Jace laughed. "See you soon, sweetheart." He hung up.

Kat sank onto the edge of her bed. Her chest pounded with excitement from listening to Jace's husky voice full of sensual promise. She opened the towel and moaned as the fibers brushed against her hard nipples. Jace had said not to touch herself, and normally that wouldn't be a problem. Kat had never been the type of person to seek self-pleasure, but last night Jace had awakened a need in her body, one that demanded satisfaction. But this wasn't the time, and truthfully she didn't want just physical release. She wanted to experience that same intimate connection she sensed last night. The one where Jace's skillful fingers on her body transcended the physical plane. Then again maybe that was her romance novel brainwashed mind acting up again.

She stood and moved over to her dresser, rustled through the drawers until she found her favorite Cardinals T-shirt and a pair of shorts. A glance back at the clock told her she had at most fifteen minutes before Jace arrived, and she'd yet to dry her hair. It was going to be close, and Kat highly doubted that a Navy man liked to be kept waiting.

She rushed to finish getting ready and ran down the stairs just as the doorbell chimed. She opened the door to find Jace standing there. The heat radiating from his gray eyes had Kat sucking in a breath and taking a quick step back. She'd never been faced with a man's desire in such an intense expression. Jace stepped into the front entry of her home and kept advancing. He clasped his hands on either side of her waist and propelled her back against the wall by the stairs. Kat's arms went around his neck and she arched against him. His mouth descended and took possession of hers. This wasn't the sweet, coaxing seduction of last night. This was a new Jace, raw and aroused. By her! Kat Martin, geeky anthropologist, had driven the hunger of one of the sexiest, most elitely trained men of the United States Navy to breaking point.

Jace cupped Kat's ass and lifted her so their heights were a closer match. "Wrap your legs around me," he ordered.

Kat did and moaned into Jace's kiss when his erection pressed against the seam of her shorts. Jace ground their bodies together while Kat tipped her head back, exposing her throat to Jace's lips. Kat was dizzy with excitement. Conscious thought became impossible. Her entire awareness boiled down to one focus—Jace. Jace's body, so large and powerful. Jace's tongue as it flicked against hers. It all felt so good, so right. Jace's hands tightened on her rear then rocked their bodies together. She'd lost her mind. She never behaved this way. Kat Martin had never been so wanton, but apparently today, she was.

A horn blasted outside three times. She looked at Jace and was satisfied to see that he was as turned on as she was. He closed his eyes and rested their foreheads together, breathing heavily.

"I hate them right now. I swear, I really do," he said roughly.

Kat ran her fingers through the crisp hairs on the back of Jace's head. "You did promise to tease and torment me."

"Yeah, unfortunately I wasn't thinking very clearly because right now I'm the one feeling tortured." He put Kat back on her feet then bent down and kissed her slowly. "Till later?"

"Promise?"

"Always."

* * * *

Kat pulled the front door to her house shut, and Jace

made sure that she'd locked the door. He'd noticed that she didn't have an alarm and intended to bring up the oversight when the time felt right. Maybe giving Kat that kind of advice was overstepping the boundaries of their relationship, seeing as how they'd only known each other a few days, but Jace knew he'd sleep better knowing she was more protected.

They walked down the sidewalk and the back door to Cory's rented SUV swung open.

"It's about damn time," Justin yelled.

They climbed into the vehicle and settled on the bench seat behind the front. Jace made sure that Kat's seatbelt was fastened then gave Cory a nod that all was secure, and they could take off.

Not even a minute had passed before Justin's voice rose above the din in the back seat.

"What were the two of you doing in there?"

Kurt, who rode beside Justin, smacked the language specialist upside the back of his head. "What do you think, moron?"

Justin rubbed the back of his head, grimacing. "Well, they can suck face on their own time. I've got a ball game to get to."

Jace growled when he saw Kat's face turn scarlet and her shoulders tense. He looked over his shoulder and scowled. "Justin, I know it's hard for you, but try not to be so much of an asshole. I remember not too long ago when we had to drag your ass away from a date kicking and screaming because of a callout."

Justin smiled. "Oh yeah, Megan. She was smokin' hot. And talented. Did I tell you about that thing she does with her tongue? She would—"

"We've heard!" the whole squad yelled.

Kat started to snicker beside him, and Jace put his arm around her shoulders as the vehicle entered the freeway.

Thirty minutes later, they were walking toward the stadium gates, weaving through the sea of red and white decked-out fans. The Cardinals were playing the Cubs, and owing to the long-standing rivalry between the teams, the streets were packed. Jace made sure to hold onto Kat's hand so there was no chance of her getting separated from him.

It wasn't long before they'd made their way down to the field-level seats.

"Jesus, Cory. Exactly who is your father-in-law and what do I have to do to get on his good side? These seats are sick!" Eric yelled over the noise of the crowd as the Cardinals lineup was announced.

Jace's eyes widened when Kat's voice cut through the melee when the name Chris Carpenter echoed over the speakers.

He leaned in and placed his lips against her ear. "Big fan of the Carp, are you?"

She turned to him and smiled. "Absolutely. He's the best pitcher in the league."

"I think some would debate that, but I'll give this one to you since we're in your home stadium."

"Oh, gee, how kind of you," she mocked.

Their group settled in to watch the game. He was amused to find that Kat cheered and jeered as loudly as any hardcore fan in the stadium.

"So, Kat, you keep up with the team or are you a 'when they're winning' fan?" Peter asked.

Kat took a sip of her beer then turned to face Peter. "I don't get to watch every game, but I manage to catch most of the televised evening games. And I try to get to the park at least two or three times a season."

"Wow. Back in the day I never got the impression you were all that into sports," Collin said.

"Yeah, well, there's probably a lot about me you never bothered to learn," Kat said under her breath, but to Collin she smiled then shrugged.

Jace winced. Sounded like Kat still held some resentment about her past with Collin and Peter. He rubbed the top of her thigh.

"So who's the player to watch this year?" Cory asked.

"Well, Wainwright and Carpenter are our most consistent hurlers, obviously. And Pujols is still the king of the stick, but Holliday and Ludwick are also having a great season. I actually have a soft spot for Yadie. He might finish above .300 this year, and you can't deny that he's the best defensive catcher in baseball."

Jace almost lost it when the jaws of six of the most battle-hardened Navy SEALs hit the concrete risers. His girl was the real deal. Being away quite often, none of them had the opportunity to follow a team's progress on a regular basis, and Jace sincerely doubted that any one of them could have summarized a group of players so confidently.

Wait a minute. *His girl?* When had he begun to think about Kat as his, and what future could they possibly have not only living in different cities but given the demands of his status on active duty? He'd better slow himself down and start to think with his big head instead of letting the little one call the shots.

They announced the seventh inning stretch, and Jace thought it was a good time to stretch his legs, grab another beer and snag a hotdog.

Hmm, beer and dogs—best baseball combo ever.

"I'm making a concession run. Anybody want something?" he announced.

"I'm going to use the Ladies room." Kat stood and slid past him with a smile and a wink.

"I'll go with you," Peter said.

Jace shuffled out of the row of seats, and waited for Peter to do the same before jogging up the steps toward the concession stands. The two of them had been in line for only a moment when Peter gripped his shoulder and turned Jace around.

"So, you and Kat still hitting it off, I see."

Jace grinned. "Yeah, she's really incredible. I find myself looking forward to whatever surprise she pulls out next."

"Has she talked to you at all about our past? Do you know

if she holds a grudge?"

He thought about the mumbled comment under Kat's breath, but was uncertain how much of her private thoughts he should divulge.

"Actually, we haven't talked about that at all. Everything else under the sun, yes, but not that. Why? Are you worried about something?"

"No, not really. I actually haven't even thought about her in so long... But after the other night at the club, I thought back and realized I'm not exactly proud of the way I used to treat her. I just noticed that you two seem to be getting really close, and I don't want that to be a problem either between us or with her."

"Why don't you ask her yourself?"

"Yeah, maybe... We'll see."

Jace had never seen Peter so uncertain. Usually he was brash and unapologetic. "I'm going to ask her to come to the wedding Saturday. I've already cleared it with Cory and Jenny. Maybe you can talk to her then. For what it's worth, I think she would really appreciate an apology, no matter how delayed it may be."

Chapter Five

Jace and Kat were at dinner later that evening when he dropped the bomb. "Will you go to the wedding with me? I'm a groomsman and will have to stand up at the ceremony, but we can stay close at the reception."

Kat looked at him, surprised. "I don't want to impose on the bride and groom. I'm sure they had to give final numbers weeks ago."

"I already asked, and they said its fine."

"Well, okay then... Thank you. What kind of wedding is it? Is it a casual or formal affair?"

"It's pretty formal. Jenny comes from a well-respected family in the city and everyone is black tie. We'll be in our dress whites. Is that a problem?"

"No, I'll need to find something appropriate."

"I don't want you to be inconvenienced. I just want to spend more time with you."

Kat reached out her hand to cup his cheek, touched at his concern. "It'll be fine, don't worry. I'll look forward to it. What time, and where is the ceremony? I should probably meet you there since you'll be busy beforehand."

After sharing the details, they sat in silence for several minutes. Kat decided it was time to broach the topic of last night since he didn't seem inclined. "Jace, about last night... What you made me feel was incredible, but why did you leave?"

"I didn't want to, believe me, but felt you deserved a little time before things went any further."

She couldn't believe how sensitive and understanding he was. Those were not emotions she would stereotypically associate with Navy SEALs. Kat decided to bite the bullet.

"I want to return the favor. Will you come home with me?"

Jace's eyes went wide and he swallowed. Kat saw the second the shock at her bold statement wore off and morphed into arousal. She really hoped she'd be able to satisfy him. She wasn't ignorant when it came to sex, but neither did she have a lot of practical experience. Most of her knowledge was theoretical, based in fantasies or taken from books she'd read over the years. Kat had been reading romance novels since she was fifteen years old, and over the years she'd picked progressively racier ones. In fact, she was eagerly anticipating finally testing out some tips and tricks she'd memorized from those very books. Based on Jace's response to the kiss this morning, she was banking on the fact that he truly did want her. Physically, at least. During the game Kat had caught her mind from wandering too far into the realm of fantasy. She had to remember that Jace was only here for two weeks. They were having an affair, not starting a relationship. She was willing to offer her body, but she'd have to be very careful to guard her heart because Kat had a feeling it would be very easy to lose around Jace.

"I can't think of anything I want more than to accompany you home, but there's something I feel is important we talk about first."

He leaned in closer. "Why didn't you tell me you were a virgin?"

Kat felt the blood drain away from her face before it rushed back in a great surge. "I was afraid you wouldn't want to continue what we were doing."

"Don't you think that should be a decision we make together?"

It was her body, but she saw his point. "If you feel it was wrong of me to not announce my most intimate secret before what we did... I'm sorry."

Jace smiled. "Kat, I love your honesty in all things,

especially your passion. Will you tell me why?"

"Why I'm a virgin? Or why I'm willing to change that status with you?"

"Both. I'm honored you want to share the experience with me. The thing is, I've always felt your first should be with someone special. Regardless of what lies in your future, a piece of your heart will always remain with the person you shared your first truly intimate experience with. I want to make sure you understand that, and you still want me to be that person."

"It's pretty simple. Nobody has made me feel the way you do. I've dated a few guys, but didn't want to go all the way with someone I was only mildly attracted to. Until I graduated from college, I was still very frumpy. I've always been on the heavy side. Most college guys are just looking for some quick action, so I was out of the running."

"After college, I went straight to graduate school for my Master's and Doctorate and didn't really have time to pursue any relationships. I've only really started dating in the last five years."

"I find it very hard to believe that not one guy was able to see the potential and passion under your surface for all these years. You must have gone to school with a bunch of idiots."

Kat was a little embarrassed that she and Jace were discussing her virginity so openly.—She had kind of anticipated that he would figure it out, but she hadn't expected him to confront her or ask if she was sure. From what her few friends had described over the years, guys simply wanted to get laid, and didn't really care what it took to close the deal. Jace's consideration for her care and feelings only solidified her resolve.

Leaning over, she whispered in his ear, "Do you have any idea what you make me want to do to you? I can't wait to get my hands on you the way you did last night. I wonder if I can make you burn the way you made me."

Jace's eyes flashed hot with desire. "You already do."

He picked up her hand and placed it under the tablecloth, letting her feel exactly how she affected him. It didn't take an expert to recognize the meaning behind Jace's erection tightening his slacks. And judging by the solid feel, Jace was very aroused. She smiled and he grinned wickedly before placing her hand back on the table. It was time to go. He paid the check and escorted her back to the car.

Once they got settled in the car, he turned in his seat and kissed her. It was not a gentle kiss. This kiss was meant to send sparks arcing between their bodies. He picked up her iPod and scrolled through the highest rated songs. Jace tapped the screen then turned the device toward her so she could see. She smiled when she saw his selection.

"You like Enigma?" he asked.

Kat leaned back in her seat and closed her eyes "I love Enigma. I have all their CDs at home, even ones not available in the States. My favorite thing to do when driving at night is turn their music up so loud I can feel the beat vibrating through my body."

Jace smiled as he hit 'play' on the device rigged to play through the car system. "Let's see how much we can make you shake."

Neither one of them said a word on the way home. She occasionally caught him glancing over at her and one time she smiled back. Jace's foot pressed on the accelerator a little harder.

Kat sat in the seat listening to the hypnotic music. She thought about how the feel of Jace's arousal had filled her palm. She had felt it against her when they were kissing before, but never realized just how large he was. The knowledge caused concern.

Will I be able to please him?

She may have read a few books over the years but not having any real experience, she felt she may slow down the night, and she didn't want him to be disappointed.

When they got back to her house, Jace softly closed the front door. Kat turned on a table lamp, but kept the room in relative darkness. *How do we do this? Should I make the first move? Oh, to hell with it.*

"Come sit here next to me," she said.

As he moved to the sofa and sat down, she leaned toward him and gently kissed his lips—a soft nibble, teasing, tasting. As Kat molded herself closer to him, she heard him groan. At first, he just sat there and let her take control, but then after a few minutes, he turned the aggressor and slanted over her, pushing Kat back into the cushions and lying over her along the sofa.

She started to protest, to remind him that tonight was for his pleasure, but what he was doing felt so good, she couldn't find the words. This was the first time she had felt his full weight against her, and it was incredible. His body was large enough to completely cover hers, but he held back enough not to crush her.

When Jace lifted his head to trail kisses down Kat's neck, she took the opportunity to get his attention. "Tonight is supposed to be about you, remember? I'm supposed to be pleasuring you."

"This is my pleasure. I love the way you taste, the way you feel underneath me."

"Please, Jace, let me up. I want to do this right."

"Now how can I possibly ignore such a plea?" He sat up and reversed their positions. They were now lying in the other direction on the sofa with her draped over his body. "Now I have my very own blanket of the sweetest, softest flesh."

Kat's breasts were pushing against his chest, her legs were between his, and his cock was cradled at their junction. Even through their clothes, Kat felt his heat. She gave an experimental rub against him and it felt wonderful.

She sat up and straddled his hips. Her knees dug into the cushions of the sofa. Slowly she undid his shirt. One by one, the buttons slipped through the holes, and she leaned forward to press small kisses as each inch of his chest was revealed. When she got to the bottom, Jace helped her pull the tails out of his jeans. He sat up abruptly and removed his shirt, and Kat fell backward so she was practically bent in half.

At first, all she could do was stare at his hard chest. His muscles were clearly defined. Obviously he had to be in good shape for his job, but this body was a work of art.

Kat pushed up and reached for the smooth skin in front of her. She ran her fingers down his chest. She squeezed his pecs and Jace let loose a soft groan. She skimmed her thumbs over his nipples and pinched them between her fingers like he'd done to hers.

"That's it. I like it just hard enough so the pleasure borders on pain."

Kat climbed off his lap and knelt beside the sofa. Jace watched with heavy lids as Kat bent her head down and touched her tongue to his nipple. She started tonguing and circling his nipples, softly at first then with more suction. He watched every second.

Maybe, just maybe he's burning the scene into his memory so he can recall this time together after we're separated. It's a nice thought, anyway.

She moved her hands down toward his jeans and as they passed over his stomach, she felt his muscles clench.

Kat found such pleasure in touching him that her hands trembled a little when she started to undo his jeans. He let her take her time. The fire burning in his eyes told Kat he was holding back. The knowledge that he wanted control, but was letting her have it was more arousing than any touch could be.

When she finally got his jeans undone, Jace helped her by lifting his hips as she pulled them and his boxer briefs partway down, finally exposing him to her view.

Her jaw slackened, and she couldn't help but stare.

Wow. I have no idea if every guy is built like this, but if so… No wonder everyone runs around having sex.

Kat's mouth watered to taste him. A small drop of fluid had built up on the tip, and instinctively she reached out with her tongue to lick it up.

"Oh, God. You're going to kill me. I know it."

Kat slipped her tongue out to lick off a drop of pre-cum, and Jace groaned.

He clenched his jaw when she gripped the base. Kat hoped it was a good agony.

She studied his penis, trying to determine the best way to do this. She wrapped her hand around his steel-hard shaft and slowly stroked up and down. It was thick and long, with large, dark veins snaking around up from the base. Jace hissed in a breath and his muscles flexed under her. Rubbing her thumb over the crown, she saw another clear drop of fluid seep from the slit. Wanting to fully taste him, she took the head into her mouth.

"Oh, God, Kat!"

Her tongue slid around the head and underneath the sensitive ridge. She was sucking on him like a lollipop, like he was a treat to be savored. It was almost too much to handle.

Taking deep breaths and letting them go, Jace somehow held off, but he knew he wouldn't last nearly as long as he wanted, not this first time as he felt her lips surrounding his cock. The heat of her mouth and rasp of her tongue were driving him insane. She slowly engulfed his length as far as she could go, fitting all but about three inches inside.

Jace threaded his hands through her hair and his thumbs caressed her jaw "Relax your throat, baby. You can take it, just a little more."

Lord, did that sound too much like I was begging?

She did and slid down another inch. Jace had experienced plenty of blow jobs in his lifetime, but never one with so much enthusiasm. He'd always felt like they were only performing in the spirit of reciprocation. Kat seemed like she actually enjoyed what she was doing.

"That feels so good. Fuck, your mouth is hot."

She continued to suck him up and down, a soft, wet glide.

Normally, Jace would guide the woman into the rhythm he wanted, but Kat seemed to sense just what he needed and when. Jace felt his orgasm building when she increased her pace.

Kat brought him to the edge then backed off enough times that he groaned as the pleasure built to near unbearable levels. "Suck my cock, honey."

He opened his eyes to watch her. Her lips were wet and puffy, her eyes bright with pleasure when she caught his gaze. "You look so incredibly beautiful doing that. I'm going to come any minute now, baby. I want you to take all of me, Kat."

Suddenly, she grabbed his balls and gave them a gentle squeeze, and he was a goner. His orgasm came on so suddenly it surprised even him, and he cried out as he came down her throat. She took everything, never stopping once until he was completely drained. He put his hands over his eyes because he felt a small tear gather and begin to fall.

When he could breathe again, Jace opened his eyes and saw her sitting on the floor, looking very proud of herself. He immediately rolled to the side, gathered her in his arms, pulled her on top of him and kissed her.

The long, drugging kiss was meant to make her toes curl, and managed to make his not quite soft dick twitch with renewed interest. "You are incredible. I hope you know that. Have you done that with the other guys you dated?" He didn't know why he asked, but felt he had to know.

"No, you were my first. I rather enjoyed it. Do you think we could do that again sometime?"

"Oh...honey... We can do that any time you want. As long as I get to taste you at the same time."

It took a second for her to process that image, but once she did, Kat let a sparkling smile light her face and eyes. "I don't want to be presumptuous, but do you want to stay the night?"

"I would like nothing better. The thought of holding you all night long sounds like heaven."

They went upstairs and settled into Kat's king-sized bed. As she curled against him in sleep, he couldn't help but think, *This feels right*.

Then he started to worry about what would happen when he had to leave next Sunday. Jace didn't get much sleep that night.

Chapter Six

Kat woke up to find Jace gone. She wasn't sure how long ago he'd gotten up, but the cool sheets told her it had been a while. She heard some banging down in the kitchen and smiled.

"He's still here," she whispered.

She had never slept in a man's arms before, and found she really liked it. It felt so secure and warm.

Unfortunately, it was Thursday morning, and she had to get ready for work. As she got out of bed to head to the shower, she grabbed her robe from the foot of the bed. Jace had insisted she wear her usual silk camisole and pants set to sleep in, warning that if she were to lie next to him naked, he wouldn't be responsible for what might happen. Kat showered, dried her hair, and put on her professor armor for her eight thirty class, then walked down the stairs with her heels in her hand.

When she entered the kitchen, Jace was sitting at the table reading a paper. His mouth was a straight line, and his brow creased a little.

"What's wrong?"

He looked up. "Oh, nothing… Another bombing in Iraq."

"Oh, does that potentially affect your team? I mean, could they deploy you?"

He shrugged. "They could, but we're probably okay unless things go real south real quick or some other incident occurs."

From what Kat knew about SEALs, they were an offensive strike team. Usually they were involved in counterterrorism, enemy snatch and grab, hostage rescue, and those kinds of operation. She thought she'd read somewhere that the teams were divided into different world regions.

"What's your team number? Do you only go certain places?"

Jace looked up from the paper. "You really want to know?"

Kat nodded.

"All right. Grab a coffee and a bagel. I picked up some fresh after my workout this morning."

She did as suggested and sat in the chair with one leg tucked up beneath her.

"Thanks. I don't usually eat breakfast, but for some reason, I'm starving this morning."

This got a smile out of Jace as he watched her over the rim of his coffee cup.

"So teams?"

"Right. I'm a member of SEAL team twelve. As you know we're based out of Virginia, but we can be deployed anywhere in the world as needed. Some of the teams specialize in a certain region, but twelve is available wherever they need us."

"Are the six of you the whole team?"

Jace laughed. "Sorry, not laughing at you. Things would be a hell of a lot simpler if that were the case. An actual team consists of about three hundred individuals made up of officers, troops, and staff. The troops are broken up into platoons then squads. SEAL team twelve actually has six platoons, and there are twenty or so squads in each platoon."

"Wow. That's a lot more complicated than I thought. I've always heard that becoming a SEAL is one of the hardest Special Forces spots to earn. So what is your estimate of the percentage of enlisted and officers in the Navy that are part of the SEAL program?"

"Not sure really because there are some units where the exact number of men is classified, but I'd wager around three to four percent."

"Top of your class," she said with a grin.

"Hooyah!" he snapped.

Kat took the last sip of her coffee. "Thank you, but unfortunately I have to head over to campus now. Sorry I have to run out on you, but you're welcome to stay as long as you want."

"I have to meet the guys soon, but I'll lock up before I go." He frowned. "I'm going to be pretty busy the next couple days so I don't know if I'll be able to see you until Saturday."

"That's okay. You have fun, and I'll see you then." She grabbed her purse off the counter and headed for the door, pausing briefly when walking by the table. She wasn't sure if it would be okay to kiss him goodbye. Over the years in all the movies she'd seen and the romance novels she'd read, a farewell kiss was typically what lovers did the morning after, but were she and Jace official lovers? And even if they were, did he want a goodbye kiss or was that too…girly. Kat didn't want to be seen as some simpering maiden, but hell, she was really out of her depth here. She needed to do some more research. By all accounts girls and guys saw sex very differently. So maybe last night hadn't been such a big deal for the studly Navy Seal.

Jace stood. He took her hand, pulled her close and gave her a kiss. The kiss was slow, sweet, and by the end of it Kat was convinced that she needed to stop overanalyzing everything. Jace seemed to be a straight forward kind of man. If he said he was going to miss her over the next couple of days then he probably would. While she was still unsure of their status, Jace's tender goodbye did a lot to calm her anxiety about what last night meant to him.

* * * *

When Kat got to her office, real life took over and she waded through her lecture with professionalism despite the butterflies in her stomach every time she thought about Jace. When she had a break around the lunch hour, she decided to call Amy. If she was going to this formal wedding on Saturday, she needed some help in the wardrobe department. Maybe Amy was available to go shopping tomorrow night.

Picking up the phone, Kat dialed and waited for an answer. "Hey, Aim, how's it going?"

"Good, what are you up to?"

"Well, I kind of need a favor. Jace invited me to go to the wedding on Saturday, and he said it's a real formal affair. Would you be available to go shopping with me? I need to find a dress, and you know how hopeless I am with that stuff."

"Sure. When and where?"

"I was thinking tomorrow night after work. I can meet you at Plaza Fontenac around six."

"Wow. Fontenac! This must be some affair."

"If what Jace said is any indication, I think so. Apparently, the bride's family is some bigwigs in the city. I think I need to look around Saks and find something appropriate. Maybe they have something on sale that won't completely blow my budget."

"Okay, I'll meet you there, and don't worry. We'll find something that'll knock his socks off."

Kat smiled as she hung up the phone.

I want to knock more than his socks off.

The next two days flew by, and before she knew it, it was Saturday afternoon and time to get ready. The wedding ceremony was scheduled to begin at six o'clock in the evening. She'd found a fantastic dress on sale—a dark blue satin strapless cocktail dress with a matching long-sleeved bolero jacket to wear during the ceremony. Amazingly enough, the dress fit perfectly, which was very unusual with her petite frame. Kat even splurged on some strappy stilettos.

After she had left Amy, she'd gone to the mall closer to her house and bought some lingerie—silky stockings and a demi-bra, garter belt and thong set made of dark blue lace.

It felt decadent to wear such things, but they made her feel sexy and desirable. Since being with Jace, she was no longer afraid to show that side of herself. With a little advice from the makeup consultant, she'd learned how to make her green eyes pop, and the lipstick she'd bought made her lips plump and glistening. Slipping on the dress and shoes, she took a look in the mirror and was surprised by the reflection facing her. The woman staring back at her looked glamorous, sophisticated and confident. Kat had always thought of herself as simple and unassuming. She knew she could dress well professionally, but always felt out of place when it came to fashion for social events.

All right, ready or not, here I come.

* * * *

Jace saw Kat's car pull into the parking lot at the ceremony location and walked over to greet her. As he pulled open her door, he heard a little gasp.

"Wow! You look incredible in that uniform," Kat said in a breathy voice.

He smiled. "Thank you."

Kat gracefully rose from the low seat of her car, taking his outstretched hand for support. They stood silently for a minute as Jace took in the beauty before him. Then he leaned over and lightly kissed her on the cheek.

He rested his lips against her ear and whispered, "You're stunning." Actually, she looked more than stunning. When Jace had opened the door, his heart had done a little jump.

He escorted her into the chapel by the back entrance so she could greet the guys. Ever since the baseball game, she had become friendly with Cory, Eric, Justin and Kurt. She was still reserved with Collin and Peter, but Jace never heard any words of hostility between them.

Music played softly as ushers escorted people to their seats. Since it was an evening ceremony, candles flickered throughout. A circular, iron chandelier softly glowed overhead, and flowers graced the pews in black iron sconces. The walls and floors were made of stone, and dark wooden arches crossed the ceiling of the chapel. Overall, the place had a very intimate feel to it even though it easily held a hundred people.

Jace was just about to show Kat to a seat when one of the bridesmaids rushed in. "We have a little crisis that's going to delay us, but don't worry. We'll sort it out."

Jace looked over at her and asked, "What's wrong? Anything we can do?"

"Not unless you can sing classical arias. The vocalist called about a half an hour ago. She was in a car accident and won't be able to make it."

"Sorry, out of luck here." He turned to everyone else with the same question. Kat kind of looked like she was going to say something, but then seemed to decide not to. Jace saw Collin and Peter glance at her then back at each other.

Collin spoke up. "Kat used to sing. She was always in one performance or another at school. Usually it was some foreign language thing."

Looking at her, Jace asked, "Is that true? Can you sing?"

Kat looked nervous but replied, "Yes, I've performed with various groups since middle school. I've never done a lot of solo stuff, though, just a friend's wedding or two."

"Well, that's perfect! Will you help them out?"

"I don't want to disappoint the bride and groom. This is their big day. I'm sure they would rather listen to beautiful instrumentals than a croaking last-minute singer."

Jace looked over at Cory. "It's your call, man."

Cory walked up to Kat. Pulling her aside, he softly said, "Jenny has talked about the music choices for months. She picked each piece out after hours of listening to recordings. I know she's probably heartbroken right now. It doesn't have to be perfect, but anything you can do would be really appreciated."

She looked uncertain for another second, then lifted her

head and straightened her shoulders. "Okay... Lead me to the loft."

* * * *

Kat looked at the sheet music chosen for the ceremony and noticed with gratitude that she knew all the pieces. It had been a while, but she figured she could handle them. It had been about a year since she'd done any real singing, but like Cory said, this was a last-minute thing. They weren't expecting a Carnegie Hall-worthy performance. The first vocal piece was Bach's *Ave Maria* about halfway through the ceremony, so she had time to warm up and refresh her memory.

Kat was introduced to the organist, who was very accommodating, saying he would just follow her with whatever happened. They had a string quartet also playing, and some horns for the processional and recessional pieces. As the service began, she kept looking at Jace. He was so gorgeous in his uniform, strong and standing tall. At one point she saw him glance up at her and wink, and her heart did a little flutter. When it came time to do the first piece, Kat stepped up to the balustrade and suddenly felt very calm.

Closing her eyes, she started singing. Everything she had went into the performance. As she reached a crescendo, her voice soared into the rafters. During the piece, Kat was completely immersed in the song. The congregation disappeared, and her fear of judgment had no place there.

After the song ended, she looked down at the front of the church and was shocked to see the bridal couple and all the attendants staring at her. She leaned over to the organist and whispered, "Was it that bad?"

He looked startled by the question, put a hand against his chest. "It was magical. I think they're just in a little bit of shock, considering the last-minute substitution."

After the first piece, everything else was easy as Kat

settled into the routine of performance that she had known for so many years.

Jace stood in the back of the church waiting for Kat to come down from the loft. He was completely stunned by her performance. He had never heard someone sing with that much feeling. Her voice was warm when she sang the low notes, but was clear as a bell when it came time to hit the high ones. He was quickly finding out that she was a very complex person, with all kinds of hidden talents.

Deciding he'd waited long enough, he started walking toward the enclosed stone spiral staircase leading to the loft. As he reached the fourth step, Kat started walking down. He stopped so that he could watch her approach.

He held out his hand and guided her down the rest of the stairs then led her down a dark corridor. Even here, there were still candles flickering along the stone walls.

About halfway down, he pulled her into his chest and held tight. "How could you sing like that and never mention it? You sounded like an angel. I stood up there and couldn't breathe as I listened to you."

Kat mumbled, "Thank you. I hope the bride and groom liked it as much as you."

Then he leaned down and kissed her. At first, the kiss was soft and gentle since he didn't want to mess up her makeup. But, as with every time their lips touched, heat flared and he was consumed with the urge to devour her. He pushed her into the wall, lifted his hands to enclose her face and swept inside her mouth, holding nothing back. Kat put her arms around his neck and threaded her fingers through his hair.

After several minutes, someone coughed at the entrance to the hallway. Jace looked up and saw Collin.

"Sorry, guys, but we need Jace for the photos. If you can tear yourselves away from each other for a few minutes, we can get this over with and find our way to the party."

They smiled at each other as they worked to get their

breath back, then Jace turned them around so his back was to Collin and quickly adjusted himself.

Kat smiled. "Go on. I'll meet you at the reception."

Chapter Seven

When Kat got to the reception location, it was immediately apparent that this wedding was a very fancy affair. She saw women wearing diamonds and formal gowns and men in classic-cut tuxedos. After leaving the chapel she'd removed her jacket and placed a rhinestone circular necklace around her neck.

My bling may be fake, but at least I still have some glitz and glam.

She located the bar, then walked over to order a glass of wine to calm her nerves a little bit. Turning around, she spotted Jace, Collin and Peter heading in her direction. They all looked a little like cats that ate the canaries.

Kat became immediately suspicious. "What are you up to?"

They all smiled.

"Nothing... Why?" Jace asked.

"Because you all look mighty proud about something, and I'm thinking you're either about to commit or have recently committed a very nefarious act."

Peter chuckled. "The whole bridal party just decorated the honeymoon suite. I would love to see their faces when they open that door."

She sternly looked at them. "You didn't do anything bad, did you?"

Collin answered, "Who, us? Never!"

Looking over to Jace, she caught the glint in his eye. He gave a slight shake of his head to say that all was okay. Her heart had started to race when she saw Jace's face light up. She'd never had a man look at her openly with affection.

Another crack formed in the protective barrier around her heart. Jace took her hand and guided her into the ballroom.

They found their table, and Kat was surprised when Jace pulled out her chair. She looked around at the other guests sharing the table and recognized that all the men held a certain kind of bearing that Kat had come to associate with military men. She smiled at them and the women, but was too nervous to introduce herself. The sound of a microphone being activated filled the room and the MC announced the bride and groom. The entire room erupted in cheers and clapping. Cory and Jenny moved onto the dance floor, and Kat smiled at the love so evident on their faces as they shared their first dance.

Jace's arm came around her waist and he pulled her back into his chest as they watched the couple dancing.

"Will you dance with me later?" he asked.

She tilted her head back over her shoulder and she saw the warmth and light in his eyes. "Yes, I'd love to."

Kat took a sip of her wine and gave a polite smile to the woman sitting across the table from her, who kept staring.

"I'm sorry," she said. "I don't mean to be rude, but you look really familiar to me. Are you a local celebrity?"

She laughed softly. "Not hardly. I'm a professor of anthropology at Washington University."

Jace placed his hand on top of Kat's. "And an incredibly talented singer, as we all heard earlier."

"That was you?" the woman's companion exclaimed.

Kat flushed and gave a small nod.

"You have a very special talent, young lady. Do you perform elsewhere? Maybe that's why my wife recognizes you. We've always been eager patrons of the arts."

"I used to perform, but it's been some time. Nowadays my shower is the most consistent audience. Today was a last-minute thing. Cory and Jenny's original vocalist had an emergency and couldn't make it."

Jace kept his hand on her knee and caressed her thigh.

"That's a true shame. You should reconsider. I'm a

supporter of the city chamber chorus, and would be happy to introduce you to the director if you want."

Kat smiled. It was nice to hear such profuse compliments, but she really didn't have time to give one hundred percent to a performance group anymore. That's why she'd quit in the first place. "Thank you. I'll think about it." She turned to Jace and leaned closer to his ear. "I need to use the Ladies room." She turned to the remaining guests seated at the table. "Please excuse me."

While it was true that she needed the restroom, more importantly she needed some fresh air. Jace's hand caressing her leg had sent her blood boiling to the point where she feared having a heatstroke caused by his touch.

Kat opened the door to the powder room and immediately came face to face with another ghost from her past. Standing in front of the mirror applying lipstick stood Serena Johnson. Kat walked past the woman, averting her face so as not to be recognized, but stopped and stiffened when the voice of her childhood nightmares said, "Hey, I know you, don't I?"

Kat decided to just get it over with and return to Jace at the table for dancing. "Yes, I believe so. Serena, right? I think we went to school together long ago."

After a brief pause, a predatory flash lit Serena's eyes. "That's it! Are you a friend of the couple? Oh, silly me. You must be. I saw you with Jace Hudson earlier. He's quite a catch."

"Yes, Jace and I met recently." Kat wanted to let Serena know that she wasn't the same helpless, hopeless girl she'd been back in school so she added, "I was also the vocalist at the ceremony earlier."

"Oh, that was you? It was a very cute performance. I'm sure the kids loved it."

She can only hurt me if I let her.

Not showing a hint of emotion on her face, Kat said, "Please excuse me for a moment."

"Oh, sure, sorry, go ahead. I'll wait here till you're done."

Oh, joy.

She walked into the restroom, and taking a very deep breath, calmed her fractured nerves. After using the facilities, she looked up from washing her hands to see Serena still there. She looked as beautiful as ever, and Kat recognized the self-confidence in Serena's expression. The woman knew she was beautiful and wasn't afraid to use whatever tools existed in her arsenal to get what she wanted.

Serena's gown was a beaded emerald sheath with a plunging neckline and thin straps at her shoulders. She exuded superiority.

Serena gave Kat a long look then said, "You know, Jace really is a catch. How do you plan on holding onto him?"

"Excuse me?"

She smirked and snidely said, "Oh, come on, *Kat*. You can't fool me. I've known you for too long. You may look a little different, but you're still the same feeble-minded nobody."

Kat stared at her, incredulous that she would assume she knew her after not associating with each other for twelve years. Standing her ground, she replied, "Correction—you used to know me. I am not the same person I was."

Serena gave her a once-over, one side of her perfectly-lined lips curling in derision, and walked right into Kat's face. "You will never be good enough for Jace to take seriously. He's just using you for a little fun. I know because he and I are *very* close, if you know what I mean."

Unwittingly, Kat felt tears gather in her eyes. "Why are you acting like this?"

"Honey, I'm just trying to protect your sensitive little feelings. You see, men like Jace are drawn to real women, ones who know how to give the ultimate pleasure, not some innocent schoolgirl playing dress-up."

Kat stood transfixed. *Is she right? Is Jace using me? I know I'm nothing special... And he represents the United States as a hero to this country. What was I thinking? Did I actually start to believe that Jace wanted a relationship with me? He must be really enjoying himself. This is his vacation, and I willingly became a pleasant diversion, a chintzy novelty that appeared to be exactly what he wanted, but when he gets home, I'll be thrown in a drawer and forgotten as he's once again surrounded by women like Serena.*

Serena stood there with victory in her cruel smile. "I can see you realize now how hopeless your situation is if you continue acting the way you are. It would probably be better if you just leave now. I'm sure he'll figure it out and not make a scene to embarrass you further." She walked out of the door.

Standing there for another minute, Kat tried to pull herself together. Slowly, she left the powder room.

I have to get out of here right now!

* * * *

Jace stood in the foyer trying to figure out if Kat was still in the restroom. Throughout the meal he'd presented his best poker face, but had constantly felt the hairs on the back of his neck stirring while the sensation of malevolence permeated his skin. She had been in there for a long time, but then again, she was a girl, and they tended to do stuff like that.

Jace was in the process of scanning the area outside the ballroom when Admiral Anderson, under whom Jace had served when he first entered the Navy, walked up to him.

"Your date tonight is quite beautiful, son, and very talented from what I heard at the service earlier. How long have you been together?"

Jace maintained an air of casualness despite the lingering unease that permeated the atmosphere. He turned to the admiral. "Only a few days, sir. We met here in town, and I asked her to accompany me this evening."

"Really? You seem very comfortable together. She's an engaging dinner companion as well, a rare find. Make sure you hold onto her."

"Yes, sir. I plan to." Just then he caught Peter's gaze over near the bar and indicated the need to talk as soon as the opportunity arose. He was unable to tell if the sensation was aimed at him or Kat, but he wasn't going to take any chances. Then he saw her walking toward him and knew right away something was very wrong.

He rushed toward her. "Are you okay?" He tried to take Kat's hand, but she stepped away from him. It hurt more than he'd expected.

Kat shook her head. "No, I think I should really go home now."

The sight of tears gathering in her eyes made him put aside any consequences of his actions. He grabbed her by the hand and walked into a corner of the room. "What's going on? Are you sick? Are you hurt?"

Kat slowly pulled her hand out of Jace's grip. "No, I'm fine."

He started to get angry. Something was obviously wrong. He needed to know if there was any relation to the threat he had felt inside the banquet room. "Kat, talk to me. What happened? You were fine when you left the table, and now you look like someone punched you in the gut."

Kat's green eyes were filled with sadness. They were the same eyes he'd seen filled with desire, that laughed, that mirrored her courageous soul.

"I ran into someone I used to know a very long time ago, and we talked. I heard some things that make sense, things about you and me that I had ignored because I was having a good time. But I need to face reality, and it's better to do so now, before things go any further between us."

Jace looked at her like she was speaking in tongues. In a harsh whisper, he asked, "What are you talking about?"

"Jace... I have had such a wonderful time with you this week. You have taught me not to fear my own desires and how to be true to myself. But you and I could never have a true relationship, and I had started to dream that was possible. This person was kind enough to remind me who

I really am. You are a national hero, and so far out of my league that it would take the space shuttle for someone like me to reach your orbit."

He started to shake his head, but she stopped him with a hand on his cheek and tears in her eyes. "Don't argue. If you take a step back and really look at the two of us, you'll see I'm right. You know, and your teammates all know it too. I'm sure Collin and Peter will talk to you and convince you this is for the best."

For a man who only days ago was convinced he didn't need anything other than his gun, his team and his own abilities, watching Kat walk away from him shattered something deep inside. He wanted to catch her and hold her here with him, but astonishment cemented his feet to the floor.

After several steps, Kat turned around and said, "The memories of this week are good ones, ones I will cherish for a long time to come. Our time together will be a very special piece in the puzzle of my life. Thank you."

And like that, she was gone.

Jace stood there with his mouth hanging open for a good two minutes before he could move to run after her. He leaped into action, running for the doors. Grabbing the valet parking attendant, he yelled, "Where is she?"

"Who, sir?"

"The woman in the blue dress!"

"She asked for her keys and wanted to walk to her car. I showed her where it was parked, and she left."

"Where was her car?"

The valet pointed down the lot. "About four rows down, center space."

Jace ran in that direction. When he got to the row and saw an empty space right in the middle, he knew he was too late. He considered leaving right away to go find her, sure she was heading home, but first he needed to find out exactly what had happened to set her off like that.

He walked back into the lobby and saw Collin heading in

his direction.

"There you are. Pete wanted to talk to you and said something about wanting to talk to Kat too," Collin said.

Jace grabbed Collin by the material at his chest and, snarling in his face, said, "What the hell did you say to her?"

Collin looked stunned for a second before he replied, "What are you talking about? I haven't talked to her since before dinner. What's going on?"

His shoulders fell and he let go of Collin's jacket.

"Kat… She…left me."

"*What?*"

"She came down the hall after using the restroom and said that someone talked to her. She started saying all this stuff about not being good enough for me, and it was better if she left now before things went any further between us."

Collin looked furious. "Who did she talk to? Who would have the balls to say something like that to her? I know that's not something she came up with on her own."

"She said that if I talked to you and Peter, you would explain things to me and make me see that she was right. What did she mean by that?"

Collin held up his hands. "I don't know, honest." He started to pace in a tight line. "The only thing that would remotely seem sensible is if she was thinking about what we used to say to her all those years ago," he mumbled. "But that is so far out in left field. I mean, why now after all the time we've spent together this week?" He looked up at Jace. "I thought she'd moved past it. I thought we were becoming friends."

Jace sighed. "I think it's time I hear exactly what did happen between the three of you. No more off-handed remarks or brushed-off explanations. Tell me everything."

Collin looked directly at him and said, "Okay, it should come out in the open sooner rather than later."

They walked over to a group of chairs and sat down. "Kat came to our school in the first grade. She was quiet, unassuming, and yes, a little on the round side. We, her classmates, started ripping into her almost immediately. It came from both sides. I know what the boys used to do, but I also know the girls gave her a hard time. We used to tell her she was a nobody, that she was fat and would never make any friends.

"She basically kept to herself and read a lot. So we started calling her teacher's pet. At recess, she would either sit alone in the playground or quietly amuse herself. If she did try to join any games, we would make sure she was the last person picked for a team, then never actually make an effort to include her.

"As the years went by and we found out she had a crush on someone, we would play nasty tricks on her to make her think he liked her too. High school was no better. The guys would blackmail her into writing their papers. The girls would ridicule her clothes.

"She never dated anyone, and everybody in our class knew it. In fact, they made it a point to make sure she knew that they knew it. What always amazed me was that despite the way we treated her, she always had a shy smile on her face and said hello if she passed you in the hallway."

After a brief pause, Collin looked up at Jace. He knew his eyes were probably ice-cold. Anger and even, at this moment, hatred steamed up inside him for the way Kat had been treated.

"Jace, I swear to you, I am truly sorry for what I did to her back then. I know I can never take back those actions. When I saw her with you that first night, I felt ashamed of myself for the first time in many years. This week Kat was gracious enough to let me see the real her, and she's an incredible person. She's warm, sharp as a tack and funny.

"I've treated her with nothing but respect this week and I will continue to do so." He paused. "Tell me something. Are you upset because she walked out before you could, or do you really care about her and want her back?"

Collin had been his friend for many years. They were teammates. They had seen serious action and lived through more harrowing experiences than two people should have to in their lifetime. He knew him better than most of the other guys.

Jace bent his head, closed his eyes, and clasped his hands together between his knees. After a few seconds, he looked up at Collin and decided to be honest. "When she walked away, I swear part of my chest felt like it was being ripped out."

Collin just looked at Jace—right in the eyes—like he was trying to see if he was telling the truth.

"Okay… We need to find out exactly what happened, if we're to have any chance of understanding why she left." He stood. "Let's go do what we do best."

Chapter Eight

They headed back into the ballroom and started scouting for possible suspects. Kat had said that she didn't know most of the people there tonight, so Jace couldn't figure it out. Then he saw Serena slithering her way toward him and grimaced. She had a very self-satisfied look on her face.

He and Serena had had a brief thing a few years ago, but he'd broken it off because the woman was cold as ice everywhere except in the bedroom. He was actually surprised to see her there, since he'd thought she was camping out in DC these days.

Serena walked up to Jace and slid her arms around his neck. "Hey, Jace. Long time no see," she cooed. "You want to go get a drink…or something?"

He removed her arms from around his neck and took a step back. "Not really. I have better things to do. What are you doing here, Serena?"

"I came with Senator Kelly. He's such a sweet old man. I think he's related to the bride's family somehow. To tell you the truth, I think he's a little hung up on me, but we both know what I really want."

"Oh, yeah, what's that?"

"Jace, don't tease me. You know I like real men. You remember how we used to burn up the sheets?" Then, in a pouting little voice, she added, "Or have you forgotten all about little me?"

Jace looked at her and said, "Frankly, there wasn't much to forget. Now, if you'll excuse me, I need to find someone."

She suddenly looked angry. "Fine, when you're done training the little schoolgirl, make sure you come looking for a real woman to satisfy you," she spat and started to walk away.

Jace grabbed her arm rather roughly. "What do you know about Kat?"

"She and I had a wonderful little chat earlier. You see, she and I are old friends. I just thought I'd better warn her. I would hate to see such a sweet little thing get her heart broken when you decide you've had your fill."

She slithered back to rest against his chest. "You know, Jace... A girl like her just isn't cut out to move in the same circles as we do. You're much better sticking with your own people, important people. Leave the innocents to little boys."

Jace shoved Serena back.

Standing right behind her was Collin, who grabbed her by the arms and said, "You know, Serena, if you weren't such a selfish, cold-hearted bitch, you might realize that when two people belong together, it doesn't matter where they come from or what they do in life. Now, I suggest you make your excuses to the senator, because on behalf of the bride and groom, you are no longer welcome here. The gentleman behind me will escort you out."

Jace watched as Serena was escorted from the room. Turning back to Collin, he asked, "How much of that did you hear?"

"Enough to figure out what was going on. Kat's actions now make a lot more sense. Serena also went to our school and was one of the girls I was telling you about."

After processing that revelation, Jace said, "What I don't understand is why would Kat believe anything she said if she knew what Serena was capable of?"

Peter walked up to Jace and Collin. "Do you remember when we recovered that POW in North Korea last year? He had been psychologically tortured for several years and toward the end he'd started doing and believing anything those bastards told him just to make them stop. Well, after twelve years of snide comments and sneaky tricks, on a child's mind no less, how do you think Kat survived? I've noticed that when you're alone together, she's vibrant and fun, but any time we join you, she closes up. I can still see that little girl in her eyes. She hides it well, but I think that part of her will always be searching for acceptance, wondering if she's good enough."

Jace felt coldness in his chest when he thought about what Kat had gone through all those years ago. Then a warming sense of pride filled him when he thought of the incredible woman she had become. She may perceive herself as weak, but he knew there had to be a core of steel under that soft skin. He had to find her. He had to have her.

Making his excuses to Collin and Peter, Jace headed toward Cory and his new wife. "I'm really sorry, but I have to leave."

Cory looked up at Jace and said, "We know. Go find her."

Jenny gave Jace a quick hug. "And tell her that we are forever grateful for her incredible gift this evening. We'll never forget how her performance made our wedding so much more personal and memorable."

Jace grabbed a cab outside and gave the driver Kat's address. The whole drive he tried to formulate a strategy for getting her to believe that despite what Serena had told her, they belonged together. He knew it would be possible to distract her with his physical presence, but really didn't want to push her that way. The best he could come up with was getting on his knees and begging her to give them a chance. How could they ever know what could exist between them if she didn't want to try?

When the cab pulled up to her house, he looked into the living room through the wide window facing the street. She had the lights turned off, but something was casting a flickering light through the room.

* * * *

When Kat arrived home, she immediately went into her

bedroom to take off the dress. It made her feel like a fraud and she could no longer stand the feel of it on her skin. Not having the energy for anything else, she'd left the lingerie on and covered herself with a black silk robe.

Coming down from the stress had left her cold despite the warm temperatures outside, so she started a fire. Needing to soothe her soul a bit, she grabbed her desired Enigma CD and turned it to her favorite track. Of course the music made her think of Jace and their car ride home the other night. She turned up the stereo to drown out her thoughts and went to get a glass of wine. When she came back into the living room, pounding at the front door startled her.

Who could be standing out there this time of night? She cautiously opened it just a crack and was shocked to see Jace on her front porch.

He snapped his head up as soon as she opened the door and put his hand out, grabbing the edge of the door to stop her from closing it again. "Please, Kat, let me come in and talk to you."

She couldn't ignore the pleading look in his eyes. Knowing that whatever he was going to say would probably hurt, she reluctantly agreed. "Okay, come in."

Suddenly, she found herself engulfed in his arms and pulled tight to his body. He spoke hoarsely, "Don't ever leave me like that again. If we need to talk about something, we'll talk it out, not make comments like that then walk away." He gentled his touch. "I found out who spoke to you, and I want you to know that under no circumstances would I ever consider anything that bitch said to you to be truth.

"If we are going to be honest with each other, it's really me who isn't deserving of you. I've hardly been a saint when it comes to my personal life, and my job requires me to do things most would consider abhorrent. Kat, I don't want to lie to you, ever. I don't know what will happen next week when I have to go back on duty, but for the time we have left, please give us a chance. Let's see where this thing between us goes."

Kat turned away from him and went to lower the music's volume, taking the moment to think since she could hardly do that in his arms. She knew that if they continued on this path, they would end up in bed together.

Do I want to give that part of myself to someone who will be leaving in a week's time? Even if we somehow managed to make a long-distance relationship work, he could be sent on some mission and be killed. I would never know. Is it worth the risk?

She decided to take a page from Amy's book and live her life to the fullest. How many times had her friend said to her, 'If you never take risks, you never gain the rewards'?

Kat turned to face him, and with a tentative smile said, "Okay."

Jace moved so quickly, it appeared like a blur. Grabbing Kat, he crushed his mouth against hers, driving his tongue inside to stake his claim. She ran her hands up his brilliant white jacket. It was a high-collared tunic with gold engraved buttons. She'd come to the conclusion over the evening that all those clichés about men in uniform were absolutely true.

He had loosened the collar at some point, and Kat slid her hands around his neck. Seeing him in this uniform with ribbons and badges, obvious signs indicating his heroism and service to their country, really brought home to Kat just what an incredible man he was. Even more incredible, he seemed to want to be with her. In fact, if what Kat was feeling was any indication, he wanted to be with her right now.

Jace slowly walked her over toward the fireplace, still placing soft kisses on her face, gentle nips at her lips, ears and neck. Grabbing some pillows and a blanket off the sofa, he spread them on the floor.

He stopped long enough to pull back slightly, looked at her and asked, "Are you sure you want this? I don't want you to feel any pressure if you're not ready."

In an answer to his question, Kat took a step back and slowly untied the belt at her waist. The robe parted enough for Jace to catch a glance of what lay beneath. Then the covering was gone, the inky black pooling around her feet.

He sucked in a breath as his gaze traveled from the tips of her toes all the way up until their eyes met once again. He slowly started to undo the buttons of his jacket, fumbling with the gold metal as his hands shook.

Kat stepped toward him again and helped him get the last two. She slid her hands inside, running them up his chest as she pushed the jacket from his shoulders. Not wanting to ruin it, she set it aside very deliberately on the sofa.

Jace walked up behind her and pulled her into his chest. "You are so beautiful, do you know that?" He ran his hands up her torso to cup her breasts. "So soft in all the right places, built to give and receive pleasure."

Kat's knees went weak.

Leading her back over to the blanket and pillows on the floor, he kissed her deeply, softly.

Kat's hands fluttered down to the closure of his pants and started to unfasten them. As they slid down his legs, she again recognized the strength of his body. Standing there in a white T-shirt and boxer briefs, he looked incredible.

She stood in front of him in nothing but lace and silk. Jace picked her up in his arms, then lay her down on the blanket. This was probably the sexist moment of her life, but what Kat really wanted was to feel all her skin against his. She sighed when he unclasped her bra and removed the lacy material. Next, he unfastened her garter and slowly rolled down her stockings.

Kat reached down and lifted Jace's T-shirt over his head, but when she grabbed for his shorts, he stopped her.

"Not yet... I want to feel you first."

He laid soft kisses and gentle nipping bites on her breasts, and his tongue soothed where his teeth abraded her soft skin. He touched her everywhere, running his hands down her legs to cup her behind her knee. Placing kisses on the top of her knee, he massaged her calf. Going down further, he actually took one of her toes and sucked it into his mouth.

Normally, Kat would have thought that kind of gross, but she felt pleasure pull all the way up her spine. He paid the same amount of attention to her other leg. Kat was panting, desperate for more, starting to ache for that peak she knew would eventually come. Kat lifted her hips in invitation, and Jace slowly slid her panties down her legs.

He moved back up her body and kissed her deeply. The weight of him against her sensitive length felt sublime. He supported himself on one forearm as his other hand caressed her breasts, lightly pinching her nipples, all the while continuing to kiss her deeply. He ground his erection into the juncture of her legs.

"Kat, I want you to feel nothing but pleasure tonight, but I know there will be a brief amount of pain. I'm sorry I have to hurt you, sweetheart."

"It's okay. I know you'll be gentle with me."

Jace wanted to prolong this first experience for her as much as possible, so he slowly slid one hand to her center. Feeling the silky, bare skin and dewy moisture was just about his undoing. "Kat, have you always shaven yourself?"

She nodded with a slight blush. "It was my little secret, made me feel sexy. Plus, I liked how it felt when I touched myself."

Hearing this, Jace just about choked.

Kat laughed softly. "You should see your face. Just because I've never done it with a guy doesn't mean I don't know how to make myself feel good."

This made Jace groan and rest his forehead against hers. "You're going to be the death of me. You know that?"

He threaded his fingers through her slickness, then slid one finger into her depths. Hot skin grasped him as Kat closed her eyes and moaned. Slowly building a rhythm, he added a second finger. Wanting to stretch and prepare her as best he could to minimize any discomfort, he was so focused on his task that he was startled when he felt her shudder and moisture pool in his hand.

Jace leaned back. Unable to wait another second, he stood, removed his shorts and pulled his wallet out of his pants pocket. Kat lay there and unabashedly watched as he rolled on the condom.

Coming back down on top of her, Jace took her face in his hands. "I want you to watch me when I take you. I want to see your eyes." He pushed two small pillows under her hips so she was at the right angle to go deeper and allow her to feel every inch of him as he slid home. Jace grasped his shaft and fit the head of his cock at the small, wet opening. With sweat beading on his forehead, he pushed the head in. Taking a moment to calm the need raging inside him to fill her completely, he looked into Kat's eyes.

She began lifting her hips for more, and Jace slid in a little further.

God almighty, she is tight and hot, feels like a satin glove gripping my cock.

Fuck. She was too tight. He was going to hurt her. He had to stop. Rocking gently in and out helped build more moisture to ease his way. When he reached the barrier, he stopped. He started circling his hips and went back to languidly moving in and out.

When Jace looked down at Kat, her eyes were closed and her hands gripped his shoulders.

She pleaded with him. "Jace... Please..."

Without stopping his gentle movements, he let out a low growl. "Open your eyes, Kat. Look at me."

As she did, he finally thrust home. Kat cried out, and although he knew she felt some pain, her cry was one of pleasure. When he reached as far and deep as he could, Jace stopped and held himself still. Giving her time to adjust to his size, he felt her muscles slowly start to relax from the unfamiliar invasion. Jace had never felt anything as perfect as Kat gripping him inside her body. He wanted to stay that way, buried as deep as possible, forever, but his body was begging him to start moving.

Kat started to squirm.

"Oh...wait... Baby, don't move... Just... Give me a minute."

When he started to thrust in and out, the feeling of Kat's inner muscles massaging him made him cry out. Never had Jace felt something so absolute. A desperate part of him wished the condom wasn't in the way of feeling her slick channel.

Each time Kat arched her hips, Jace went deeper. Jace slowed down his movements. Bending down, he suckled Kat's nipples. Her moan was music to his ears. He reached between them and found her clit. He stroked and rubbed it between his fingers. He could tell she was getting closer. The flutters were beginning to ripple down his cock as he continued to thrust.

"Oh...God... Jace, I feel like I'm going to explode."

"Don't fight it. Just let the pleasure take over. I want you to come for me. I want to feel you explode around my cock."

He felt the seed building in his balls, desperate for release. He pulled almost all the way out then thrust strongly, feeling her swollen tissue rasp down every inch. Kat's cries were getting louder, and her hands were gripping his back as her hips instinctively rose to meet his.

Changing his rhythm, he began to drive quick, hard thrusts high up inside her. He grabbed Kat's hips and with four more plunges, he groaned, "Now! Now, Kat!"

He vaguely heard her shout out her release but definitely felt her tighten around him in the strongest contractions he'd ever felt, almost bruising in their intensity. The waves continued endlessly, the sensation milking his cock till there was nothing left. Finally, he collapsed and pulled her close.

He didn't want to let her go, ever. He knew that now. Unfortunately, he had to take care of the condom. So, gently disconnecting them, he went to the first-floor washroom to dispose of it. He dampened the hand towel Kat kept in there with warm water and went back to Kat to apply the soothing moisture.

She sighed as he lifted her in his arms and carried her

upstairs. The fire had long since gone out, and he couldn't recall when the music had stopped. Placing her gently under the covers, he went around the other side of the bed and slipped in, gathering her close, spoon-fashion. With his chin resting on the top of her head, Jace breathed in the scent of her shampoo and slid into sleep.

* * * *

Jace awoke some time later to the feeling of soft lips encircling the head of his cock. His eyes flew open and he partially sat up, looking down his chest and stomach to see Kat slowly sliding him down her throat. He fell back on the pillows with a loud groan.

"God, that feels good. But if you keep that up, I'm going to want to come inside you again, and I don't want to hurt you. Are you too sore?"

Kat sat up and crawled on top of Jace's body. "No, I feel wonderful. Nothing would be better than to have you inside me again."

"What about a condom? I don't have another one and I want to make sure you're protected. I have a clean bill of health—don't worry on that end—I just don't want to risk getting you pregnant... Yet."

That word 'yet' hung in the air, and he saw Kat tremble. Was it with excitement, fear, or simply arousal?

"I bought some a few days ago. They're in the bedside table. I wanted to be prepared in case we got this far."

"I was pretty rough on you earlier. Are you positive you're okay?"

Kat reached into the drawer, opened the foil pack, then slid the condom down his shaft. "You know, Jace, I may have been a virgin, but in my mind that was more of a physical technicality than a defining sense of self. I'm thirty years old with the desires of a grown woman, not some simpering maiden. I feel as though our time together has finally given me the courage to reveal my true colors.

Everyone is innocent at some point in their lives. Just as everyone has someone who teaches them about the pleasure that can be found by sharing your body with another. So how about it? Will you teach me to fly?"

He looked at the amazing woman in his arms. "It'll be *our* pleasure. Come up here and I'll teach you a new trick right now." Jace lifted her up and slowly impaled her on his cock. Teaching her how to move, he gripped her hips and met every slide down with an upward thrust of his own, and they flew as high as the heavens all night long in each other's arms.

Chapter Nine

Kat slowly opened her eyes to find a rising sun outside her bedroom window then rolled over to discover what true beauty looked like at the sight of Jace still sound asleep in her bed. They'd only fallen asleep for the last time about three hours ago. Even though her body was still tired, her mind spun a million miles a minute. She decided to take this opportunity to study Jace without his constant awareness of what was happening around him.

When some men slept, they looked very peaceful. She had seen this with family and friends over the years, but when Jace slept, his features never completely relaxed. His brows remained slightly furrowed, and his jaw still looked like granite. Since the sheet was pulled down to his waist, she inspected his impressive chest again. She noticed for the first time in the morning light that it wasn't as perfect as it had first appeared. There were small scars in numerous places, but they only served to enhance his magnetism.

Jace must have subconsciously sensed her scrutiny, because he turned over, revealing to Kat more evidence of his hard lifestyle. In fact, it looked like there might be two healed-over bullet holes — one in the left shoulder, and one in the center of his back, frighteningly close to his spine. She was so wrapped up in her inspection that she started when she heard his voice.

"You know if you stare hard enough you can make your eyes go cross."

Kat shook her head and smiled. "If my eyes do go cross, it'll be from pleasure so extreme I can't control my body any longer."

Rolling back over, Jace smiled. "Now, that is a sight I definitely want to see."

Kat tucked the sheet around her body. Maybe it was silly to be modest after the night they had shared, but she wasn't ready to flaunt her naked body. She knew she'd made the right decision. Kat had never felt the complete closeness to another person as she did with Jace. Giving up her virginity to him had been very special, and a memory she would treasure for the rest of her life, regardless of what happened to them.

She stared up at the ceiling, enjoying the quiet, and grateful that she didn't feel the need to fill the space with nervous chatter. Suddenly, Jace's face loomed above her and he bent to kiss her. She was afraid she had horrible morning breath, but he didn't seem to care. In fact, when she tried to squirm away, he grabbed her by the waist and pulled her closer to his body, deepening the kiss.

After several mindless minutes, he pulled back. "Don't ever be afraid to touch me or kiss me. It doesn't matter to me if you've eaten a dozen onions or are covered in mud from your head to your feet. I will touch you and kiss you every chance I get, regardless of what we're doing. Understood?"

Kat was mildly amused, picturing various scenarios of stooge-like proportions, but simply responded with, "Yes. I need to get up and shower, then I imagine you'd like some breakfast."

"You're right on the breakfast part, but I think I'd like a shower first as well." A wicked gleam lit his eyes. "Do you want to share one?"

As tempting as that sounded, Kat wasn't sure her body could handle another round just then. Her heart was definitely willing, but she felt a little sore from last night's exertions. "I'm not sure that would be a good idea. If we shower together, I don't think I'll be able to keep my hands off you, and as much as I want to, I don't think my body could respond with the same passion."

"I'm such an ass, sorry." He threaded his fingers through

her hair. "You have so much passion inside you, and I consider myself the luckiest man to have the opportunity to share in that. I have a better idea. Do you only have a shower, or do you have a bathtub as well?"

"Actually, I have both. That was one of reasons I bought this house—the master bath had been remodeled not long before the previous sellers put the place up on the market. I have my very own spa retreat, including a steam shower with multiple jets and a soaking whirlpool deep enough to swim in."

Jace grinned then leaned down and gave Kat's lips a soft kiss. "Why don't we draw a bath and we can both relax. We'll let the warm water and jets sooth all our tired muscles. I'll even wash your hair."

Kat sighed. "That sounds like heaven."

They went into the bathroom. Jace realized she wasn't kidding about the whole spa atmosphere of the place. The water closet was separated from the rest of the room. They each used it to relieve themselves in private. Coming back into the main part, Jace noticed an amazing stained-glass window above the tub. The flooring all looked like slate, similar to what was on the fireplace downstairs. The walls were painted a warm honey-cream color, and the room smelled like apples and cinnamon.

She turned on the faucet of the tub, and as she did, he was rewarded with a very appealing view of her backside. He had yet to really pay proper homage to that particular curve. That was something he was going to remedy when he got the chance.

As Kat adjusted the water temperature, Jace found towels and placed them on the heated towel rack. Switching it on, he turned around and found Kat at the sink. She had taken out her toothbrush and gave him an impish grin in the mirror. He could hear the water filling the tub in the background, but was completely fascinated with watching her wash her face, comb out the tangles in her long hair and brush her teeth.

Jace noticed that when Kat rose up from washing her mouth out, she studied his nude body in the mirror. Under Kat's watchful eyes, one part of his anatomy predictably reacted. His cock started to waver and bounce as blood began to fill it.

He caught her gaze in the mirror and shrugged. "I can't help it if he has a mind of his own. Any time a beautiful woman looks at him with a warm, appreciative glint in her eyes, he responds." He stepped up to hug her from behind, his lips curling as she let out a little gasp. "Do you have a spare toothbrush? I know I said I'd kiss you regardless, but I never did like the feeling of cotton mouth."

Kat handed him an unopened spare brush. "You know, if we're going to be spending as much time together this week as I hope, then you're welcome to stay here with me. I mean, it seems silly to keep a hotel room and never stay there. Unless you don't want to or can't cancel your reservations."

Jace turned off the water flowing into the tub. He stepped over the ledge and sat down. "I'm sure it would be no problem to check out earlier than expected. Are you sure you want me underfoot all week long?"

Kat sighed blissfully as she sank into the tub, her back resting against Jace's chest. "I'm sure. In fact, the house feels a lot warmer with you here for some reason. I don't know quite what it is, but having you here makes it feel more like a home. I kind of like it."

* * * *

After their bath, Jace managed to convince Kat that a big, home-cooked breakfast was just the ticket. Fortunately, Kat's brothers had been in town recently, and she still had bacon and eggs in stock. So they made a hearty breakfast. He was surprised to find that working around each other in the kitchen was easy. Jace was actually a good cook.

He enjoyed and knew just what spices made the eggs taste delicious. But normally having another person in the kitchen while he worked his magic annoyed him. With Kat it was comfortable.

"Where did you learn how to whip up food like this?" Kat asked after they'd sat down and started to eat.

"When all you eat on mission are MREs if you're lucky, you become desperate to learn how to make real meals when you finally make it home."

"What's an MRE?"

"It's a pre-packaged meal that can be eaten out in the field when there's no mess or kitchen."

Kat made a face, and Jace laughed.

"They're really not that bad," he explained. "My favorite is actually the pasta with spicy sausage and vegetables."

"How do you cook them if there's no kitchen? I imagine there are times you're in a situation where you can't exactly announce your location with a campfire."

Jace smile. "That's for sure. It comes with a thermal heating pouch. You toss in your entrée that's sealed in a bag, add water, and bingo—instant chemical reaction. A few minutes later you get a steamy breakfast, lunch or dinner."

"Interesting. I'd actually like to try one sometime. Just to see."

Jace picked up Kat's hand and kissed the back. "I'll liberate one after our next mission and bring it home to you."

Kat laughed and shook her head. "You're nuts. So do you want to maybe go to the hotel after breakfast and pick up your stuff?"

The sooner he moved in the more time they had together. Jace was ready to leave right now, but Kat would probably appreciate it if he cleaned up his mess first. He stood and moved to clear the dishes.

Kat stepped up behind Jace and wrapped her arms around his waist. She went up on her toes to kiss the back of his neck. "You cooked. I'll do the dishes. Why don't you go check your phone? I've heard it going off a few times since we came down."

Jace had heard the alert tone that he'd missed text and voice messages, but he wasn't worried. He knew if an emergency had come up and the team was being called in that the boys would call Kat's house. It was most likely Collin or Peter checking in after last night's drama.

He turned in Kat's embrace and wrapped his arms around her. "How would you feel if I invited Peter and Collin out to lunch with us?" Kat's body tensed, and Jace started to rub her back. "They sat down and told me last night everything that happened between you and your former classmates. They are truly sorry for the pain they caused, and I'm not trying to butt in... Well, maybe I am a little, but I think the air needs to be cleared between you. You're becoming very important to me, and I literally trust those two guys with my life."

Kat rested her head on Jace's chest. "You know, it's funny. Before this past week I really truly thought I'd put all the old anger and resentment behind me. I hadn't thought about those kids in years, but then Collin and Peter were at the club and Serena at the wedding. Guess I'm not as evolved as I thought."

Jace continued to caress Kat's back as she nuzzled against his chest. "Putting bad experiences or negative emotions into a mental box and locking it tight isn't the same as dealing with it. As a soldier, I've seen and done things during battle that have to be compartmentalized in order to survive, but I know that if I don't eventually take those same experiences out of the box and lay them to rest, they'll eat me alive from the inside. How about today, you and I go together and lay your demons to rest? Give Collin and Peter a chance to apologize."

Kat let out a long slow breath. "Okay. Go make the call."

* * * *

Kat had to grade some reports before they left for lunch, so Jace decided to turn on the TV and see if he could find a ball game. She was sitting in the overstuffed chair next to the sofa with papers spread out all over the table. As she read a research paper written by one of her students, a chagrined look appeared on her face. Even though he was watching the game, he occasionally looked over at her. She looked very cute with her legs crisscrossed underneath her, reading glasses perched on her nose.

Completely absorbed in her work, Kat jumped when Jace cheered loudly for a home run. He laughed at her reaction, but apologized. "Sorry, didn't mean to startle you."

She smiled. "That's okay. I take it we're winning?"

"Yeah, five-three now. Pujols just hit a two-run homer. I don't want to distract you. Do you want me to go somewhere else?"

She looked surprised that he would offer.

"No, I like hearing the game in the background. Normally, I'd have it on anyway when grading papers. It's easy for me to get lost in my reading. People have told me that a herd of buffalos could run past me and I wouldn't notice. Having some noise in the background helps ground me to reality."

He looked at her and chuckled silently as he pictured her sitting in a field with a herd of buffalos running past her while she read.

After the game ended, Kat looked up and asked, "Do you know what time it is?"

"It's 1200 hours. We're meeting Collin and Peter at 1300 in the hotel restaurant. What time do we need to leave here?"

"Do you want to get your belongings before or after we meet them? If you want to get them before, we should probably leave in the next ten minutes. If you want to wait till afterward, then we have about thirty."

"Logistically I'd say we should get my stuff before. Plus I'd like to go to lunch in something other than my dress whites or your brother's sweat pants and T-shirt."

Kat rolled her eyes. "Sorry, I wasn't thinking."

Kat currently wore a pair of stylish jeans, forest-green V neck top and heeled boots. When she'd come down the stairs a little while ago, Jace had had to shake his head. It seemed that no matter what she was or wasn't wearing, his head spun.

* * * *

When they arrived at the restaurant, Collin and Peter were already at the table. Jace guided Kat over to them with his hand on the small of her back. She smiled warmly at Collin and Peter, noting that the tension evident in their bodies instantly relaxed.

They were all seated, and Kat nervously fidgeted with the napkin in her lap.

"Kat, I see you decided to give our fearless leader a chance to prove that scheming bitch wrong. He was rather intimidating in his determination to find out what had happened," Collin said.

She looked over at Jace and saw that he actually blushed a little bit then glanced at her out of the corner of his eye and shrugged.

Kat took the opportunity to put her hand on Jace's denim-clad leg. "Well, he was very convincing. He spent hours enumerating every little point."

She wasn't sure what had possessed her to make it known exactly what had happened between her and Jace last night. Maybe it was her way of staking her claim. Judging by Collin's and Peter's smiles, the two men were happy. When she looked over at Jace, she saw warmth in his eyes that spoke volumes more than words.

After ordering their drinks and lunch choices, they began talking about what they planned to do that week. Collin and Peter still had family in the area and planned on spending it with them. Justin, Eric, and Kurt were taking a side vacation rock climbing in Osceola. And Jace announced that he planned on spending the week with her, which sounded perfect.

Finally the purpose of the lunch couldn't be put off any longer. Kat opened her mouth to say something when Peter jumped in before she could.

"Kat, I want you to know that I am immensely sorry for the way I treated you when we were children, and I sincerely hope that you will give me the chance to show you that I'm a much better man than I was a boy. I don't want you to ever feel inferior to me, and if I ever do something to make you think that, I want your promise that you will let me know."

Collin also chimed in with, "He's absolutely right, Kat. Over the past week, we've come to know you better than we ever took the time to do as kids. We know that our actions can never be reversed, and the damage that was done cannot be erased, but we would feel honored if you would forgive us."

Kat sat in silence, processing. She had anticipated everything from condemnation to the possibility of a modest apology, but these heartfelt declarations surprised her. She had thought she'd let go of her anger years before. As Jace had said, there was no way for her to move forward if she continued to live in the past. Nonetheless, at their words she still felt something in her soul being set free.

"I appreciate the sentiments, gentlemen. I know that you have to be honorable men if you serve in Jace's company. He would never allow anything else. Therefore, I propose a toast. Starting today, right here, we all vow to keep moving forward, never letting the past control our present."

Jace, Collin and Peter smiled and lifted their glasses to meet hers.

"To the future."

Chapter Ten

After they had finished lunch, Kat and Jace decided to take a drive out to the wineries. The sky was clear with large puffy white clouds, and the temperature was comfortable with a light breeze. As the attendant pulled Kat's car around to the curb, she looked at Jace as he started to open the passenger side door to assist her inside.

Pausing at the curb, she said, "Why don't I drive? I know the way, and you acted as chauffeur this morning."

Jace enjoyed driving Kat's car. It was sleek and sporty, easily maneuverable through the city traffic, with more power than he would have thought possible. With a little mental reluctance, he said, "Okay, I have no problem with that. It is your car, after all."

He walked over to the driver's side door and held it open for Kat as she sank down into the bolstered seat and put on her seatbelt. Bending down, he gave her a light, teasing kiss. After adjusting the seat and mirrors, she gripped the leather-wrapped steering wheel. Kat pulled out into traffic, and Jace took advantage of the situation to observe the old converted brick warehouses flying past the window. The power of the engine threw him back when she shifted into second gear, and he smiled.

Kat maneuvered onto the freeway with ease. Jace could tell she was completely comfortable behind the wheel, and it was obvious she enjoyed driving. When they reached the outskirts of the county, before heading into the countryside, Kat pulled the car over.

Jace looked at her, raising an eyebrow. "Why are you stopping?"

Kat turned in her seat to look at him. "How would you feel about having a little fun?"

Jace's mind immediately turned to the type of fun he wanted, but he restrained himself. Kat most likely wasn't talking about having sex on the side of the highway. "What did you have in mind?"

"The roads to the winery are secluded and very curvy. Last night, you taught me to fly. Today, I want to show you what it feels like to soar. That is, if you trust me."

Trust was not something that came easily to Jace, but in that moment, he felt completely safe in her control. He knew that she would never physically endanger them, plus she knew the limits of her own vehicle.

"Why not, as long as you don't break too many laws. It wouldn't look too good to my superiors if I ended up in jail on my vacation for hot-dogging."

She had a very mischievous glint in her eyes as she leaned over to place a gentle kiss on his cheek and whispered in his ear, "It's not how fast you go, but how you handle the curves."

Jace desperately wanted to handle her curves and moved to do just that, but she stopped him.

"Oh no, I'm going to need my wits about me if we do this, and that's impossible after experiencing your touch."

Kat merged back onto the country road, and Jace sat back in his seat. After about five minutes, he noticed that the scenery transitioned to rolling hills and valleys. When the road began to get curvy, he started to really enjoy himself. Once again, he was amazed that Kat drove a car like this. It had obviously been modified, and he had a feeling she knew every nut and bolt on it, had probably even helped turn a few.

He settled down into his supported seat, and just like that, Kat downshifted, and the car shot off. He looked at the speedometer and was surprised to see they were only going ten miles per hour over the speed limit, but somehow it did feel like they were soaring. She pushed a button on the dash, and the engine started to roar louder. He felt more horsepower being generated by the now-open exhaust.

Kat maneuvered her way through the gears and around the curves with skill that would do a rally racer proud. He saw the absolute concentration on her face and at the same time could tell she was having the time of her life. She drove that way for about thirty minutes until they started to see signs for the turn-off.

After pulling into the vineyard, Kat shut off the car and blew out her breath. She turned to look at him.

"That really was fun," he said.

"I'm glad you enjoyed it. Most people get scared when I suggest we take a drive."

Jace got out of the vehicle and came around to open Kat's door. They strolled hand in hand to the entrance. Jace held open the door to the tasting room. His gaze automatically traveled down to watch her ass as she walked in.

"Welcome to Nautinghaus Winery."

Jace nodded to the attendant. "Hello." He and Kat walked toward the counter. Kat ran her fingers down the age-worn wooden counter, the tips gliding over the smoothly rounded curve.

My little sensualist.

"Are the two of you here to experience a wine tasting or would you like a tour of our cavern?"

Kat turned to Jace. "The tour sounds fun. I've always wanted to see if reality matches my imagination."

"Then a tour is what we shall do, followed by a nice drink and maybe a snack while relaxing on the grounds. How does that sound?"

Kat nodded. "Sounds perfect."

The attendant smiled. "Excellent. It's quiet today, so the two of you'll get to experience a private tour. It can be crazy busy during peak leaf season. I'll take you myself. Let me call my brother to come man the desk."

A few minutes later, Kat's hand was in his and they made their way down into underground cellars. Their tour guide flipped a switch and antique sconces drilled into the stone walls came to life.

"It's beautiful. Makes me wish I had my camera," Kat whispered.

Jace tried to look at the space from an artistic point of view. He supposed the natural stone walls had a primitive appeal and the large oak barrels that lined either side could be viewed almost as sculptures. The low lighting created a lot of highlights and shadows that, under Kat's talented fingers, would probably make the photograph appear very dramatic. He actually wished Kat had brought her camera. He'd like to see what she could do with the space, and have a memory of their day together.

He absently listened to the tour guide as she talked about the wine-making process and why oak barrels were used instead of hickory, how the humidity and temperature of the cellars were monitored and adjusted with exacting detail. They wove deeper into the labyrinth and when the tour guide stopped for an extended oratory, Kat began to shiver. Jace wrapped his arm around her waist and brought her in against his body. He was glad when the tour ended and they climbed back up into the sunshine. They made their way through the grounds and back to the tasting room.

"So did you enjoy the tour?" Elise the sommelier asked.

"Yes, thank you," Kat said.

"You're welcome. Now comes the fun part—sampling the merchandise."

Elise brought out several varieties of both red and white wines. Jace was pleased to discover that Kat also enjoyed whites with a slightly dry taste. Kat made several funny faces when the wine steward poured very sweet wines. They chose a crisp Pinot Gris and purchased several types of cheese and sausage. They left the tasting room with their wares in hand.

"I have a blanket in the back of the car. Would you like me to grab it before we go find a spot to relax?"

Jace nodded and Kat took off. He saw a worker heading

in his direction. "Excuse me. Can you tell me where the best spot for a quiet picnic would be?"

The young man looked over at Kat who was still walking toward the parking lot. "You want somewhere quiet and secluded, I imagine."

"It would be nice." They shared an understanding smile.

"Head down the gravel path. When you reach the end, go to the left through the grove of trees and you'll find a nice spot that overlooks the river."

* * * *

Jace spread out the blanket on the grass underneath a huge oak tree. He had to admit, this was nice countryside. It wasn't the same as Virginia, but Missouri had a charm all its own. They opened their bottle, put together a plate of meat, cheese and crackers, then Jace leaned back against the tree and pulled Kat into his arms. They sat quietly just looking out at the scenery.

He occasionally lifted a bite to Kat's mouth, and on one of those times, she took a small bite out of the pad of his thumb. It made his heart quiver and he closed his eyes in bliss. He sat under the tree and felt her pulse quicken as he leaned down to kiss her neck.

His hands trembled a little as he slid them into the edge of her neckline. Gently cupping her breasts, he pulled at her nipples in soft tugging motions.

Kat leaned back further into his chest and sighed, closing her eyes. His erection grew against the small of her back, and she nestled closer between his legs. She lifted her head up for his kiss, and he obliged, slowly, gently gliding his tongue across hers.

Needing to be closer, they lay down on the blanket. Kat lay on her back with Jace on his side slightly over her. The sun highlighted her eyes and made her hair shimmer with threads of red. He took a few moments and just looked at her, softly touching her face with his fingertips.

Kat reached up and wrapped her hand around his neck and pulled him down to kiss her again, and they stayed that way for long minutes, just caressing and kissing like a couple of teenagers making out.

Finally, Jace pulled up and in a husky voice said, "The sun is about to set. We should probably head home soon."

"Yeah, we should... Soon." Then she leaned up to kiss him again.

He was painfully aroused, but today, their actions felt sweet and tender, where last night he had burned like a fire unable to be extinguished. Now she felt like sunlight in his arms.

As he thought about it, he realized that with Kat there was a closeness, a sense that they connected in more ways than just physical. He thought about last night and how they'd shared their bodies. Was it still just sex when you felt like your minds and souls were blending in the way your bodies did? When did having sex turn into making love? When did lust turn to love? Were the two mutually exclusive?

He couldn't seem to get enough of her, and it was more than the incredible physical pleasure they shared. He loved seeing her smile, making her laugh, making her moan. She was constantly surprising him with different sides of her personality, although that wasn't too hard, since they had only known each other a week.

When he had to leave Sunday, they were going to have to figure out how things were going to work. He had to report for duty on Monday. There was no choice. Kat couldn't just leave in the middle of a semester, or he would ask her to come home with him. He'd been honest with her when he said he didn't know what would happen when he had to leave, but he was quickly trying to find a way to make it work so they could stay together.

Kat looked up at him, blinking against the setting sun at his back. "What are you thinking?" she asked softly.

"I'm thinking about how much I want you. I don't mean

just physically, even though that is pretty obvious right now, but how much I want all of you. I want you in my life, Kat. I need you in my life. Even if we are separated by thousands of miles, promise me you won't forget what we've shared this week. I just want to hear the words, so when I'm lying on the stone-cold ground in some godforsaken country, I can remember the warmth I feel in your arms."

Tears shimmered in Kat's eyes. "I promise you, Jace. I will never forget our time together, however long that may be." She raised a hand to his cheek. "Why don't we go home?"

After quickly gathering their things and walking to the car, they went back to her house in silence. Jace drove this time and soft music flowed through the speakers. He recognized it as Deep Forest. It was a perfect selection for a drive through the countryside at night. They rolled down their windows and let the scents of the night-time air waft over them. Jace inhaled the remnants of honeysuckle and clean country air. Being out in the country always relaxed him.

Once they got back to the main highway, Jace was able to leave the car in fifth gear and take hold of Kat's hand. Even though it felt delicate in his rougher one, he knew she was a strong and capable woman, a woman he hoped would be strong enough to be his partner.

It was not easy being with a Navy SEAL. They worked difficult situations full of danger, often out of the country for long periods of time. So many of the guys remained single or were divorced for that very reason, but somehow Jace sensed Kat had the strength necessary.

He would have to teach her caution, because even if he didn't like to think about it, some of the dangers he faced could potentially leak into their personal lives. Just last year one of the guys on another team had to evade an assassin that came after him at home after he had been forced to kill the man's brother in Columbia. Jace didn't think he would survive if Kat were hurt because of him. This was something he was going to have to think about very carefully.

When they got back to Kat's house, Jace closed and locked the door. Without turning on the lights, he checked all the windows and searched for any sign of another presence in the house. Then Jace took her hand and led her upstairs to the bedroom, still leaving the house dark. The wooden shutters on her windows were open, and the light of the full moon gently cascaded across the bed.

They undressed each other slowly. Kat pulled Jace's shirt out of his jeans and spread her hands across his abdomen. His muscles clenched under her light touch. He stood still while she pushed the shirt up toward his head, but when she was only able to get it as high as his shoulders, Jace lifted it the rest of the way. The shirt was tossed away but Jace didn't see where it landed. He only had eyes for Kat, whose gaze traced his exposed skin.

"The moonlight makes the ridges of your muscle definition starker. I've never done nude portraits, but right now I'm feeling very inspired."

He hissed as her fingernails slowly raked down his chest, lightly flicking over his nipples. Right now he was letting his little cat explore, enjoying the tiny bite of her claws. But soon it would be his turn to make her hiss, his turn to make Kat feel as though she were unraveling from the intensity of his possession.

Jace reached for her sweater. Once he got the top off, he leaned down and kissed her neck and collarbone, sucking the skin over her pulse points hard enough that Kat groaned.

"Do that again. I want the whole world to know that I've experienced a night of pleasure in an amazing man's arms."

Jace moaned and made a matching mark on the opposite side. "You want to wear my marks, little cat? You want to explore the darker side of passion?"

"Yes," she moaned. "I want it. I need it. You. I need it with you."

The breathy words tested Jace's restraint. He'd intended to show Kat how to embrace her submissive side little by little, but it seemed his professor was aching for some extra lessons. His hands slid around to her back, and he unhooked her bra. His palms caressed her shoulders, lowering the straps simultaneously. Her bra fell to the floor. She stepped in so their chests rubbed against one another. Jace buried his fingers in her hair while he strived to send her mind spinning out of control with his kisses.

Kat sucked on his tongue as though to absorb his taste. Her lips were sensual, yet demanding. He loved how Kat didn't allow him to give half measure. But he never would. Kat deserved all the soul-shattering pleasure she could handle. And he planned to give it to her.

Grabbing for the button to her jeans, he pulled them down her legs with a hard tug, taking her panties with them. Jace knelt on the floor, placing gentle kisses all over Kat's stomach and tracing a path lower. When he got to her center, he breathed deeply.

"Do you know there is nothing like your scent of arousal? It's been burned into my senses. It's uniquely you, a heady combination of vanilla, peaches and pure Kat."

Jace leaned down and took a slow lick right up between her labia. Spreading her lips with his fingers, he began to circle her clit. Then he alternated between short little stabs and deep plunges of his tongue into her heat.

Jace took her little bud of nerve endings between his lips and suckled. Kat moaned, grabbing onto his hair to hold him closer. Kat cried out in pleasure and shuddered as she came in Jace's mouth.

With Kat's flavor still on his tongue he walked over to his bag and snatched up some lengths of silk rope and a small velvet bag. If she wanted to further explore her limits, then he was more than willing.

He turned back toward the bed. "Kat, remember the other night when we talked about control?" Seeing her nod, he continued, "Well, tonight we're going to test that control. I am going to blind you and restrain you. I will touch you and take you any way I see fit. You will make a move unless I give you permission. You will not come again until I say you may. Do you understand?"

"I understand."

He recognized the signs of Kat's arousal. Her pulse pounded in her neck, her breathing became shallow, and her nipples tightened. She wanted this.

"Good. Before we begin, we need to establish a code. This code will serve to protect you if you feel threatened in any way. You will only use this code if you become scared and want to stop. It must be a word that you would not normally say, especially in the heat of passion. What is your word, Kat?"

"Adagio."

Knowing she wasn't likely to blurt out musical composition terms during sex, this seemed a safe choice.

"Excellent. Now walk over to the bed." She did, but remained standing next to the mattress.

"Very good. You waited for my command to sit. I am going to blindfold you now. The blind is not a form of punishment. It's designed to heighten your senses. By taking away your vision, I'm forcing your other senses to tell you what is happening."

He secured the blind he removed from his bag earlier. "I want you to lie in the center of the bed. Spread your arms to your sides and bend your knees to open your legs wide."

As she did so, he reached around the post of her headboard and secured each wrist with a bowline knot. Smiling to himself, Jace reflected that his naval training came in handy for more than just sanctioned operations.

He made sure that the ties allowed her sufficient movement. By this time, Kat was breathing hard, and he sensed just how aroused she was. He leaned over her and said into her ear, "I'm going to make you scream for me tonight, Kat. I'm going to make you lose control. The night I bound your wrists gave you a taste of what heights you can reach when you give up control, but tonight, your real training begins."

He stood up and removed his pants and shorts. He walked

over to the bedside table to take out a condom and noted that they had managed to go through more than half the box already. He was definitely going to need to buy some more. He opened the packet and rolled it down his hard length.

Jace had not anticipated sharing an experience like this while on vacation, so he had not brought all his toys, but he had thrown a few things in his bag just in case. He brought them over to the bed, letting them rest against Kat's leg so she could feel their presence but not figure out exactly what they were.

He leaned down and took her right nipple into his mouth, sucking on it so it hardened further on his tongue, and continued his ministrations until Kat's breasts became swollen. Then he took one of the clamps and secured it around her nipple to trap the blood in the tip. Kat gasped and tried to jerk her hands toward her chest, most likely as an instinct to protect the vulnerable and now pinched flesh.

"Shh. It's okay. Relax and breathe. The pain will ease in a moment. The clamps create a delicious hypersensitivity in your breasts. When I remove them, the blood will rush back in a surge so powerful you'll thrash and beg for my mouth to ease the ache." He gave her other breast the same treatment. "Can you feel how swollen your breasts are, Kat? Can you sense how the clamps make your nipples tight and achy?"

"Yes."

"Do you like it?"

"Yes."

"What do they feel like?"

"My nipples feel huge. They're sensitive, but at the same time starting to go numb. I want... I want you to touch them, lick them."

She moaned when he rewarded her with a drag of his tongue over the nubs.

Jace opened a small bottle of oil and held it under Kat's nose. "What do you smell?"

After inhaling the tangy aroma, Kat responded, "It reminds me of sandalwood incense."

"What you smell is special oil that is designed to stimulate blood flow. It will make your skin tingle and slightly burn. The sensations are only relieved by friction. I'm going to put some on your nipples and between your pussy lips."

After applying the oil, Jace waited a few seconds for the effects to stir through Kat's body. She squirmed.

"Remember you're to lie still unless I tell you to move."

"But, I need... I need..."

"What is it you think you need, Kat?"

"Something... Anything... Just touch me!"

Jace picked up a soft latex tickler. He made sure to apply lotion so it would glide across her skin like silk. He started at her lips and slid it down the length of her body. When he passed over her nipples, Kat gasped.

"Tell me what you feel," he ordered.

"It feels like a thousand tiny fingers touching me all over."

Jace reached that part of her that desired him most, and could tell the oil was working. She was so wet that her thighs glistened with moisture. Taking mercy, he slid his fingers inside her hot sheath. "Baby, you feel so good around my fingers. You're so soft and wet. I can feel you trying to suck me deeper."

Kat let out an almost feral growl. "Jace, please, I need you. I can't take any more, it's too much."

He crawled over her and growled, "It's never too much."

He fit himself to her entrance and entered with one strong, smooth thrust. Holding himself completely still, he allowed her to adjust to his invasion. She was still so tight he didn't want to hurt her.

Having none of that, Kat bucked up against him, trying to force his movement.

After counting to twenty, Jace started to move in long, firm thrusts. "Oh, Kat... I wish you could know how this feels. It's so good, so good." He continued to move inside her tight, hot body. With every thrust, he felt her get wetter, and he could hear the slap of his body against her.

Jace pulled out quickly, and Kat whimpered. He removed the silk ties, flipped her over onto her stomach then reattached them. Jace pulled her hips into the air. She was completely exposed to his touch. Remembering how he wanted to pay homage to that delectable round bottom, he slid his hands down and squeezed her, then gave her a gentle slap, just enough to sting.

"You know, someday I'm going to spank this little ass of yours to a beautiful, blushing pink, but I think we'll wait for that another day."

Jace grabbed her hips and entered her once again, and had to grit his teeth to keep from coming right then. At this angle, he could reach all the way to the deepest part of her channel. Picking up the small vial of oil, he let a few drops fall on the tight ring hidden between the round cheeks of her ass, and used his fingers to massage the oil into her skin. He leaned over her and lightly bit into her shoulder. "Can you feel the oil seeping into that delectable asshole of yours?"

"Yes, it tingles and burns a little."

"Do you want me to make the burn go away?"

"Yes."

"Are you sure, baby?"

"Yes."

"Tell me how you want the burn to go away."

"I want you to touch me."

"Where, sweetheart? Where do you want my touch?"

"Oh, God... My... My hole... Please, Jace... Please stroke my asshole. Make the burn go away!"

"Your wish is my command." He slid one finger inside her and started massaging her, mimicking the thrusts of his cock. Adding a second finger, he stretched her a little more. So many of his previous lovers hadn't let Jace play with this dark and most intimate part of their body. But his Kat cried out and tried to thrust back onto his hand, demanding he give her more.

"Your muscles are clenched around my fingers so tightly. They're gripping and sucking them deeper into your amazing heat. You like my fingers and cock buried inside you at the same time?"

"Yes," she whimpered. "So full. So good."

"Hmm, yes. Imagine what it's going to feel like when I get my cock back here, and I fuck your hungry little pussy with a dildo."

Kat's shudder, moan of pleasure, and a fiery wash of cream dripping onto his balls told him that she wasn't averse to the idea.

"Are you ready to come, Kat? Are you ready to explode?"

"Yes!"

She was so close. He had her begging, crying for release.

Jace reached around to her breasts and pinched her nipples. The combination of the oil and clamps had enlarged them to twice their normal size. He knew that the sensitivity made the gentle motions of his fingers border somewhere between extreme pleasure and pain. He continued to drive his cock deep inside, each hard thrust forcing her hips forward.

Countering his motions, she pushed back against him.

"On the count of thirty, we come together... One, two, three... Oh, God. Sweetheart, you're so perfect... Ten... We were made for each other. I wish...there was nothing between us... Twenty... I can feel you tightening around my cock... Twenty-five... I can feel you pulling me in... Thirty!"

Jace pulled the clamps off Kat's nipples, and she screamed as her orgasm ripped through her body.

"Fuck... Yes," he shouted.

Jace's release pulsed into the condom, and once again he wished there was no barrier.

After they'd caught their breath, Jace leaned up, untied Kat's wrists, and removed the blindfold. "Are you okay? Did you enjoy our little game?"

She opened her eyes long enough to answer, "I've never

been better."

Kat lay on her stomach in the twisted sheets. Her body started to tremble, and Jace pulled her in closer. The warmth from his body stopped the chills coursing through her as the adrenaline left hers. He caressed one hand up and down her back, while the other held her head on his shoulder. Her breaths slowed and her limbs went lax over him, until her eyes slowly closed and she fell asleep in his protective arms.

Chapter Eleven

The next week seemed to fly by. Kat kept to her routine with classes and grading papers during the day, but her evenings were filled spending time with Jace. They stayed in and rented movies a couple of nights. She took him go-cart racing and to a few more of the sights of the city. Most evenings, they ended up back home early.

On Wednesday, Kat had to go up to the school, despite not having classes scheduled. She was working on putting together a grant for the following summer and needed to finalize some details. The look of surprise on her face when he suggested that he join here was priceless.

"I'd like to see where you work. It gives me another opportunity to see a different side of you."

"All right, but there's not much for you to do. You'll probably be bored. Unless, of course, your intention is to join me simply so you can ogle co-eds," she said, smiling.

"You, sweetheart, are the only co-ed I have any desire to ogle. Actually I'm living out every young man's dream."

"What's that?"

Jace leaned down and whispered into her ear, "I'm sleeping with the hottest professor on campus."

She rolled her eyes and smacked him in the arm. Jace's laughter rang out in her kitchen.

* * * *

Jace pushed open the door to the building housing the Department of Anthropology. Kat was working on her grant proposal, and while Jace loved spending time with her, sitting in her office and watching her type on the computer was not his idea of entertainment, no matter how sexy she looked in those reading glasses.

He stepped through the stone arch of the building's portico and followed the flagstone pathway that led between buildings. All of the structures he'd seen so far had a very old-world feel to them. The stone and brick façades were embellished with lots of carvings and stone reliefs. It was a very nice campus. He walked around the back of the building and found himself in the large grassy area that made up the center of the campus. It seemed that the buildings were all placed in a basic rectangle surrounding the green space. This would make securing the campus easier than if it was scattered amongst buildings in the middle of the city.

Jace noticed that across from him was a small chapel, to the west were the athletic fields and to the east the school's main library where he knew Kat spent a good amount of time.

He decided to walk in that direction. Taking this little tour of the campus would give him the opportunity to study the layout and inspect the overall security. The main campus of the university was far enough away from downtown that he didn't think street crime would be an issue, but when it came to Kat's safety, no precaution was too much. He wanted to make sure that the campus and her building were as secure as possible at a large university.

Although he hadn't felt any further threats since the wedding, Jace refused to let down his guard completely. It was possible that he had sensed the hate from Serena aimed in Kat's direction, but then again, there are always other unknown sources. He always searched the house when they came home at night, double-checking the locks on the doors and windows. All this was done casually, since he didn't want Kat to become alarmed or sense this was anything out of routine for him.

His phone rang, and he looked down to see Kat's name

on the caller ID.

"Hey! Miss me already?" he asked, smiling.

"It's only been five minutes, but a colleague of mine just came into my office and asked if I could cover one of his classes. Do you mind? It'll only be for an hour or so, then we can go grab some lunch."

"No problem. What time is the class? Can I sit in and listen, or is that not allowed?"

"I'm sure it's fine, but you have to promise to behave yourself. It starts at eleven o'clock, and is in our building, room B7."

"I'll have you know that I am an ideal student — attentive, and I absorb information like a sponge." He looked down at his watch. "If the class starts at eleven then that gives you two hours to work and me time to explore. I'll see you then, Professor," he said with a smile.

Jace toured the campus and managed to grab a seat in the back of room B7 just before class began. He listened as Kat presented a lecture on the effects of violence, trauma, and their political and subjective consequences. She was fascinating to watch. Her students looked genuinely interested in what she was saying and asked very insightful questions. About three-quarters of the way through, Jace couldn't restrain himself. He raised his hand to ask a question of his own.

Kat, seeing his hand, raised an eyebrow, but continued in a professional manner. "Yes, Mr Hudson?"

"Using history as a retrospective model, how do you feel the current conflicts of the Middle East are going to affect the distribution of global power?"

He was impressed that Kat was able to school her shocked expression so quickly. She probably hadn't expected him to talk at all, let alone hit her with a question so in-depth. Jace hadn't been lying when he told her he was a good student. Back during his days at the Naval Academy, he was consistently ranked in the top group of his class

"Mr Hudson, that's a very complicated question and the

answer is highly dependent on global market strategies. If you'd like to learn more, I believe Dr McKennzie's business and government class is over in McDonnell Hall." She paused for the chuckles in the room to stop. "However, using anthropological evidence from civilizations of the past, we have determined that power was often awarded either to the conquering nation or those which were able to successfully assert their independence. Therefore, I would speculate that if the people of the Middle East are able to self-govern, then any power that would be gained by those nations wishing to subjugate them would be transferred to them, thereby creating a wider global distribution."

Jace nodded and smiled at how professional she sounded, very different from the casual Kat he'd come to know. He also gave her a little wink after the heads that had been turned in his direction had faced the front of the room again.

It's actually rather sexy.

* * * *

Jace had just taken a bite of his sandwich when Kat put down her fork and gave him a look of frustration.

"I realize that you have much more real-world experience in global political conflicts and their violent consequences, but were you trying to test me this morning with that question?" she asked.

He gave a slight shake of his head. He didn't like the accusatory tone of Kat's question. He hadn't meant any harm earlier, but obviously she didn't see it that way.

"Not really. It just sort of popped into my head as I listened to your lecture, and I felt it was a good opportunity to find out your viewpoint. I will admit, though, it was fascinating to watch you process the answer, which was a good one by the way. I could almost see little wheels spinning in your head.

"I had no intention of trying to embarrass you or make you feel uncomfortable on a topic you didn't prepare for.

I'm sorry if you felt that way."

Kat's features smoothed out, and she gave him a weak smile.

"I'm sorry. It's not your fault. I have to put up with a lot of chauvinistic males in the world of academia."

"Is there someone in particular who is giving you a hard time? Making your life difficult here at the university?"

Could this be related to my unease?

"Not really hassling me, per se, but the head of the department always tries to make getting grants difficult for me. I don't know why, but he always manages to arrange my schedule so I get class times people attend as a last resort."

"Does it make you want to leave the university?"

"Not yet, but if things don't improve, I may reconsider. Anthropology is a relatively small community, but I've made a lot of good contacts over the years, and if it came to that point, I shouldn't have difficulty finding another position. It may need to be more research than academic at first, but that's fine with me. I love working in the field."

She's open to change, but how big? Would she be willing to completely give up everything she has here? She loves her home and has good friends. Is the risk to her safety worth keeping her close to me? Then again, it would be easier to protect her if she lived closer to me – like in the same house.

With a mental sigh, Jace acknowledged that regardless of the arrangements, he would do everything in his power to keep Kat safe, but if he never saw her again after this weekend, his life would feel very empty.

* * * *

The abrasion caused by the rough bark is worth being able to spy on the two lovebirds walking around campus. They can't possibly see this hiding spot. Watching their wide, flashy smiles and bright eyes oozing happiness makes me sick to my stomach. Just look them, meandering in ignorant bliss with their arms around each other,

This just will not do. It's time to intercede, time to shatter Jace's happy little world. There is nothing like causing torment and terror in the hearts of people... The magic of watching a plan come together like a well-tuned orchestra... It's the best high I could ever ask for.

Yes, I will enjoy this. Proper balance must be restored. Failure is not an option.

* * * *

Kat held Jace's hand as they walked down the broadway inside the casino. Earlier she'd called up Amy and invited her and her fiancé to go out with them, along with Peter and Collin. Kat had no intention of losing a lot of money so she'd requested a credit allowance of only twenty dollars from the cashier when they had ordered their playing cards. She'd never been lucky when gambling, but there was always a first time.

Their little group headed through the casino. Kat followed Amy over to one of the bars.

She placed her order for a spiced rum and coke then turned to her best friend. "You promise not to turn this night into some kind of grand inquisition?"

Amy took a sip of her beer. "I promise," she said. "Mostly," she added under her breath.

Kat accepted her drink from the bartender with a "Thanks". "Hold on, what do you mean 'mostly'? I didn't bring Jace here for you to interrogate. Remember we're taking this one step at a time. He leaves Sunday, and I really want to enjoy the time we have left, so please be good."

"All right, all right. No third degree, but if things get more serious between the two of you, remember he has to pass the best friend test before you're allowed to walk down any aisles."

Kat rolled her eyes as they walked off to join the boys at the poker table they'd all gravitated to.

Kat and Amy watched as the boys played a few hands of poker. But she didn't come out tonight to be an observer.

"You want to go find a blackjack table with me?" she asked Amy.

"As long as the minimum bet is less than ten dollars," Amy said with a smile.

"I think we passed one on the way over from the bar." She leaned down and whispered in Jace's ear, "Good luck."

Jace tilted his head back and gave her a quick kiss. "Don't get into too much trouble," he said with a smile.

"Me? Never."

Amy scoffed and started to laugh.

"Shush! He thinks I'm sweet and innocent," Kat scolded.

Jace set his cards face down on the table then turned to look at Kat and Amy. "Sweetheart, I know there are horns holding up your halo."

Kat stepped in closer to Jace and situated herself between his legs. "So you don't mind if I have a naughty side?" she asked softly.

Jace put his hands on either side of Kat's waist then nibbled on her neck just below her ear. "If you want to play the naughty girl tonight, I'll have to stop by the toy store on our way home. I didn't bring my handcuffs with me."

Kat shivered with instant arousal and she locked gazes with Jace. The heat smoldering in his smoky gray eyes told her that he was turned on too. The sound of someone coughing dissolved the moment. Kat looked over at Peter who was looking down at his cards and trying to hold in his laughter. She gave Jace a slow kiss then stepped away. When she passed behind Peter, she smacked him upside the back of his head, as she'd seen Jace do earlier when Peter was being a smartass.

She and Amy walked away as all the guys at the table, including the dealer, started laughing.

* * * *

When Sunday rolled around, Kat woke up feeling very morose, but didn't want Jace to see how distraught she was to see him go. She'd known when they started seeing each other that their time was limited, but she hadn't expected her feelings to grow as quickly as they did. So she put on a happy face and went about the morning in her usual manner.

When she came downstairs and saw Jace sitting at the kitchen table with his paper and coffee, which she had learned he did every morning whenever possible, she put on a breezy smile and cheerfully said, "Good morning. Did you sleep well?"

Then she turned her back and grimaced because she knew full well they hadn't slept much at all the night before. It had been their last night together, and where in previous nights their lovemaking had been explosive, last night was very tender. They'd savored each other slowly, and when exhaustion finally took over in the dawn hours, Jace had gathered her in his arms and held her.

Jace looked up from the paper with a slight frown on his face. "I slept fine, thank you." Actually she suspected he had gotten about as much sleep as she had since she'd felt him stirring beside her after they'd collapsed in sated exhaustion. She had just pretended to sleep in order to enjoy the feeling of Jace's arms around her. Periodically his arms would tighten and his lips would caress the back of her neck or her temple. It seemed neither of them had wanted to waste a single second of their last night together with anything as mundane as sleeping.

"You seem very chipper this morning."

Too much, idiot. He knows you don't have conversations containing more than five words until you have at least one cup of coffee.

"I just woke up feeling like it was a great day. The weather looks beautiful, and I'm hoping to get a lot of work done around here."

"Well, I don't want to hold you up, so if you would prefer

that I have the boys pick me up here versus you taking me to the airport, I can call and ask them."

A wave of disappointment swamped her. "Oh... Well... If that's what you want..."

"If you have a lot of plans, I don't want to inconvenience you."

Kat heard frustration taint his voice. She carried her coffee over to the table then crumpled into the chair across from him.

"Okay, I give in. The last thing I want is to see you leave even earlier than you need to. I was just trying to put on a good face so you wouldn't think I was being too clingy. I knew going into this that our time was limited, but... I don't want to let you go."

Jace got up out of his chair and came over to kneel before her. "I don't want to leave either, but I don't have a choice. We'll work something out. I can visit again or you can come out to see me over your holiday break. There's video conferencing and email. I'll talk to my commanding officer and see what our options are."

Kat sat there with trembling lips and tears pooling in her eyes. "All I ask is that from time to time you send me a note or something letting me know you're safe. If I can't see you, just knowing you're okay will make a big difference."

When Jace gathered her in his arms and kissed her, she tried to explain to him through touch all the emotions she couldn't express out loud—her desire for commitment, her unquenchable lust, her love.

Chapter Twelve

Jace stepped into his commanding officer's office. The sun was barely over the horizon but he'd been told to report first thing this morning.

"Commander Hudson, nice to see you again. Did you have a good vacation?"

Jace stood at attention. "Yes, sir."

"Good because it's time to get back to work. We have a personnel recovery in Bolivia that your team has been selected for. Some goddamn senator's aide was stupid enough to go out into the jungle without a security detail, and now he's being held hostage by a revolutionary faction. We've got a C-130 standing by for take-off today at 1300. You and your squad will be flying in dark and perform a nocturnal HALO jump then meet up with an informant who will give you the most up-to-date sit rep."

Jace felt his adrenaline already kicking in. Flying in the dark meant the transponder on the plane would be disabled, and being able to perform a night-time high-altitude, low-opening drop was one of his favorite parts of being a SEAL.

"Sir, is there already an extraction plan in place, and do we know anything about the package's condition? Is he ambulatory?"

"Our last communication with the informant indicated yes, but plan for every contingency by the time you get down there."

"Yes, sir."

"All right. Go inform your team and get ready."

Jace saluted then turned to walk out of the office. They had seven hours until take-off. He was actually glad they had an immediate objective.

Prep work and briefing the guys on the plan kept his mind focused on the details and not constantly thinking about Kat until he made it on the plane.

The rumble and drone of the plane threatened to put him to sleep. They'd been in the air for six hours and had about another two to go. Now that he wasn't running around, his mind started to drift back to the days spent in Kat's company.

Getting up from the seat across the aisle, Collin sat down next to him. "Hey, you okay?"

"Yeah, I'm fine. Why?"

"You had a faraway look on your face."

"I was just thinking about Kat."

"You do realize that we need you here with us right now, don't you? Some nasty shit could go down on this, and we can't have you wool-gathering when it hits the fan."

Jace looked over at Collin, offended that his teammate would even for a second think that Jace would put the men's lives at risk over a battered heart. "I know my job. I know your lives depend on my judgment. I'd never give you second-rate efforts."

Collin put his hand on Jace's shoulder. "Hell, Jace, I know that. I wanted to make sure you remembered it. Just think about it like this—when we get back, you can call her and recite prose and sonnets to her beauty as much as you want."

Jace laughed. "You can be such an asshole, you know that?"

A huge smile cracked Collin's face. "Absolutely. That's why you all love me."

* * * *

Getting into the jungle was the easy part. Now they had to get the hostage and get him out with as little fanfare as possible. According to the intel, the suspected syndicate of revolutionaries holding him was rumored to have been responsible for several dozen bombings and execution-style murders over the last fifteen years. Things could get very complicated very quickly if not handled right.

Jace positioned himself in the foliage and kept an eye out for their contact. The man was supposed to meet them at this location within the next five minutes. So far there was no sign of him. Jace looked down at his watch then over at Peter positioned next to him who was keeping watch through the binoculars.

"Any sign of movement?" he said, keeping his voice low pitched and soft.

"Negative."

"This fucker better show, otherwise we're going to have to implement plan B."

"I hate plan B," Peter grumbled.

"It's better than plan C. That one's a real bitch."

"Movement, ten o'clock, twenty yards."

Jace looked through his night vision goggles at the spot Peter indicated. Sure enough, a man was heading in their direction. He waited to see if the man gave the pre-arranged signal then stood.

He walked over toward the contact. "Nice night for a walk."

The code was a secondary level of security. If this man was their true contact then he'd respond with the right phrase.

"Yes, the moon lights the path well."

It was a go.

"Tell me, what's the latest?"

"Your package will be ready for pick-up within twenty-four hours." The contact pulled out a map. "Your targets have a staging area outside Oruro, and like to use it for storage. The best spot to intercept is along the isolated roads leading from Sucre."

This was good news. They would be able to get in and out quickly then rendezvous with an extraction team just north of the roads in Cochabamba.

* * * *

With the team in place, Jace sat silently just off the track of land that could barely be called a road. It was black as pitch under the canopy, and he had the distinct honor of lying in a muddy pile of decaying undergrowth. The smell of rotting jungle reminded him of the stench that would occasionally waft over the base from the sulfur chemical plant a few miles down the peninsula.

Hearing a vehicle approaching, he signaled to Peter who was positioned five yards south of him. When the truck came around the bend, he knew it wasn't the one they were waiting for, so speaking into his com-link, he ordered the team to stand down.

Suddenly, Jace heard a noise like someone running. Remaining still so he didn't give their position away, Jace followed the sound with his ears and waited to see who had decided to join the party. He saw a short, thin man emerge onto the road. The man appeared to be holding an MD-97L, a Brazilian assault rifle, and looked to be searching for someone.

After making sure he wasn't going to be joined by any friends, Jace quietly walked up behind him and slid his knife under the man's chin. *"Tomemo una caminata."*

It's obvious the man has no training. There is no way I should have been able to walk up right behind him. Is he one of the revs?

"Quién son tú que busca?"

The man smelled like tequila and unwashed body. Jace felt the oil from his hair smearing onto his face.

The nasty things I have to touch for the good of my country.

The man swallowed and said in broken English, "I looking for you. You are to meet trucks, no? I come to tell you bad idea, they know you are here."

"I don't know what you're talking about. I'm simply out here enjoying the stars."

"Yes, yes. I heard man talking. He tell Sanchez you plan to ambush and steal their guest."

"Why should I believe you? I don't know you from Jesus and you're holding a very lethal weapon. You could be working for them."

"I could, but why would I reveal myself if I worked for them?"

"Are you familiar with the word 'bait'? Besides, you were running through the forest like a herd of stampeding buffalo. Anyone within half a mile could have heard you."

"Please, Lieutenant, you really should believe me. They will be coming down this road any minute."

Jace tightened the knife against the man's neck. "What makes you think I'm a lieutenant?"

"That's what man told Sanchez. I heard him say 'lieutenant plus seven others will be waiting.' Since you come to me, you're in charge, no?"

Jace weighed his options. If what this man said was true, then it would indicate that there was a leak in the operation somewhere. However, their primary objective was to rescue a hostage. "Do they still have the hostage?"

"Yes."

"Are they still planning to move him?"

"I do not know."

Jace snarled into the man's ear. "Guess."

"I think it will be a trap."

Jace had to make a decision, and he had to make it fast. Did his team attempt the rescue knowing there was a potential for entrapment, or did they retreat to investigate the possibility of a mole and grab the hostage at a later date?

He looked down the road toward where his teammates were still hidden in their positions, weighing the costs of further endangering their lives if the convoy was a ploy. Without any definitive intelligence to indicate their initial plan was faulty, he could not alter their objective based on what this one man said. Speaking into his com-link, he used their code names to relay commands.

"Hickok, come pick up our visitor and hold him for further questioning. Gadget, Ace and Webster, you're clear to move on target alpha."

Jace moved back into position and prayed he had made the right decision. About five minutes later, a large cargo truck with fabric sides came around the corner.

"We have enemy on approach from the north," Jace reported.

The truck looked like a relic from the 1940s. The axles were bent and wobbling back and forth, and it had more dents than a pockmarked teenager. Noting that the driver actually appeared to slow down as he approached their position concerned him, but Jace did not sway from his resolve.

On his signal, Hickok, aka Peter, blew the explosive planted to fell a tree in the path of the vehicle. The truck skidded to a halt, and men jumped out of the bed armed with assault rifles. As he moved into position, Jace felt the heat of several close shots whiz past him, but it seemed that the men in the truck were firing sporadically.

Amateurs. Don't they know don't pull the trigger till you have a shot?

Jace crouched low and gradually worked his way to the back of the vehicle. He had to take out two of the assailants with close-range shots to the head.

Better not to take any chances.

Peering inside the canopy, he found a terrified-looking man who looked like he belonged on the pages of *GQ*, not hog-tied in the back of a smelly cargo truck.

Politicians are such morons.

Grabbing the senator's aide, he pulled him out of the truck.

"Target secure!"

He led the package through the jungle to the pre-arranged location.

Jace held onto their rescued hostage while Peter kept the tipster under control. Jace heard the sounds of feet running through the foliage and kept his weapon ready. Justin acted as point and Eric was at the rear. Eric acknowledged that everyone was accounted for and ready to move.

It was time to get out of Dodge. Jace loaded everyone up in the truck and set course for the extraction site.

Something else was in play here, but what? Why did the driver slow down? None of the men in the truck had aimed to kill. The hostage was basically gift-wrapped and placed at their feet. What was the purpose behind their visitor who knew exactly who was waiting there and why?

The roads leading to Cochabamba were not exactly well maintained, and Jace grimaced as his spleen got jammed up into his lungs again.

"Jesus fuck! Are you trying to hit every pothole?" Cory yelled over the roar of the engine.

"Nope, just the small ones!" Jace shouted back. He keyed up his radio. "Control, this is Raven. Do you read me?"

"This is control. Go ahead, Raven."

"Control, package is secure. All boots are running. We are plus one."

"Copy, Raven. Your bird's ready for flight."

Jace signed off with the command. He kept a sharp eye out for anything unusual as he drove. They wouldn't reach the pick-up zone until 1700 hours the next day. He was working on little to no sleep in the last forty-eight hours but needed to stay alert.

Something in his gut told him that the whole operation had been too easy.

* * * *

Jace waited outside Captain Marshall's office. He'd already turned in his operational report and been debriefed, but he still had concerns. Something stank in Bolivia, and it was more than their smelly little friend who joined them in the jungle.

The door to the office opened. "Jace! Welcome back. Come

on in."

He walked through the door and stood in front of the captain's desk.

"I understand you needed to speak with me about your latest mission. I read your operation report, but didn't see anything that was a concern."

"No, sir. I wanted to speak to you about something that wasn't included in the report."

Captain Marshall sat up straight. "You left something out?"

It wasn't necessarily a reprimand. The operation report was an official document, but sometimes things happened in the field that weren't official.

"Yes, sir. But nothing about the action."

"I see. Well, go ahead and spit it out. And for heaven's sake, Jace, at ease! Good Lord, son, this isn't a congressional hearing."

Jace smiled at the man who was not only his superior officer but also mentor and close friend. He sat in the chair opposite the captain's desk. "I have a feeling that not everything is as it appears."

Marshall fiddled with a pen sitting on his desk. "How so?"

"It was too easy, sir."

Marshall chuckled and shook his head. "That's because you're good at what you do. It's not a bad thing for a mission to go off without a hitch."

"You're right, sir. But, how many times does that actually happen? Down there? *Nothing* went wrong. When I watched that road, I could have sworn the targets slowed down when they approached our position. Then of course there was our uninvited guest. Any word on when his interrogation is scheduled?"

"I hear you, Jace, and I share your concerns. Rest assured, the safety of our teams is priority one. I want you to go home. Take a shower, eat some food, and get some sleep. You look like shit."

He couldn't think of anything better. Except maybe hearing Kat's voice again.

Chapter Thirteen

It had been a week since Jace had left, and Kat desperately missed him. Her home felt empty without his presence. Her bed was somehow colder at night. She had probably yakked Amy's ear off during the past week just looking for something to fill her hours. It was closing in on ten o'clock, and after flipping channels on the TV for an hour, Kat decided it was time to call it a night. At least she still saw Jace in her dreams. As she walked around the house making sure all the doors and windows were locked, a habit she'd picked up from him, she heard the phone ring.

Amy's working the night shift tonight. Who else would be calling me so late?

She picked up the phone. "Hello?"

"Kat?"

Oh Lord, his voice sounds good. "Hi, Jace. It's good to hear from you." Kat leaned against the wall by the stairs and smiled.

"I didn't wake you, did I?"

"No, I was just locking up and heading upstairs to read for a little bit."

"I'm sorry, this is the first chance I've had to call. We were called out of town almost as soon as our plane landed last Sunday."

"That's okay. Is everyone safe?"

"Yes, we're still trying to work out the details of what brought about the situation, but the higher-ups handle that. So how was your week?"

There was tension in Jace's voice, but Kat didn't want to ask any questions that might put him in an awkward position. Although he'd probably just say something like 'that's classified' and change the subject.

She started up the stairs to her bedroom. "It was okay. The chair of the department accepted my proposal for the grant. I sent the request off to the Jeffersonian. Now I just have to wait to see if I get funding."

"That's good. When will they let you know?"

She heard him moving around, and wondered if Jace was calling her from his home. Did he have a house or apartment? They never got around to talking about that kind of stuff.

"It'll be a while, probably after the New Year when the financials for next year are established. If I do get funding, that means I'll be on site pretty much all next summer."

"Where would you be going?"

"Peru and parts of Bolivia. We're specifically looking at the sites around Machu Picchu and Lake Titicaca."

"You know there are parts of that region that are very unstable right now. Will you have safety measures in place?"

She smiled at the concern so evident in Jace's voice.

He really does care about me.

"Oh, yes. Safety is always our first concern, but where we would be going is heavily traveled by tourists and as safe as possible. Trust me, I'm not going to be traipsing around the jungle all by myself."

"So you would be down there the whole summer?"

"Well, I actually wrote the grant requesting enough money to fund the project for a year, but they rarely approve grants as written. Most likely, if they approve it at all, they'll give us a restricted timetable of a few months at the most. That's why I'm guesstimating three months."

"Just promise me that you'll stay safe."

She sat on her bed and fell back against the pillows. "I promise... Jace, I miss you."

Kat heard him sigh into the phone. "I miss you too, baby. I wish I were there with you, tucking you in next to me as you fall asleep. You know that was one of my favorite times with you—holding you in my arms at night."

She looked over at the side of the bed Jace used. "Me too. My bed has felt cold all week."

Kat wasn't going to admit it out loud, but she'd even bought one of those large body pillows so she could place it along the side of the bed where Jace had lain.

"Well, I guess I'd better let you go. You have class in the morning, right?"

"Yes, eight o'clock sharp. I'm sure you have to report in early too."

"0700 for additional debriefing. Would it be okay if I called or emailed you later this week?"

She smiled at the hesitancy in Jace's voice. Who knew that the Navy SEAL could be insecure?

"Yes, I'd like that. Tell Collin and Peter hello for me. And, Jace…?"

"Yes?"

"Stay safe, okay?"

"I will, I promise. Goodnight, Kat."

"Goodnight," she whispered.

Kat hung up the phone and grabbed her pillow to her chest. Rolling onto her side, she forgot about opening her book and fell asleep with the sound of Jace's voice in her head.

* * * *

Jace arrived on base early the next morning. He wanted to request permission to be present at the interrogation of Emanuel, the jungle visitor. He knew that Master Chief Campo was the one who was going to do the interrogation. That was a good thing in Jace's book because Campo was the best. The man had ice running through his veins. He could sit across the table from the world's most despicable human beings, and within minutes have them blubbering about how they killed thousands because their mommas didn't love them. Most of the time Campo appeared deceptively calm, but under the façade was a brain constantly analyzing angles and calculating probabilities. It was a real bitch to play poker against him. His chances of getting into the observation room were decent. Plus Campo owed him one.

At the detention center, Jace signed the log and was given a badge indicating his status. He entered the observation room behind the one-way glass that looked into the interrogation tank. Normally his team wouldn't be involved at this stage, but Jace had a hunch that things were much more complicated than they had initially appeared. If that was so, there was a good chance it would affect his team in the very near future, and he wanted all the intel possible. It was important to listen to what was said and what wasn't said.

An armed master-at-arms led Emanuel into the room. The jumpsuit and bad fluorescent lighting did nothing to hide his sallow complexion. He looked very nervous and had sweat beading on his upper lip.

Campo sat across from Emanuel and opened with, "Why would you risk your life to warn our guys of an impending ambush?"

Emanuel just sat there.

Campo took a sip of the coffee he'd brought in with him. "Why warn our guys? What did you get out of the deal?"

Emmanuel smirked. "Is that not obvious? I got out. Your boys packed me up and carted me back here without ceremony."

"How does that make a difference in your life? You know we're just going to ship you back when your usefulness is at an end, or we might make a reservation for you at Gitmo."

"Well, then, I will just have to remain useful, won't I?"

"You mentioned to our boys that you overhead men talking about the location of the interception for the convoy. Who were the men?"

"Sanchez and some American."

Campo took another sip of his coffee and waited in silence.

Jace saw the moment Emmanuel began to crack. Staring into Campo's freakishly pale eyes did that to all of them.

"I don't know the American's real name. We just called him *Tio*."

"You called him Uncle?"

"Yeah, you know, like Uncle Sam."

Jace cursed under his breath. This was bad. He had a feeling the situation was way bigger than they had initially thought.

Campo stood and walked around to Emmanuel's side of the table. He leaned down, bracing one hand on the table, and used the other to grip the back of the suspect's chair. "Are you sitting here asking me to believe we have a leak from an official in the United States government?"

Emanuel shrugged. "You can believe whatever you want. All I can say is what I know. Is it really that surprising? You got your hostage, none of *your* men was hurt or killed, and the mission was a success."

Campo slammed his palm on the metal table. Even through the glass Jace's ears rang.

"Our mission was a success due to preparation and having the best-trained soldiers available."

Emanuel gave a little smirk. "Who said I was talking about your mission?"

Jace had heard enough. He left the observation room. As much as he hated to admit it, the little worm's words were making sense. If a US official had turned, the first thing the revs would want to do is test his ability to provide accurate information. What better way than to kidnap a senator's aide on vacation, have the official set it up so that a SEAL team would come in to extract, and be able to tell them exactly where the interception would take place?

That would explain why the driver slowed down as if he were expecting them and why the armed men in the truck seemed to randomly fire without obvious targets. They just wanted to give the appearance that they gave a shit. The transporters were considered expendable, and the hostage was just a patsy to them. They didn't care if he was picked up or not. By having his team go ahead as planned, Jace had confirmed whatever information the mole had provided.

Things were going to get very complicated if this assessment was accurate. It appeared that there might be a leak within the government concerning the movement of Special Forces personnel. That could lead to serious consequences for any operation. Jace couldn't even contemplate the fallout if someone was selling information to the highest bidder regarding strategy and operation details to the very people being infiltrated. First things first—they had to determine whether the presence of a leak was true. From where he sat, Jace could only think of one way that could be achieved. He headed directly for his captain's office to fill him in.

* * * *

Jace was shown into the office to await the return of his captain. At least it had a window overlooking the bay so he could entertain himself watching the ships while he waited. The walls were painted a soft blue and there was a large world atlas on the back wall. Most of the room was commanded by a large desk and credenza in a dark-stained wood.

Continuing to stand at attention, he looked around the office and noticed pictures of Captain Marshall's family on the desk and credenza. He glanced at the one sitting closest to him and saw a happy man with a loving and obviously adoring family. It made Jace both jealous and hopeful that someday he could share his life with a family like that. He had never known what a real loving home felt like.

Jace looked around some more and saw another photo of Captain Marshall at what appeared to be his daughter's high school graduation. Jace wasn't sure if he could picture that in his immediate future, but found the idea of raising children surprisingly pleasant.

Hearing the captain enter the office, Jace snapped, "Good morning, Captain."

"Good morning, Lieutenant Commander. At ease." Marshall indicated the chair Jace usually sat in. "Please have a seat, Jace. How did the interrogation go this morning?"

Jace relaxed into a leather armchair in front of the desk. "I think we may have a serious problem, sir."

Marshall looked up from the papers sitting on his desk and looked at Jace. "You believe the allegations?"

"I think it's highly plausible, considering the details of the operation."

"Well, that certainly makes things complicated right now, doesn't it? The logical course of action would be to establish definitive evidence that a leak exists." Both men sat in silence for a few seconds. "Jace, I want you to convene with your team and come up with some possible scenarios."

"Sir, I can only think of one way to do this."

Marshall reflected for a moment. "You want to set up a false operation."

"Yes, sir, unless you know of an alternative."

"You realize the risk of such a plan?"

For the first time, Jace thought about his personal safety. If he was to have a future with Kat, then he was going to have to be more careful about taking reckless chances, something he was quite known for. However, that did not take precedence over national security.

"The potential to discover a leak outweighs any risk. I believe my men would agree with me."

"Without a doubt. Your men will follow you into hell. That's why you're such a good leader. However, I wasn't thinking of your men."

Jace's brows knit in confusion. "Sir? To whom are you referring?"

"I understand that you became very close with a young lady on your recent vacation." Jace just sat in silence, refusing to confirm or deny the comment. Marshall continued as though the silence did not exist. "I may be locked away in this office most of the time, but I still have ways of finding out what's going on in my men's lives. Our little circle is not a good place to try to keep secrets. Talk to me, son. Are you serious about this one? Who is she?"

Jace sat in front of the man he respected and admired. For many years now he had considered the captain a surrogate father, and knew the captain thought of him as a son. Once again he glanced at the photos on his desk. "Yes, I am serious. Her name is Kat, and she's a professor of anthropology. I don't know how we are going to work things out logistically, but I very much want to keep her in my life."

Marshall smiled. "It looks to me like you've finally been bitten by the love bug." Jace squirmed a little in his seat. "This is a good thing. To be honest, I've been a bit worried about you. You're thirty-five years old and we both know your family life growing up didn't exactly have a *Leave It to Beaver* quality. It's not good for a man to spend his life alone with only a career to keep him company. I've seen it often enough and it leads to a very cold existence.

"Logistics always work themselves out. If this girl really means something to you, then you'll find a way. Does she have any problem with you being in the service? Knowing what you do? Would you be put in a position where you had to choose the Navy or her?"

"No, sir. In fact, all she asked when I left was that I write her from time to time and let her know I'm safe. However, if I plan on keeping her in my life, I can hardly have some lunatic selling details of SEAL operations to the targets we're infiltrating. That would make situations suicidal that are already considered dangerous. I have no desire to die. So before Kat and I come to a decision about our lives together, I need to stop this, assuming the leak exists."

"Good, then I'll pass on the word of your proposed course of action and let you know accordingly when the time comes."

Jace stood up and snapped to attention. "Thank you for

your time and indulgence, Captain."

Marshall stood up. "I noticed you looking at my photos when I came in, Jace." He picked up the picture of his daughter at graduation and smiled. "Having the love and support of a family is more fulfilling than any job."

Jace walked out of the office, thinking about Marshall's last words. Having a family to come home to did sound ideal, especially if it was Kat waiting for him. Once this whole leak issue was taken care of, he would have to think about how he was going to get them back together again. On a permanent basis, he hoped.

* * * *

Jace rolled over and squinted up at the low ceiling of his tent. The ground was chilly, but dreams of Kat had kept him warm as he slept. They'd spent the last two months dealing with one situation after another. After Bolivia came an all-expenses-paid trip to a North Korean arms site suspected of building a nuclear arsenal. That one had been strictly an intelligence mission. The targets were to have no knowledge of their presence.

However, during the mission, Jace had come very close to being seen when one of the armed guards had deviated from his usual patrol. He was heading directly for Jace's position when Collin created a diversion to call his attention away.

He scrubbed his face and wiped away the sleep. He'd gotten a full four hours of sleep last night. Compared to the catnaps he'd grabbed over the last few days, the consecutive sack time made him feel like a new man. Next to him lay Peter, who still snored away. He crawled out of the tent then stood, sighing as his back popped when he stretched.

"Jesus, Hudson. That was almost as loud as the crack from my M4. Didn't realize you were getting so damn old."

Jace flipped off Collin—who'd taken last watch—before digging out an MRE. He sat beside Collin who was drinking coffee. "Nice morning."

"Yep, but winter is coming. Would really love to get out of here before the snow starts."

Jace looked out over the mountains in Afghanistan where the squad had been camped out for the past few weeks. They'd initially been sent to provide support for a team of Rangers trying to identify and capture a group of insurgents. However, a few days later, word came down about a cache of weapons being stored in a cave. Nothing like an insurgent one-stop shop. Jace and his crew were ordered to locate the cave, identify the weapons, and blow it to hell before the rounds found their way into more American soldiers.

He and Peter had been setting the charge when they were suddenly fired on from multiple directions. For a while, Jace had been pinned literally between a rock and a hard place. It had taken some very fancy footwork and precise shots to get out of the situation. He knew that no mission was guaranteed to go exactly as planned, but why their team's objectives were suddenly apparent to the targets both aggravated and concerned him.

He added his food portion of maple sausage meal to the ration heater bag, dug his canteen out of his assault pack and poured the water, then sealed the pouch. While his food cooked he ate the pouch of granola. He carved up the apple that came with the meal using his SOG Seal Pup knife then wiped the blade on his trousers before sliding it back in the sheath. He smiled as he remembered that morning in Kat's kitchen when he told her about liberating an MRE for her to try.

"What has you grinning?"

"Told Kat I'd bring her home one of these." He shoved a bite of granola in his mouth.

Collin stared at him. "I thought you loved her."

"I do. Why?" He fought with the hot beverage bag to make his French vanilla cappuccino that tasted nothing like the five-dollar variety at Starbucks. "Jesus, I miss my coffeemaker."

"If you love the woman, why do you plan to poison her?"

He pulled out his meal pack from the heater and opened the sealed bag, took a sniff and grimaced. Okay, so it wasn't gourmet, but it was edible. For the most part. "You hate them so much, give me your rations."

Collin held his food away from Jace. "I said I didn't like them. I never said anything about willingly starving myself."

Jace heard some rustling behind him and a soft curse.

"Will the two of you shut up? It's oh-fuck-thirty in the morning. I'm tired, I'm dirty, and I'm horny. I need food, coffee, and to take a piss. Not necessarily in that order. Then maybe I'll consider not placing a chunk of Semtex under your pillows tonight."

Jace chuckled. "Good morning to you too, sunshine."

Peter grumbled as he walked away to take care of one of his problems. Jace looked over on the other side of Collin. The rest of the squad settled down to breakfast. Hopefully sometime today, orders would come down as to when they'd be cleared to leave their little mountain love nest and get back to a base camp so he could email Kat. He tried to send messages when he could, but knew that they were sporadic at best. However, each time he received a response, his heart felt lighter and his stress level dropped for the time it took to read her words and imagine the sound of her voice, reading them to him. He had no idea when they'd make it back CONUS, but each night before he sacked out, he prayed it would be soon.

Chapter Fourteen

Kat inhaled the crisp fall air as she walked from the parking lot to her department building. The leaves above her head were vibrant red and orange and yellow.

Jace's team had returned to Virginia over the weekend, and according to him, planned to be stateside until some type of investigation got cleared up. As elated as she was to have Jace back on American soil, she'd heard the tension in his voice. Something was bothering him, but she didn't think it had anything to do with their relationship. In fact, they'd spent hours on the phone over the weekend reconnecting. It had been so good to hear his voice after several weeks.

No, whatever was bothering her man was work related. And that worried Kat. But she knew that she couldn't exactly ask Jace how his day at the office went. While he was away, she and Jace had sent emails back and forth whenever possible. She told him over the weekend that she looked so forward to reading his notes that she'd gotten into the habit of checking her email every morning when she got to work. Jace had responded with a teasing comment about passing notes in class and asked if she'd circle 'Yes' or 'No' if he asked her if she liked him.

Her pace sped up as she entered her building. Maybe there'd be a note waiting for her this morning. Kat logged on to her email and smiled when she found a message waiting for her. She clicked the link and her screen flashed a bright white.

"What the hell!" she exclaimed.

Her monitor went black then filled with a giant skull

and crossbones. Bright red lines that looked like blood ran down from the top of the screen. A loud static sound came from her speakers then an evil-sounding voice echoed, "Do you believe in the ultimate sacrifice? You will!"

Kat frantically tried closing the computer window, but the system appeared to be frozen. The message kept playing over and over, the skull changing from bones to flesh like decomposition in reverse. It ended with the skull transforming into an image of Jace, his eyes blank in death, a giant hole in the center of his forehead. Gasping, Kat hit the switch on the power strip to the computer, no longer caring about improperly shutting down the system.

She sat in her chair and stared at the now-dark monitor. *Why would he send something like that?* She didn't think Jace had that twisted a sense of humor.

Then she thought about all the stories she'd heard of people's email being hacked into and sending viruses to those who open the files. She looked at her desk clock. Kat had to teach a class in five minutes. She didn't have time to worry about this at the moment. She would tell Jace the next time they talked. She supposed she'd have to call the IT department to have someone make sure she didn't damage the computer. Fantastic, that would really get her on the Dean's good side. Maybe everything would be fine? It was just a nasty email. A cruel prank. She picked up her notes and left the office. She'd probably power up the computer next time and be greeted with her pretty background image.

* * * *

Kat sat in her living room grading term papers, avoiding the black Friday shopping insanity. The phone sitting next to her rang and she jumped.

"Damn, I did it again." She looked down at her watch. She didn't realize it had gotten so late.

The phone trilled a second time. She picked it up. "Hello?"

"Hi, sweetheart, how are you?"

She threw the papers onto the table and held the phone closer to her ear. "Jace! Oh, it's good to hear your voice. I've been worried sick all week."

"Why? What's going on? I told you I haven't been deployed on any operations with this investigation going on."

"I know, I just... It's silly, I guess... I really shouldn't have read as much into it as I did."

"Kat, what are you talking about? Did something happen to you? Why haven't you been responding to my emails? Is something wrong?"

Kat heard a frantic quality to Jace's voice and wanted to quickly reassure him. "No... At least, not with me. I'm sorry, Jace. I got so caught up in work this week, I forgot to call and tell you that I had a little computer issue on Monday. Someone sent me an email with a virus attached, and it spooked me a little. I found out later from the IT people that it totally fried my computer at the office. I've actually been afraid to open my email at home for fear of the same thing happening."

"What kind of email was it?"

Should she tell him about the video attached to the email? She didn't want him to worry. He had enough on his plate.

"Kat? What was in the email? Remember what I said about talking things out?"

That was Jace's dominating voice. She sighed. "You're right. I should have told you earlier."

Kat told him what happened when she had opened the message that had been addressed from him.

"Kat, has anything else out of the ordinary happened this week? Anything unusual, doesn't matter how small?"

"Well, in the spirit of honesty, I've felt a little creepy all week—like someone's been watching me—but I figured it was because I was paranoid after seeing the message."

Jace expelled a loud breath over the phone. "Baby, why didn't you call me? I can't help you if I don't know what's going on."

"Well, I knew you were busy, and I had a hectic week, and honestly, I didn't want to think about it. I trusted that if anything had really happened to you one of the boys would call me... I hope they would call me. I'm sure it was nothing and my paranoia will go away. Can we talk about something else? I don't want to spend what time we have together arguing about pointless pranks."

She knew Jace wasn't going to forget what she had told him. Most likely the second they hung up the phone, he'd get to work on determining the source of that email.

"Sure, what do you want to talk about? I know... What are you wearing?"

She laughed. "You are so bad."

He gave a husky chuckle. "Are you telling me that you haven't missed me? I must not have left as much of an impression as I hoped."

"You know I've missed you dreadfully," she said softly.

He loved her laugh. He hadn't planned on this when he called but suddenly he desperately wanted to hear Kat cry out in passion again. He missed her presence more deeply than anything, and wanted back that closeness they shared.

"I most definitely am thinking about you, and how you make me burn. I miss you, sweetheart. Will you make love with me, Kat? Right now?"

Her breathing sped up and became shallower. "Okay, let me go upstairs."

He heard her feet hit the stairs and the click of the light switch in the bedroom. The rustling sound of fabric made him picture Kat stripping and he cut off a deep moan. Then there was a slight squeak from the springs of her mattress.

"Okay, I'm ready."

"Oh, no, Kat, you're nowhere near ready, but we'll get there. Are you still in your clothes?"

"No."

"Good, I want you to rub your fingers across the tops of your breasts, very softly. Now imagine that it's my fingers touching you. Pull gently on your nipples, make them hard, and give them a slight pinch."

He knew Kat was following his orders, because he heard a soft moan. "Kat, does your phone have a speaker on it?"

"Yes, I've already turned it on. Your voice is filling my room just like you were here with me."

Hearing that admission made Jace get even harder than he had been a moment ago.

"Believe me, I wish I was there with you. I love watching you come alive with desire. Your eyes get dark, your skin gets warm and flushed. You're so goddamn beautiful."

"I want you to keep massaging your breast with one hand and reach the other one down between your legs. Slowly slide your fingers between your lips. Feel the wetness I know is gathering and rub it into your skin. Slide your fingers up and down to spread that lovely cream around. Now, take your index finger and lightly circle your clit. Go around it ten times then flick it with your nail."

Her cry echoed through the receiver as he unzipped his jeans, pulled out his cock, and began stroking himself. "Now, take two fingers and slip them inside you. Move them slowly in and out, just like I would. Feel that sweet slickness gather on them, feel your muscles clench around them like they were my cock. Can you feel the pressure building in your blood, Kat?"

On a slight whimper, she answered, "Yes, but I need more, Jace. I don't think I'll be able to come this way. Can I use the vibrator I bought?"

Jace sucked in his breath, then his voice deepened even further. "You bought a vibrator?"

His cock was flushed dark red and leaking. Using his pre-cum as a lubricant, he stroked faster. Running his hand up and down the length, he gave a little squeeze on the upstroke over the top of the head

"Yes. I was missing you so badly and went to the store last week to pick one out, but I haven't used it yet."

"What kind did you get, sweetheart?"

"It's pink and has little beads in it that rotate around when I push a button. The shaft vibrates and moves in circles too. I loved it when you would circle your hips inside me so I thought that might feel similar."

The image of Kat lying on her bed pleasuring herself with a vibrator and imagining it was him drove him crazy.

"Go get your toy. We'll play together."

Jace heard Kat shift, and what sounded like her bedside drawer open and close.

"Okay, I've got it."

"Do you have any lubricant to put on it?"

"No, I didn't think about that."

"That's okay. We'll make sure you're nice and wet before we put that inside you. Now, turn on the vibrator and just lay it against your pussy. Press it against your clit and adjust the speed so you're just on the verge of over-sensitizing yourself. I want you to slowly circle it around the little bud, placing just enough pressure to make you squirm... Are you getting wetter, baby? Are you ready to take it inside you?"

He heard her pleading voice. "Yes, Jace, please come inside me now. I need you desperately."

Hearing her refer to the vibrator as him, Jace released his own groan. He was stroking himself with slow, strong pulls. "Move it slowly down to your opening and push just the head inside you. Take your clit between your fingers and pull slightly just like I do when I suck on it. Push me a little deeper inside you. I want you to alternate between short and medium thrusts but don't go all the way to the hilt yet." He heard a soft cry escape from Kat's lips.

After several minutes, she pleaded, "Please, Jace..." in a breathless whisper.

"Okay, baby, all the way. Push me all the way in, nice and hard and deep."

Kat hollered and Jace closed his eyes to savor the sound of her pleasure.

"Turn on the rotator and tilt the shaft up into your body.

Keep rubbing your clit with that finger. Don't stop. Move me in and out of your snug, wet body... A little faster now, sweetheart, a little harder. I'm there with you. Feel me thrust deep inside of you. God, you are so tight and hot and wet. I love feeling you explode around me—feeling that sweet cum gush down my throat, soak my hand, or wash over my cock."

Closing his eyes, he recalled the hot liquid feel of Kat's channel around his cock and the intoxicating taste of her orgasm. Pulling hard, he shifted his hips and thrust up into his hand. He heard Kat's moans and pictured the toy cock sliding in and out, wet with cream, her pussy lips spread open and flushed, her clit swollen and desperate for release. His toes curled into the bed as his climax approached. He needed a little something more to send them both over the edge.

"Kat, I'm so hard for you. I'm imagining you fucking yourself right now. I can see it in my mind. You're so beautiful—my ultimate fantasy in living color. I'm close... I can tell by your cries that you are too. Let's come together. I'm right there with you. I have you in my arms. I can feel your skin against mine. Your panting breaths are whispering in my ear. Oh, God... Here we go, Kat. Come with me." He felt his orgasm rolling down his spine and pooling in his balls. He followed the path, continuing to thrust. He grabbed his balls and gave a squeeze. With a roar, he threw his head back and felt the hot release erupt over his fingers.

Jace heard Kat scream, too, and knew she had climaxed. After several minutes, he asked, "Kat? You still there?"

"Yeah, I'm here."

"Are you going to fall asleep on me now?"

"Yeah, but will you stay on the line with me for a little while, Jace? I just want to feel your presence a little longer."

"I'll stay right here, okay? Just imagine that I'm pulling you into my arms and against my body under the covers. We'll fall asleep together."

Jace heard Kat's breathing even out and slow down.

Sensing she was asleep, he whispered into the phone, "I love you," and hung up.

* * * *

Jace entered his captain's office the next morning, his mood dark as the sky with the current storm that threatened to unleash hell on the base. He had been tempted to barge in and start yelling, but the years of training and discipline forced him to observe protocol.

After he got off the phone with Kat last night, he'd spent hours trying to organize his thoughts into a concise and logical argument to present to Marshall. The problem was, when it came to Kat, his emotions kept trying to kick him into panic mode every time he thought about a threat against her. It was a good thing that the Navy had beat panic mode out of him years ago. Otherwise, he would have been on a plane to St. Louis first thing this morning.

"I think someone may be either targeting my team or, more specifically, me personally."

Marshall looked startled for a moment. "What makes you think that, son?"

"First of all, we haven't received any reports of other teams' operations being anything other than routine. Second, it looks like someone hacked into my email and sent Kat a threatening message. I spoke to the rest of the guys last night, and none of them reported anything out of the ordinary."

"Have you been able to confirm the message origin?"

"No, not yet. I found out last night when I called her. I was concerned that she hadn't returned any of my emails this week, and she confessed to receiving the message." He ran a hand over the top of his head. "A week ago," he grumbled. "She told me that the university's IT guys suspected a virus was attached to the email. Her office computer got fried in the process, and she didn't want to risk opening any email from me at home."

"What would be the point of sending a threatening message to someone clearly not connected to any operations?"

"It wasn't threatening her. It was threatening me. They only sent it to her. If someone were targeting me specifically, it wouldn't take a genius to know the best way to get under my skin would be to terrorize Kat. Especially if the person is as closely related to operations as we suspect." He stopped pacing and turned to look at Marshall. "I understand if you feel the need to replace me within the team, Captain. I don't want this situation to endanger any other members."

"Nonsense, Jace. You know the team sticks together no matter what happens. We'll work this situation out together. Is there any way we can get our hands on that computer? Then we could trace the email back to the IP address, right?"

Jace thought for a moment. "I have no idea, but I'll ask Kurt. He's called Gadget for good reason. She said that the IT people claimed it was trash, and already put in a request for a new one."

"Can we get in contact with her right now and ask? This is the first possible lead we've had on the situation, and I don't want to lose it."

"It's 1000 hours here, that means it's 0900 there. She should have just finished a class. If you want, I can call her cell right now."

Marshall sat back in his chair. "Well, go ahead."

Jace took out his cell and gave the number to Marshall, who punched it into the base unit of his desk phone. A ringing sound was amplified and broadcasted into the office through the speaker.

"Hello?"

Jace knew the smile that crossed his face wouldn't escape Marshall's notice. "Hey, Kat, how was class?"

"Good. The kids were really excited about today's lecture. Blood, fighting and all matter of fascinating gore. Hey, what number are you calling from?"

"I'm here in my CO's office. We have a question for you.

First I want to know what your lecture was about."

"We were discussing ancient Mesopotamia and how aspects of Assyrian warfare can still be seen in military training programs throughout the world. With photographic and illustrative support, of course. I think the little heathens just liked the bloody pictures."

Jace and Marshall both chuckled. "Unfortunately we're short on time so I have to ask our question and run."

"Okay, shoot."

"Do you still have your computer that got fried by the virus?"

"Yeah, the IT people took a look at it, said it was hopeless. I've put in a requisition for a new one, but it hasn't arrived yet. Why?"

"Well, we think there could potentially be a link between whoever sent you that email and what we've been working on. The only way we can trace it back to the sender is to have the actual hardware. Do you think the school would allow us to have it?"

"I don't see why not. It's of no use to them. I thought we decided it was just a prank and to let it go?"

"No, sweetheart, you decided that. I never agreed. I would really appreciate it if you just go with me on this."

"Okay, I'll box it up and send it to you, but from what the IT guys said, you won't find anything useful. The hard drive was completely fragmented."

"Well, we may have secrets they don't know about."

"Somehow, that would *not* surprise me."

Marshall scoffed, and Jace glared at him. Lowering his voice he asked, "Did you notice anything unusual this morning on the way to school? Like you were talking about last night?"

"No, everything was quiet. I told you it was probably just my imagination. Now that I know you're safe, I'm fine."

"Promise me that you'll call right away if that changes, okay? Doesn't matter what time it is, day or night."

"I promise, worry wart."

Marshall signaled to Jace to let him talk. "Dr Martin, this is Captain Rich Marshall. I appreciate you going to the trouble of sending us your computer remains. Unfortunately, I can't divulge the nature of our investigation, but you may be providing a very valuable clue."

"Whatever I can do to help, Captain. All I ask in exchange is that you keep an eye on Jace and make sure he stays out of trouble."

Marshall gripped Jace's shoulder and gave it a squeeze. "I'll do my best, but he can be a very stubborn man when he puts his mind to it."

Kat huffed. "Don't I know it."

Marshall smiled at Jace. "I'll give you a moment to say your goodbyes." He walked out of the door.

Jace and Kat talked for another minute or so, then he told her that he really did have to go. After he hung up the phone, he waited for Marshall to return. It was nice of him to give them some privacy, but now Jace was standing here twiddling his thumbs. He wanted to get out there and do… something. Unfortunately, until Kat's computer arrived, they didn't have any other evidence to examine.

The door to the office opened while he stood beside the window looking out at the thunderheads rolling in off the bay.

"She'll do just fine, son. Out of curiosity, what was that about her telling you if she felt threatened?" Marshall asked.

"She said last night that she felt like she was being watched all last week. She's convinced it was paranoia in reaction to the email, but I'm not willing to bet her life on that."

Marshall walked over behind his desk and flipped open a file folder. "Do you think we need to send a detail to watch over her?"

Jace ran his hand through his hair as he answered. "My heart wants to say yes, but my instincts are uncertain. She's a smart girl with a healthy dose of self-preservation." Once again thinking about everything Kat had overcome, he added, "She's also a fighter. However, if I sense a real threat, you can bet my commission I'll find a way to protect her. Sir, unless it's absolutely necessary I'd like to request that we keep this investigation within our squad. I don't want NCIS or any unnecessary personnel to go stirring up trouble we haven't bought yet."

"I'll do what I can, but if the threat is global against the teams they have to be called. You know that. And when we catch the bastard they're the ones who will be taking custody of him. I'm not going to allow you to go all vigilante on me, Jace. I need you here, not rotting in the brig at Norfolk."

"Yes, sir."

Chapter Fifteen

It was only three weeks until Christmas. Jace loved this time of year on the base. For a place that was never really quiet, this time of year always seemed peaceful. He had received Kat's computer a week ago, and Kurt had been working on it ever since, trying to trace the source of that email.

Since his return to Virginia, Jace and Kat had talked on the phone almost every night. They'd had phone sex more than a couple of times. Even though their interludes left him briefly physically satisfied, Jace couldn't help but feel something was missing. He was also starting to get concerned.

Every night he asked Kat if she had noticed anything unusual going on and every night she said no, but last night Jace had had a gut feeling that she wasn't telling the complete truth. He couldn't stand to think about Kat being in danger or someone targeting her just to get to him. He would have felt much better if he'd had a chance to check things out himself, but right now that was impossible. Now instead of half a world separating them, there was only a thousand miles, but they were still no closer to spending time together.

He needed to feel her in his arms, to hear those breathy sighs against his neck when they loved each other, to actually see her smile light up those expressive eyes. He hadn't said the words to her yet, but he knew he loved her. Somehow, saying something like that over the phone didn't seem right. He wanted to be holding her when he said the words for the first time.

His pager, sitting on the coffee table, started to buzz. *That can't be good.* The pager never went off unless the team was being called in for an emergency. He stood to grab the kit he kept at the ready. As he was walking over to the closet, his cell phone went off and his landline rang. *This is definitely not good.* Jace picked up his cell so he could run and talk at the same time. He opened the door to his town house and started running toward his bike still parked in the driveway.

"Hudson."

He heard Kurt's voice come over the speaker. "You need to get over to the office right now."

"I'm on my way. What's going on?"

"I don't want to say without a secure line. Just get here as fast as you can."

It didn't take long to get to the SFO building riding his motorcycle. The 865cc engine sped through the streets on base like a bat out of hell, and this late he didn't have to worry about traffic. Five minutes had passed when he pulled into the parking lot.

As he got off the bike, he saw Commander Jefferson walking into the building and, just behind him, Captain Marshall.

What the hell is going on?

CDR Jefferson, although technically Jace's commanding officer, was rarely found out in the field.

If he and the captain are here, they must have broken the IP address of the email on Kat's computer.

Jace picked up the pace and ran to the conference room where they were gathering.

Kurt nodded as soon as Jace walked in the door. "Okay, everyone is here, so let me begin by saying that all information in this room is strictly classified. Jace, I've been able to reconstruct the email sent to Kat, and I think you should see this."

Kurt hit a key on the laptop in front of him. The wall at the end of the conference room was lit up from the projector overhead. Jace sat in silence as the video that Kat must have seen so many weeks ago played in all its gory glory. He clenched his fists and ground his teeth. The vein on the side of his neck began to pulsate. It wasn't the fact that it was his face up on the screen that made him so mad. It was the fact that Kat had been subjected to watching it. Hearing her describe the graphics did not remotely compare to seeing them with his own eyes.

"Now that we've had show and tell, I can inform you that the IP address this message originated from was isolated to a public terminal on base. Since it originated from Jace's personal email, we can't trace it specifically to the sender. However, when we confiscated the terminal, we found that he had left clues.

"By hacking into Jace's email account, he left little electronic fingerprints throughout the system. So we are either dealing with someone who was following orders and didn't realize he was leaving evidence, or someone who was banking on the fact that, with the virus frying Kat's hard drive, the source couldn't be traced."

Looking down the table at Jace, he said, "That's not all. We were also able to determine that while the virus was being uploaded to Kat's computer, it was simultaneously hacking into her hard drive. They got everything. They know who she is, where she lives and works, not to mention any personal information she had stored on her office computer."

A cold fear entered his chest as Jace listened to this news. *They know how to find her!*

CDR Jefferson spoke up. "I've only recently been briefed on the situation, but who is this woman, and how is she connected to us, exactly?"

Everyone looked to Jace.

"She's a professor of anthropology at Washington University in St. Louis. We met while I was on leave for Cory's wedding. We've since…become close."

Collin chimed in with, "He loves her but hasn't told her

yet. Peter and I also happen to know her from our childhood days, but that's just pure coincidence."

Jefferson responded, "Okay, so why go after her? What's the strategy? If the goal is to sabotage SEAL missions, why even contact a woman who has no direct connection to base of operations?"

Kurt answered, "We suspect with this new evidence that Jace is the primary target, sir. Our last several missions have not gone according to plan, and each time Jace's position or objective was actively compromised. Jace, has Kat mentioned anything to you about feeling threatened?"

"No, I keep casually asking but she denies it. However, I get the feeling that she's not telling me the whole truth. I'm not sure if she's trying to hide it from me because she feels I have no power to help, being a thousand miles away, or if she doesn't trust her own instincts."

Speaking for the first time, Marshall said, "I think we have no choice now but to initiate the plan Jace suggested to flush out the target. I don't think we can ignore the evidence that something is afoot within our ranks."

Jefferson responded, "Putting aside the fact that Jace seems to have questionable abilities to achieve his objectives, we'll devise a plan and advise you accordingly, Captain."

If he'd been capable of amusement at the moment, Jace would have had to hide his smile at the look Marshall gave Jefferson.

Marshall stood and braced his hands on top of the table. "Let's have a plan in place at fifteen-thirty tomorrow." He looked directly at Jace. "May I speak with you privately?"

Jace stood and exited the room with the captain. They stopped a short distance from the door. "Sir?"

"I know you must be upset with the information presented here tonight, but I want to remind you to keep a level head. I know how hard that is when someone you care about is being threatened, but we still need to figure out exactly what is going on here, okay? Also, just ignore Jefferson. He's cantankerous because his new baby has prevented him from getting a decent night's sleep for the last two months."

"Yes, sir."

Marshall put his hand on Jace's shoulder. "I can make a few calls and make sure that she's being looked after, okay?"

"Appreciate that, Captain."

"Don't worry, son. We'll keep her safe."

* * * *

Ah, here she comes. So good to see the effect of my little email on her. Quick steps, little feet scurrying across the pavement trying to reach the safety of the car. Look how she dresses, displaying herself to be noticed by every passerby.

Well, let's see how she likes it now that I've taken notice. Oops. She's on alert. Must've stepped too heavily... How cute, the way she weaponizes her keys.

You think those can stop me? Oh, no, my dear. They won't save you. The time for an introduction has come.

* * * *

Kat crossed the dark parking lot of campus. A minute ago, she'd thought she'd heard a noise like someone running, but when she'd turned around, there had been nobody in sight. Not that people running were unusual around campus. Lots of the students jogged at night but that particular sound didn't seem like a co-ed out for a late-night jog.

Finals were scheduled next week, and she was still preparing her exam for two classes and had two Doctoral theses to review. It didn't help her nerves that she hadn't been sleeping well at night. Even on the nights when she talked to Jace, as soon as she hung up the phone, the air around her always felt wrong. She didn't know what was making her feel disturbed, but the anxiety was always there. Still, she had no concrete evidence of any foul play, so every time Jace asked her if things were okay, she said yes.

She'd debated about finding some way to protect herself, but didn't want to have a gun in the house, especially when she had no training with how to use it. She could get some kind of big dog, but adopting one purely to turn it into a canine bodyguard hardly seemed fair to the animal. No, if she was going to adopt an animal, she'd do it because she wanted to share her life and love with a companion.

As she neared her car, the light post above her flickered and shut off.

Great. Just what I need.

She clutched her keys a little tighter and used her thumb to feel for the unlock button on the key. Suddenly she saw the shape of someone standing behind her reflected in the car window. She spun around to confront the person, but didn't react fast enough.

The attacker shoved her against the car. Her back arched painfully. Her neck strained as her hips stayed pinned to the car and her shoulders were crushed into the intruder's chest. One hand clamped over her mouth and the other around her neck.

"Don't say a word!"

The whisper left no doubt that she should obey. Kat's eyes widened, but she didn't dare move. She shivered in cold and fear as a gust of icy wind blew across her face combined with the menacing presence of the assailant pressing against her.

"I know who you are. You're Jace Hudson's little tart. If you want to save his life, the next time he calls, you tell him it's time to break things off. You tell him you need more than what he is capable of giving. Now, he's going to try to talk you out of this, but you'd better do a damn good job of convincing him. If Jace does nothing else, he'll follow your orders like a good little soldier. He has to think this is your decision, so you can't tell him of our little meeting here tonight, and I'll know if you do. Should that happen, you and I might need to get better acquainted. Oh, and leave the police out of this, otherwise there will be more blood on your conscience."

There was the alien sensation of a hot tongue licking the back of Kat's neck, making her cry out under the gloved hand. Then her attacker released her and ran out into the darkness surrounding the parking lot.

Kat stood frozen, shaking, tears streaming down her cheeks. He'd said not to call the police, but isn't that what you were supposed to do after something like this? Then again there was no surveillance video in this lot, and all she had was her word about what happened. Plus, what if the attacker hadn't been bluffing, and she was truly being watched? It wasn't worth the risk.

Climbing into her car with shaking hands, she turned the key in the ignition. Sitting in the darkness with the doors locked, Kat took several deep breaths. She had to get home. She had to find some way of warning Jace without her attacker recognizing the signal. Putting the car in first gear, she drove off the lot and headed for her house.

* * * *

Kat sat in her living room thinking about how to tell Jace what had happened without telling him. Just as the phone rang, it came to her.

"Hello?"

"Hey, princess, how are you tonight?"

Taking a deep breath, Kat started her speech. "I think we need to talk about something."

She heard the tightness in her voice, and knew Jace would pick up on it.

"Okay, what's going on?" he said hesitantly.

"It's time to break things off. I need more than what you are capable of giving."

Please don't believe me. Please don't believe me!

"Why the sudden change of heart? I thought things were

going well between us."

"I was leaving school tonight and I realized that you are too overbearing to suit my quiet, reflective personality. You are always trying to manipulate me, forcing me to do your will. I need space and air to live my life the way I see fit. I feel like you're choking me. I don't want to be responsible for what happens if I continue to feel threatened."

"Kat, this doesn't sound like you. What's going on? Is someone there? Are you being forced to say this to me? Come on, sweetheart. You can tell me. I can have somebody at your house in less than five minutes if need be."

Oh, God, what do I say? He knows something is wrong but I can't tell him. What if that guy is watching, listening?

"I've said what needs to be said," she answered in a raised voice.

She heard a sound like a gasp on the other end of the line. *I'm sorry, Jace. I'm so sorry.*

"Well, if that's how you feel, I sure don't want you to feel *threatened* by me. I'm sorry I'm not there so we could talk this out like adults. Is there anything you want me to tell Collin and Peter, since you won't be seeing them again, either?"

He believes me. He actually thinks I'm breaking up with him! No! Listen, Jace, listen to my words. Don't give up on me.

"Yes, please tell them stay safe. It's a dangerous world out there and you never know who you can trust." With that, Kat hung up the phone.

She ran up the stairs into her bedroom and cried into her pillow, praying Jace would calm down enough to read between the hateful words and pick up on her message.

The phone rang again. She didn't want to pick it up in case it was Jace calling back. She didn't think she could talk to him like that again. Hearing the machine kick on downstairs, she tensed and heard an electronically altered voice. "You think you're so smart? That pathetic ploy won't help you or save him. In fact, you disobeyed me." *Click.*

Oh, my God, he heard our conversation! Is my phone tapped?

Was he close enough to hear what I was saying? Is he in my house?

She picked up the phone to call the police. She didn't care at this point. Her finger shook as she tried to read the numbers through her tears. The tone as she hit each digit seemed loud in the dark room.

"9-1-1 emergency."

"I... I think I need to report a break-in."

"You think, ma'am? Are you in the house now?"

"Yes. I heard. Over the phone. A man. He threatened me."

Kat heard the operator sigh on the other end of the phone. "Have you heard any sounds in the house? Has anything been disturbed?"

Kat pulled her knees up to her chest. "N...no. But—"

"It was most likely a crank caller."

"I don't know. There's been—" Wait, she couldn't tell the operator about Jace or his status as a SEAL. What if that broke some kind of national security code?

"I'll have a patrol car drive by your address to make sure everything is quiet. Please refrain from using this line unless you are experiencing a life-threatening situation."

The line disconnected and Kat stared at the receiver making loud obnoxious buzzing sounds in her ears. The 911 operator had hung up on her. Were they allowed to do that?

She climbed out of bed and closed her bedroom door.

* * * *

Kat squinted against the sunshine that came through the kitchen window the next morning after spending the night locked behind her bedroom door, wide awake. Two police officers had come knocking on her door not long after 911 had hung up on her. They'd checked the house and told her everything was secure, but it hadn't helped Kat achieve any amount of sleep. In fact, after they left, she'd locked her bedroom door, looked at the chest of drawers and, after some mental debating, decided, *fuck it*. It took some maneuvering and determination, but eventually the heavy piece of furniture rested in front of the door. Unfortunately, she ran out of household barriers in the bedroom to block the window. Subsequently, she'd spent the remainder of the night in bed, hugging her 'Jace' pillow to her chest.

Now, the sky outside said it was time to go to work, and Kat's eyes were gritty and her muscles ached from being so tense all night long. But she still had to work. This time of year there was no such thing as sick days. However, there was no way in hell she'd be able to function without some caffeine. Kat went to get the coffee out of the cabinet and froze. There was a note sitting on the counter by the coffee machine.

Don't try that again, or he will suffer the consequences.

She let out a weak scream. He *had* been in her house! Why hadn't the police seen anything? Who cares? She had to get out of here!

Kat grabbed her purse and made a dash for the front door. She jumped into the car and didn't even blink when the tires squealed as she reversed out of the driveway. A horn blasted, and she looked in the rear-view mirror to see another vehicle right behind her.

Was that him, or had she just almost hit a neighbor on their way to work? Kat hit the accelerator, not wanting to take any chances.

* * * *

Four hours and five cups of coffee later, Kat sat at her desk. The calendar in front of her blurred and she shook her head to clear her vision. She'd been looking over her shoulder all day, startled by every little noise. The phone on her desk rang, frightening her and making her jump. Her latest cup of coffee turned over and she cursed. She swiped at the hot liquid, trying to get it off her desk and into the trash can. The phone wouldn't shut up so she grabbed the receiver.

"Dr Martin," she answered, aggravated at the intrusion.
"Kat? You okay?"
She took a deep breath and let it out slowly. "Yes, sorry, Grant. I just spilled my coffee all over my desk."
"Uh-oh. I'll send a graduate student with some more, ASAP."
Kat fell back into her chair and laughed softly, "I'm going to need it." Her hands started to tremble, but she wasn't sure if it was residual nerves or maybe the fact that she'd actually had too much caffeine.
"I noticed you were looking a little flustered earlier. You do know that it's the students' jobs to freak out about upcoming finals, not yours, right? You're a professor now. We get to sit at the front of the room and laugh while we watch the sweat drip down the foreheads of all our students who didn't bother to learn anything all semester until pulling a cram session eight hours before the test."
Kat tilted her head back and closed her eyes. "Did you just call to harass me? And why are you calling me from down the hall? Are you really that lazy?"
"No. And yes. Like I said, I saw you a little while ago and you looked stressed. Thought I'd offer my services with any help you might need on the thesis you still have to review. I owe you one from back in September."
"I appreciate the offer, but really I haven't been sleeping well. That's why I'm so frayed. I think I'm going to head home. Make an early night of it."
"All right, but give me a shout if you need anything."
"Will do." Kat hung up the phone then stood and gathered her papers. She was useless until she got some sleep.

****

She couldn't relax. She'd tried tea, she'd tried music and she'd tried reading. She thought about getting a hotel room, or calling Amy to ask if she could crash at her friend's house. But hotels cost money, and Amy would pester her about why Kat suddenly felt the need for a sleepover. Besides, she didn't want to put her friend in danger. So now it was dark outside and Kat sat in her living room. She didn't turn on any lights. She waited, her legs pulled up against her chest. She wasn't sure exactly what she was waiting for, but she knew something was coming. Every sound in the house had her jerking upright.

She'd picked up the phone to call Jace and tell him what was happening so many times, but clearly whoever was stalking her also had intimate knowledge about her boyfriend's movements. And Kat would never forgive herself if her cowardliness got Jace killed, not when he survived war and terrorists on a regular basis.

Just as she was starting to doze off, a shrill sound cut through the air like a siren, and she realized it was her cell phone. Looking at the caller ID, she noticed it flashed a number she was not familiar with.

"Hello?"

Kat didn't hear anything on the other end, just heavy breathing and a click as the call was disconnected. A few minutes later, her home phone rang. Seeing the same number on the ID, she picked up the receiver.

"What do you want?"

"I want you to suffer, just like he will."

Click.

When Kat finally crumpled owing to sheer mental exhaustion that night, she dreamed of dark reflections and shrilling phones with no answer.

* * * *

She woke up with a start in the middle of the night. The wind blew hard outside, making a God-awful moaning sound. She looked over to her clock. The number twelve blinked repeatedly, taunting her. The power was out. She covered her ears and shouted when a loud bang echoed in the dark room. She looked over to her bedroom window and saw a tree branch hitting the windowpane. She removed her hands, feeling like an idiot. A scuffling sound had her looking up at the ceiling.

It's just squirrels or leaves. There is nobody up there. Get a grip on yourself!

But then, a loud thump sounded just outside her bedroom door.

Kat jumped out of bed and ran to the bathroom, where she grabbed a can of hairspray. It wasn't the best weapon, but if someone came in, she might be able to temporarily disable them. She stayed there the rest of the night, crouched in the darkness, holding her can like a weapon.

* * * *

The rest of the week went much the same way. The phone would ring, but nobody would be on the other end. Kat finally stopped answering her phone. Her voicemail box filled up. Many of them were from Jace. He wanted to try to work things out. He sounded upset, almost pleading with her not to shut him out. Just knowing that he was hurting and it was her fault only made things that much worse.

Every night, she walked through the house checking the locks on the windows and doors two or three times. If she happened to fall asleep, she would come awake terrified that someone was in the house. Every morning, she would go downstairs and something would be moved from where it was the previous evening or a note would be left on the counter, but the locks were never disturbed.

* * * *

From the shadows of a car parked two houses away, a gaze followed Kat as she checked the locks on the windows again.

Tonight's the night. I can feel it. The time has come to proceed.

The lights in each room went off, one by one.

I'll give her time to get settled in bed. In the dark of night is when the nightmares come.

He opened the front door, silently, and slipped inside. In front of him were the stairs leading to the second floor and his girl. He pulled out a cell and dialed the number to the house. The ringing phones crashed through the silence. From upstairs the sound of Kat screaming caused laughter to bubble out.

Oh, this is just too good.

Having identified the light switches during previous trips, he grasped the desired one in gloved fingers and made the lights in the upstairs hallway flash on and off. The effect looked like a cheap strobe.

A loud thump echoed down through the floorboards overhead, then the sound of feet running. A door slammed. He ran up the stairs and shoved against the closed bedroom door. The wood cracked then gave way. The barrier crashed into the wall behind it. Kat was perched on the windowsill. She'd gotten one leg outside the window and was attempting to escape.

She must be stopped.

Kat tried to push her way out of the window. It was situated in an eave of the roof. If she could get out, then she could cross the roof to reach the large tree and climb down to safety. Cold, biting wind hit her face.

He rushed toward the window. Her hair flowed down her back, and he grabbed it, twisting it around his hand.

Her head was yanked backward and twisted at an unnatural angle. The intruder's fist remained wrapped in her hair. Her head was slammed against the window frame. Pain exploded throughout her skull. Darkness was quickly closing in, but she fought the sensation.

She slumped, allowing herself to fall onto the roof. The intruder made a grab for her arm. The bones in her wrist felt like they were being crushed, then the sensation was gone, and Kat fell backward. She felt herself rolling down the roof, but couldn't seem to stop the motion. Kat vaguely felt herself hit the ground. The darkness finally closed in.

Chapter Sixteen

Jace knew he had to get to Kat. He knew something was wrong. After he'd calmed down, he'd realized that Kat's words coming through the phone on the night she'd broken up with him had been some type of code. He'd tried calling both her cell and home phone numbers and he'd emailed her, but had never got a response. Checking his watch, he saw that it was just after 0900. He knew Captain Marshall would be in his office. They needed to discuss the situation. The team had planned on setting up the decoy operation for the following week.

He'd started running toward the SFO building when his pager went off again.

Shit! Now what?

Detouring to the same meeting room as the other night, he walked in to find Captain Marshall, Collin and Kurt sitting at the table.

Jace executed the courtesies necessary to his superior then asked, "Sir?"

Marshall looked solemnly at Jace. "Son, I think you need to sit."

Jace did not like the sound of that. "Why? What's wrong?"

"At 0300, I received a phone call from St. Joseph's Hospital in St. Louis. Dr Martin was attacked last night."

Jace nearly jumped out of his chair, but was pushed back down by Collin. Marshall held up his hand when Jace opened his mouth.

"She's okay, just banged up a little. In fact, they released her from observation early this morning. She told them she tripped on a rock and fell down her front stairs. The only reason they called me was because they didn't buy her story, and she listed my name as an emergency contact."

Taking a breath, Marshall continued. "That's not all. Later, I received a package with what appeared to be a digital voice recorder inside. I brought the package directly to Petty Officer Jamison, and using some fancy equipment I know nothing about, he downloaded the file. This is what we heard."

As Jace listened to the audio file coming out of the speakers of the computer, the bottom fell out of his stomach. That was Kat's voice, and he stilled as he remembered what came next. Just then the sound of his voice filled the room.

Jace was surprised that he was capable of feeling both burning hatred and embarrassment at the same time. The conversation that played was one of the times they had been intimate over the phone. Collin coughed to hide what was undoubtedly embarrassing for him as well.

Then they heard a digitally altered voice. "She's a sweet little thing, Jace. I love watching her get off when she talks to you. Her skin gets all flushed and her breathing quickens. But then, you already know that, don't you? She feels real good too.

"Her neck is so soft and supple. It fit perfectly in my hand. I know she tried to warn you the other night, Jace, and because she disobeyed me, she has to be punished. Oh, don't worry. I'm not going to hurt her too badly, just enough to make her see reason. I fear that because of her recklessness there will be consequences."

I knew something was wrong with Kat! I felt it in her voice. How long has this son of a bitch been terrorizing her? How many days has she lived in fear and not told me?

He couldn't sit still another second. Standing up, he paced over to the window.

"Jace, we've got you scheduled on the next flight out of Norfolk. You'll be there by this afternoon. Obviously, with this turn of events, we need to postpone the operation, but once Dr Martin's safe again, we will proceed as planned. Is that understood?" Marshall said.

Jace looked over at Marshall. "Yes, sir. Thank you, sir. Does she know I'm coming?"

"No, we haven't contacted her yet. It's apparent that her phone lines are tapped, and we don't want to give her admirer any advance warning of your arrival. You bring her back here, and we'll do what needs to be done."

* * * *

Jace picked up his rental car at Lambert Airport. He'd thought about just grabbing a cab, but didn't know exactly where Kat would be. He figured she would want to stick as close to her normal schedule as possible. Kat would never abandon her students this close to the end of the semester, even if she wasn't operating at one hundred percent. His little professor's body may be banged up, but her heart was strong. Her loyalty and dedication to both the university and her students were very similar to the constitution of a SEAL. The SEAL motto 'Ready to Lead, Ready to Follow, Never Quit' seemed to describe Kat well. Maybe that's why the two of them were such a good fit.

Looking at the time, he decided to head straight for her office. She would be starting a lecture right about now, assuming she went in. Pulling into the employees' lot that they had parked in before, he saw her car in the assigned spot. He walked toward McMillan Hall, remembering where her office was from the time they'd come to campus together. He figured the best place to wait for her was there.

A perky little blonde sat at the department reception desk. She must have been a student working there as a part-time job because textbooks were spread across the desktop, and she was furiously writing notes. Jace cleared his throat and she looked up.

"Can I help you?" she said with a smile.

He didn't know how much Kat had told her colleagues about their relationship, but regardless, it was highly doubtful that she gossiped with a student worker. It was probably best to circumvent.

"Can you direct me to Dr Martin's office?"

"Yeah, it's the third door on your left, but she's not there right now. She's in class, but should be done shortly. If you want, you can wait here."

Jace pulled up his killer smile. He could be charming when the situation called for it. "Actually, I'm a good friend of hers. Would it be okay if I waited in her office? I'd kind of like to surprise her."

The blonde looked Jace up and down. "A good friend, huh? Go, Dr Martin! Wish my good friends looked like you. I guess it's okay, if you promise not to mess with anything."

Wow, they make kids rather brazen these days. "Thanks, I appreciate it."

The walls of Kat's office were brick, and the windows had old-fashioned wood frames. It smelled of old books and lemon furniture polish, but also the lingering scent of Kat. He breathed deeply, not realizing until that moment how easily a simple smell could trigger memories of their times together.

The last time he'd been here, Jace hadn't really taken the time to look around the room. Kat's various degrees hung on the wall, interspersed with more evidence of her love for photography. He walked up to a grouping of framed photos. These were more geared toward famous archeological sites, a few of which he recognized. He wondered if she had taken these, as well. If so, she had traveled pretty extensively for still being early in her career.

Moving into the corner, he perused the books on the shelf and was so engrossed in the titles that he didn't hear her enter until she let loose a little scream. Whipping around, he saw her standing in the door.

Realizing he was backlit by the window and she couldn't make out his face, he quickly said, "Kat, wait!"

She took a step forward, squinting to see. "Jace?"

"Yeah, it's me. God, I'm sorry. I didn't mean to scare

you like that." He walked toward her, and taking her right hand, noticed it was ice-cold. He also noticed that it was enclosed in a splint, and his gut tightened at the thought of her attack the previous night.

How much pain is she in?

He gently pulled her over toward the window where a beam of sunlight slanted through.

Kat meekly followed. "What are you doing here?" she asked softly.

Jace didn't like how weak her voice sounded.

"I had to come... I heard about what happened last night, and some other things have been brought to my attention." Cupping her face in his hands, he leaned his forehead against hers and asked, "Sweetheart, why didn't you call me? I said any time, day or night, remember?"

Kat took a moment to respond, as if she was having trouble processing the question.

"I couldn't take the chance. I didn't know if that creep would be listening. I figured the doctors wouldn't buy my story of falling down the stairs. I still had Captain Marshall's number saved in my cell phone and figured he would get a hold of you. That's why I put his name as an emergency contact."

Hearing this made him both proud at her ingenuity and that much more livid at her having to experience the terror in the first place.

As if suddenly realizing he was truly there, she exclaimed, "What are you doing? You have to get away from that window! He watches me. He'll know you're here. You're in danger!"

Jace humored her, turning them and placing her back against the wall next to the casement. "Honey, if he's as good as I'm giving him credit for, he knew the moment I stepped off the plane."

Suddenly, as if she had lost all her strength she fell against him, wrapping her arms around him tight.

"I missed you so much... I've been so scared... I'm sorry

I couldn't tell you what was going on, but I didn't want to risk your life any more than you already do."

Jace held onto her as tightly as he could without hurting her. "I missed you too. It terrified me to suspect there was something wrong, but not be here to protect you. Then when the captain told me what happened, and I heard that bastard's voice, I decided I'm taking you back with me. No arguments. The other professors can handle your classes until the end of the semester."

He leaned down and kissed her. He started out softly with gentle kisses so as not to frighten her further. Then he pulled her close and molded his lips to hers. After months of not holding her, it felt like coming home. He couldn't stop. His tongue moved over hers, encouraging her to respond, and when she did, they went up in flames. Kat grabbed the back of Jace's head to hold him close and fit herself tightly against his body.

He reached up to run his hand through her hair and suddenly felt her stiffen. "What's wrong?"

"Sorry. It wasn't you." Kat lifted her hand and touched the back of her head. "That's where I conked my head…or was hit. I'm not sure at this point. Things are a little fuzzy."

Jace turned her around and, separating her hair, found a knot the size of an egg on the back of her head. It looked like she had received a few stitches there last night as well. He leaned down and kissed the little spot, then gathered her back in his arms and just held her for a moment.

In a choked voice he said, "I'm so sorry I wasn't here."

"It's okay. I really thought I was protecting you."

Jace kissed her temple and rubbed her back slowly. "What do you need to do in order to leave?"

Kat lifted her head. "I'm not even sure if it's possible."

"Make it possible, sweetheart. I'm not leaving this campus without you, and I have to be back in Virginia tomorrow night."

"All right. Let me think. I have three more classes to teach today. They're the last ones of the semester and my students will freak out if I cancel because there will be questions about the final. Then I suppose I can ask Grant, Dr Kendzior, to proctor my exams." She smiled. "He did say he owed me from when I covered for him back in September."

"Do you have to give notice to anyone?"

"How long do you plan on me being gone?" she exclaimed.

"I'm not sure at this point. How hard would it be for you to take a leave of absence if necessary?"

"Jace, what's going on? Why is all this happening?"

He sighed. "We don't know. Not exactly, anyway. So far, you and I are the only individuals who have been targeted. But whoever this is has hit us at home. It's not safe for you here without me, and I can't be in two places at once. So however long it takes to resolve the situation is how long you'll be gone."

And if I use the time to convince her to move to Virginia, then so be it.

"Then I think the best thing to do would be to inform the dean of the department what's going on. If you wouldn't mind coming with me so I don't sound like the crazy person I know I appear today, that would be nice."

Jace followed Kat down the hall to the dean's office. He could tell she was nervous, and he really didn't like putting Kat in a difficult position with her job but her safety came first.

Kat knocked on the doorframe of the dean's office. "Dr Fitzgerald, do you have a minute?"

"A brief minute. What can I do for you, Dr Martin?"

Kat walked in and gestured to Jace. "This is Lieutenant Commander Hudson of the United States Navy." She looked over at Jace and said, "I guess you could call him my personally assigned bodyguard."

Dr Fitzgerald looked Jace over. "US Navy, huh? Why is the Navy interested in one of my professors?"

Jace stood at attention. "Actually, sir, it's a little more complicated than the normal US Navy. I'm a SEAL, and we believe she may be directly linked to an internal investigation surrounding a leak exposing Special Forces operation details. Her safety has been compromised, someone has been terrorizing her, and she needs to return with me to base immediately." He smiled and took Kat's hand. "At the same time, she's mine… And I protect what is mine."

Dr Fitzgerald looked over at her. "Is this true, Dr Martin?"

Kat gave Jace's hand a squeeze. "Yes, sir, every word. Last night, I was attacked in my home after a week of more subtle threats." She showed him the splint and explained her trip to the hospital. "Jace and I have also been in a relationship since September." There was no need to go into the long-distance details.

Sitting behind his desk with his fingers in a steeple, Dr Fitzgerald gave them a once-over. "Well, I suppose I don't have much choice in the matter. If the Navy is ordering the presence of Dr Martin, she is obligated to present herself. However, what about her responsibilities here?"

"I'm prepared to speak with Drs Brown and Kendzior about proctoring my final exams later this week. My work with the Doctoral candidates is complete. The update reports are in your inbox. Once I receive the exam results, I'll process the course grades and submit them through the university system."

"You sound awfully sure I'm going to release you, Doctor."

"On the contrary, sir. I figure it's in my best interest to cooperate with Lieutenant Hudson. I don't see how disobeying a direct order from his commanding officer, a captain of the United States Navy, would be in either my or the university's best interest."

"Very well, you may go. I expect this business to be concluded as quickly as possible. I know you are up for tenure, and would hate for an incident like this to inhibit that achievement."

* * * *

He followed Kat home after she was finished finalizing arrangements at the university to return for the winter semester, making sure to keep an eye out for any tails. They stood outside her front door. Kat turned the key, but Jace stopped her before she could push the door open.

"Wait here until I give the all clear."

Jace slid inside. After checking each room downstairs, he went back to the front door and let Kat inside. He put her on the sofa. "Don't move. I'm going to check the upstairs."

He walked up and cleared both spare bedrooms, the master, and guest bath. In the master bedroom he stood by the window. Kat had escaped through there. There was a single strand of long dark brown hair caught in the frame and a smear of blood from where Kat had hit her head. Jace's body got hot, the blood rushing to his ears. He took a deep breath and let it out slowly.

He went back downstairs. Kat sat on the sofa where he had left her. He could see that she was fading fast. He held out his hand. "Come on. You're going to soak in a hot bath while I find something to cook for dinner."

Jace walked her up and they went into the master bath. He turned on the water for the tub and switched on the towel heater. He turned to face Kat while the water filled the bath. "Do you need any help getting undressed?"

Kat shook her head. "I'm fine."

"All right. Then I'll be right back with some food. Try to relax. I'm right here. Nothing is going to happen to you."

When he came back upstairs, Kat was in the tub. It was then that he really noticed how exhausted she looked. Her makeup had been applied very carefully, but he saw the hollowness of her cheeks, the black circles under her eyes, even the paleness of her skin. There hadn't been any food downstairs, and looking at her critically now, he saw that she had lost significant weight since he'd last seen her. Slightly alarmed, he went over and sat on the edge of the tub, gently shaking her alert.

"Kat? How long has it been since you really ate or slept?"

It took her several seconds to respond. "I'm not sure. I stopped sleeping through the night a while ago. I knew that if I fell asleep for long, he would come into the house, and that was worse than not sleeping. Food just became unimportant. I ate when I got too hungry to think clearly."

Jace could tell she was on the verge of falling asleep as he sat there. He didn't want her to pass out in the tub, so he gently washed her, avoiding her stitches, being very tender around her scrapes and bruises. Gathering her up in a warm towel, he carried her over to the bed. He had laid out a soft, oversized T-shirt for her to wear. Sitting her down in his lap, he dried her off and slipped the T-shirt over her head as she slept in his arms. Then, after turning down the blankets, he slipped her underneath and covered her back up.

Kat reached out for his hand and murmured, "Don't leave me... Please."

His heart broke a little at the pleading sound of her soft voice. Reaching out, he gently cupped her face and kissed her cheek. "I'll be right back, I promise."

He went back into the bathroom and cleaned up their mess, then came back into the bedroom. Sitting on the edge of the bed, he removed his socks and shoes, jeans and shirt. Then he crawled under the sheets and pulled her into his arms. He softly kissed her temple and whispered into her ear, "This is where you belong."

Chapter Seventeen

When he woke up the following morning, Jace was relieved to see that there was at least a little color in Kat's cheeks. She was still sleeping soundly, curled against his chest. He lay there for a few moments and enjoyed the feeling of her in his arms again. He slowly stroked her hair, which slipped like silk through his fingers. He felt her stir against him, and looking down, saw her eyes open. At first, they had the confused blur of someone not yet aware of their surroundings, then the haze cleared and the green brightened like he remembered.

He smiled down at her. "Good morning."

Kat looked up at Jace. "Hi. I still find it difficult to believe that you're really here." She stretched while releasing a low moan. "What time is it?"

Jace looked over at the clock. "0900. I hope you can pack quickly, because our flight leaves at 1530 hours."

With a mischievous glint in her eye, Kat looked up at Jace. "So, what you're saying is that we have about four and a half hours before we have to leave. Whatever shall we do with our time?"

Kat's husky words caused Jace's body to awaken as if a gong had been struck. "I'm sure we can find some way to occupy ourselves."

Mindful of her head, he rolled Kat on top of him. Her shirt bunched up, and he felt the silky smoothness of her stomach against his own hard abs. He reached his hands underneath the bottom of the shirt and slowly slipped it upward.

Kat sat up and straddled his hips. Reaching for the edge

of her top, she lifted it over her head. Holding it daintily in her fingertips, she dropped it over the side of the bed.

Jace held in his breath as Kat's nakedness was revealed. Seeing her in the morning light, he was once again stunned by her beauty. He felt as if it had been years since they'd been together like this, not just months. She was all soft curves and gentle swells. He had dated women who were twigs and women who were as ripped as him, but he found Kat's simplistic allure addictive.

Her real beauty was in her warm spirit and giving nature. He realized that now was the time he had been waiting for to tell her how he felt. Jace wanted to do this right, so he sat up. Keeping Kat's legs locked around his hips, he took her into his arms and kissed her deeply. Careful of her head, he took her face between his hands, leaned his forehead against hers and looked straight into the depths of her beautiful green eyes.

"Kat, I love you." He saw tears gather in her eyes and continued, "I don't want you to think I'm going to push you for a commitment, but I just needed to tell you. In case something should happen to me on a mission at some point, I wanted you to know."

She put her fingertips to his lips. "I love you too, Jace. I don't expect anything from you. But should anything ever happen to you, I want you to know someone will always remember you. I will always remember you. I will always love you."

That last sentence meant more to Jace than any medals for extraordinary heroism or distinguished service. Regardless of what happened to him, someone would remember him with love.

With tears in his eyes, he kissed her again, this time holding nothing back. He caressed her back with his hands and pulled her hips as close to his own as possible. He rotated their bodies so she was underneath him. "Is your head okay? I don't want to hurt you."

"I'm fine, just don't stop."

"You don't need to worry about that. If everything goes according to my plans, I'm never going to stop." He leaned down and kissed her neck in that sensitive spot he knew she loved. He slid his lips down to her collarbone then circled his tongue around her left nipple, getting close, but never taking it between his lips, even as she arched up seeking his warmth. He moved over to the right side and repeated the treatment. Finally, he gathered both breasts into his hands and pushing them together, took both nipples into his mouth and sucked hungrily.

Kat cried out, gripped his shoulders and kneaded them in her hands. Her nails dug into his skin, and Jace thought of the half-moon impressions now embedded in his skin as his most treasured badge.

He continued sucking and tonguing her nipples for long minutes. He loved the taste of her skin, especially warm and freshly awakened. He released her breasts and trailed kisses down her stomach, nuzzling her belly button and making Kat laugh out loud at the tickling sensation. Before he could go any further, she surprised him by hooking a leg over his and rolling them over so she was back on top.

Where did she learn that maneuver?

She looked down at him with a very self-satisfied smile on her face.

She latched her lips around one of his small, flat nipples, and sucked him into her mouth like he had done to her.

Jace let out a deep groan. She moved to the other side, and this time used her front teeth to scrape across the little nub. He hissed in a breath but said, "Do that again."

She did, and afterward used her tongue to sooth any lingering sting. Taking his boxer briefs between her teeth, she pulled them down, making him laugh at her antics. Kat placed little kisses on the five sensitive spots she'd learned he liked—just below his navel, on the arch of each hip, in the 'V' leading to his groin.

He looked down as Kat hovered above his cock. The flesh strained toward her, silently begging for attention. She took the wide plum-shaped, dark red head between her lips and swiped her tongue around the sensitive rim, then, without warning, sank the thick length down her throat, causing Jace to clench his hands in the sheets and groan, "Oh, Kat!"

She alternated between short, hard pulls and deep slides. She was driving him out of his mind with pleasure.

Not able to take another second, Jace lifted her off him and reversed their positions once again. "I want to be inside you. I need to be inside you." He reached down between their bodies to test her readiness. Finding her meltingly soft and very wet, he slid one finger inside.

Just like I remember – hot, tight and perfect.

He added a second finger and slowly stretched her. When Kat's hips started lifting into his hands seeking more, he removed his fingers and guided the head of his cock to her entrance. He sank partially into her hot depths and held still. Slowly he began to rock back and forth, never completely filling her, but never leaving her empty, either.

"I need all of you," Kat cried out.

He reared back and sank his remaining length in one long stroke, and both of them let out a deep sigh.

"Oh, baby, you feel so good. You surround every inch of me like a velvet glove."

"You feel incredible too. I've missed this. Nothing could ever substitute for the feeling of you inside me."

Needing to move, he began thrusting in slow long glides, moving almost all the way out before sliding back into her. After several minutes, his pace began to pick up. Kat's hips lifted to meet every down stroke, and he began to move more forcefully.

Their bodies moved and their arms clung to one another as they reached for climax. Kat got there first. The sound of her cry and the feel of her body rippling around him had Jace groaning as his release shot hot seed against her womb.

Jace stiffened above her. "Oh, honey, I'm so sorry. I didn't use protection. I didn't even think about it."

"That's okay. It's not the right time anyway. I just started a new cycle the other day."

Hearing this, he felt both relieved and slightly disappointed. The thought of Kat carrying his child was far from unpleasant. He knew now was not the right time to be dealing with potential fatherhood, but the image of her round and waddling through his home singing sent a smile to his face.

They made love again in Kat's massive multi-jet steam shower, this time with her legs wrapped around his hips and braced up against the tiled wall. He had always thought of showering as a utilitarian necessity — it always felt good to get the grime of the day or the mission off his body — but he was quickly coming to appreciate Kat's spa-like amenities.

When they moved in together — and he had no doubt they would — they'd need to find a place with a bathroom just like this, or one where they could design their own. Up to this point, he had lived on base simply because he didn't see a point in paying outrageous rent or mortgage payments for a dwelling he would rarely be in town long enough to make it feel like a home.

As they dried and dressed, Jace thought about how nice it would be to have a home. He smiled as he cooked breakfast with Kat's help. He managed to find some frozen waffles and fruit shoved in the very back of the freezer. That, with a hot cup of coffee, went a long way to making Jace feel better about Kat's ability to function.

Following breakfast, Kat headed back upstairs to pack a suitcase while he called Captain Marshall, using a cell phone with a secure line, to update him on their progress.

"Our plane is scheduled to leave at 1530 hours, so barring any delays we should be back in Norfolk by 1900 hours."

"Good to hear. Any unwanted attention?"

"No, sir. Which considering Kat's report of what she's been subjected to this past couple of weeks is ironically disturbing."

"Maybe since he knew you were there, he didn't think

she would be as vulnerable. This type of guy plays on the vulnerability of his victims."

"Maybe, but I definitely don't think we've seen the last of him."

"How is she? Holding up under the circumstances?"

"Yeah, like I said before, she's a fighter. Physically, she took a beating—stitches to the back of her head, a fractured wrist, plus various other bumps and bruises. Mentally, it was a good thing I came when I did. She was holding her own, but I can tell the strain has taken a toll."

"You take tonight to get her settled, then report at 0600 tomorrow morning. I assume she will be staying with you."

"Yes, sir."

"Very good, I'll see you tomorrow. Good afternoon, Jace."

"Good afternoon, Captain."

* * * *

Kat and Jace landed at Norfolk airport right on time. The exited the jetway and Jace took her hand. Which was fine with her, because the terminal was crowded. All the bumping and running bodies made her slightly nervous.

"Peter and Collin should be waiting for us, since I was dropped off prior to my departure."

Part of her was actually excited to see the two men again, which made her smile because only a few months ago that would have been the last thought in her head. The other part of her was nervous. She knew despite getting a good night's sleep last night and Jace's amazing lovemaking this morning that she still looked worn around the edges. The way her clothes fit told her she'd lost weight and she was sure both Peter and Collin would be able to spot the dark circles under her eyes from a mile away.

Jace waved when Peter's hand shot up in the air. They wove their way through the other passengers and people waiting for them. Kat smiled in greeting while Jace shook hands with his teammates.

"Thanks, guys, for playing chauffer."

Peter smiled and said, "No problem but this means you have to let me take the bike out for a ride." He turned to Kat and placed his hand on her arm. "Hey. Nice to see you again."

Collin started to acknowledge with a similar response, but at the last minute, he grabbed her into an embrace. "To hell with it. I'm glad you're okay. If there is anything you need, just let me know, okay?"

Jace looked a little surprised at Collin's outward show of emotion. He gave him a disgruntled expression and put his arm around Kat's middle to tug her back to his side. "Yeah, we'll be sure to do that."

Collin backed up and looked at Jace. "What? I'm just offering to help when you're not around."

"And just where the hell am I going?"

"I don't think that is something that should be discussed under present circumstances. Why don't we get Kat's bags and head back to base?"

Kat took the opportunity to interrupt the battle of wills being instigated. "I only have one bag." She held up her splinted wrist. "But I would appreciate the help."

Peter responded, "No problem. What carousel is your baggage coming in on?"

"Honestly, I was asleep when they announced it. Your commander makes for a very good pillow." She looked over at him. "Did you hear the announcement?"

He looked at her and smiled. Putting his hand up to cup her face, he leaned down for a kiss. "I was too busy watching the sleeping beauty on my chest. But I think we can manage to find it."

Peter rolled his eyes and grabbed Collin's arm. "Oh, geez. Let's go before they start making out like horny teenagers." As he walked away, he turned and gave a little wink to Kat.

They found Kat's bag without trouble and headed back to Jace's town house on base. Seeing his home for the first time, she was pleasantly surprised. She had expected to see a very utilitarian dwelling with some basic furniture and a TV, but the place actually looked like a home. The walls were a basic white. There was a small gas fireplace with a watercolor of a yacht in stormy weather. A blue and white striped area rug ran underneath a chest that doubled as a coffee table. The furniture was overstuffed, with clean, simple lines, and navy tab-top curtains hung on the windows. It was also spotlessly clean.

Seeing her quick assessment, Jace said, "I can't take too much credit. It came furnished."

She glanced over. "I like it."

He escorted her through the two-cent tour, and they walked into the simple galley kitchen. "There's not much in the fridge, so we'll need to do some shopping. You're welcome to poke around and get used to the organization of the cabinets, but it's pretty basic." They headed down a short hallway. "There's small utility closet, laundry area and a half-bath." He gestured up the stairs. "My bedroom and full bath is at the top of the stairs. You want to go up and take a look?"

She nodded. "Will I be sleeping there with you?"

He looked surprised. "Where else would you be?"

She shrugged. "The couch? I don't want to be an imposition to you."

In an answer to this statement, he swung her up into his arms and carried her up the steps, into the bedroom, and tossed her onto the bed. Then he stalked her across the bed on all fours.

"You will be no further than two feet from me at any point. Is that understood? I've waited too many months to get you in my bed, and I'll be damned if I'm going to let you sleep on the couch versus in my arms, where you belong."

Kat lightly kissed him and scooted up the bed to rest against the headboard. "Good. Now that we've settled sleeping arrangements, I have one last question."

"And that is?"

"How soon can I take advantage of you?"

He gathered her in his arms and slid her down so she was lying partially under him. "Anytime, anywhere you want to."

She scooted down a little further on the bed and looped her arms around Jace's neck. "Hmm, I like that answer, but you may regret it later on. You've turned me into an insatiable fanatic. I have this constant urge to feel your body next to mine. You never know, I may grab you and haul you into a dark utility closet for some nookie at any moment."

He laughed. "Not if I grab you first." There was no gentleness or hesitation in the kiss he gave her. His lips and tongue possessed her mouth just as his heart possessed hers. Kat responded in kind. She owned him, just as much as he owned her.

The phone next to the bed rang. Jace groaned. "The only people who have my number here are the team and my commanding officers. Sorry, honey, but I should take that."

Kat reached over, picked up the phone and handed it to him.

Looking at the caller ID, he saw Peter's number. He picked up and answered, "There had better be thermonuclear war breaking out right now."

Peter chuckled. "Catch you at a bad time, Lieutenant Commander?"

Jace responded in a warning tone. "What do you want, Peter? I've been given orders by Marshall to report at 0600, and I plan on using this brief liberty wisely. I would suggest you do the same."

"Oh, don't worry about me, but I thought you might like to know I found out Jefferson is joining us in the field

"All right, I appreciate the warning. Now you pass the word along that no one is to bother us tonight unless someone is dead or the world is about to end, got it?"

"Sure. Whatever you say. You'd better tell Kat to take it easy on you tonight, though. We need you still capable of walking in the morning."

"Jackass." With Peter's laughter still ringing in his ear, Jace hung up the phone.

* * * *

It was 0500 when Jace heard the alarm go off beside the bed. He rolled over and hit the off button. Then, looking to the other side of the bed, he leaned over and gently kissed Kat's cheek. He climbed out, then tucked the covers tighter around her. He knew she would subconsciously feel his absence, and he didn't want her getting chilled in the unfamiliar house. Even though she looked immeasurably better than the other day, he could tell she was still physically and mentally exhausted after the stress of the last couple of weeks.

After showering, he scribbled down a quick note telling her that he should be back that afternoon. He wanted to take her around base and show her the area he'd made his hometown since being assigned to team twelve. If the weather held out, maybe they could even ride his bike. He thought Kat might get a kick out of that, considering her penchant for speed and performance. Locking the front door behind him, Jace headed over to Captain Marshall's office.

They needed to finalize the details of the plan to flush out the leak. Thinking about various scenarios, he found that he was still concerned about Kat's safety, especially considering the suspicion that someone on base was involved. He would ask Cory if his wife would be willing to keep Kat company while they were gone. He didn't want her to be alone, especially in an unfamiliar place. The more he thought about it, the better that idea sounded.

Jace and Marshall exchanged acknowledgments before Jace heard Marshall give out his usual order, "Have a seat, Jace." He did. "Everything okay with Dr Martin?"

"Yes, sir, she's resting comfortably at my house."

The door to Marshall's office opened, and Jace watched the rest of the squad come in.

Peter quipped, "Oh, good, he's still walking."

Jace looked over at him and scowled. "What is your problem, Hampton? Every chance you get you're making some smartassed comment. Is there something we need to talk about privately? Because I'm getting damn tired of your crude and harassing remarks."

Peter looked affronted. "Hey, man, I'm just having a little fun at your expense. You know me. I've always been like this. Damn. I've never seen you so defensive before. I thought I made it clear to both of you back in St. Louis that I think you and Kat are a good thing. Hell, she's better than a leech like you deserves, but for some reason she seems to like your old, slightly sagging ass."

"Maybe the reason I'm defensive is because you can't seem to plug that giant hole in your face. From now on, I only want to hear effusive remarks about how I'm the best commanding officer you've ever had. Otherwise, I'm going to stick you with every shit job I can think of for the next six months, *and* I'll take away your explosive privileges after school." Then he broke into a self-satisfied grin. "That's an order."

"But, *Daaad*," Peter whined and winked.

Everyone in the room was silent throughout the exchange, but he heard one or two quiet chuckles at the end.

Of course Jace's luck would have it for Jefferson to walk in during his and Peter's exchange.

Jefferson looked around then scowled. "What's going on? Hudson? Are you having a problem controlling your team?"

Jace looked at him "No, sir. We were having a personal discussion."

Jefferson gave him a stern look, and in a reprimanding tone said, "I think you've wasted enough time lately on personal issues, Hudson. Maybe with your indulgence, we could do some real work now?" Jefferson turned to Kurt.

"What's the status on the electronic analysis of the voice on the recorder?"

"It was done via a digital manipulation available in many audio/video editing programs. There's no way to break it down any further. I was able to isolate and identify some environmental sounds in the background, specifically a ship's bell and a horn, as well as what sounded like train cars being locked together."

"So, what you're saying is that the recording could have been made within close proximity to any body of water large enough to support boats and close to a rail yard. *That* narrows it down." Jefferson sneered. "I thought you were supposed to be some kind of technical wizard."

Kurt appeared insulted by Jefferson's attitude. "Actually, sir, I proceeded to do an analysis of the ship's horn and the acoustic signature is identical to that of military craft. So, really, we are looking for a location in close proximity to a naval shipyard and train tracks."

Jace processed this information. "So it is possible that the recording was actually made here, on base. Captain Marshall, what was the postmark on the envelope it was delivered in?"

Marshall took the envelope out of his desk. It had been sealed in a bag to prevent contamination of any trace evidence. "It was mailed from St. Louis, Missouri. This would then indicate that the recording was done premeditatedly."

"Look, we can speculate all we want, but it's not going to solve the issue. And unfortunately, until this personal issue of Hudson's is resolved, this team is useless to the US Navy. So what is the plan to flush this guy out?"

Jace frowned at Jefferson's callous remark.

"You got a problem with something I said, Lieutenant?"

It wasn't like this was a problem of my making. What did I do to piss this guy off? "No, sir."

As acting commander of the team, Jace took the responsibility to inform Jefferson of the plan. "We've considered several possible scenarios. However, the most logical is to set up a false interception operation. The primary objective would be to infiltrate a secure location and prohibit the off-loading of a cache of weapons and drugs. We set up a decoy dealer and see if our man contacts him with an offer."

Jefferson thought for a moment. "If our man is as smart as he thinks he is, wouldn't he be able to tell the dealer was a decoy? Anyone worth their salt knows who's a real player in the weapons game."

"Our thinking was not if we use a real dealer. It just so happens that Margolis is being extradited to El Salvador this week. It would be simple enough to work out an arrangement to delay his delivery by a couple days. We put the word out that he's eluded authorities and has arranged for a meeting with a buyer to dump a stash of weapons and drugs at a location of our choosing. Our team would be assigned to intercept the deal and complete the extradition."

"What makes you think our man would go to Margolis in person? Why not just use telecommunications?"

"So far that does not follow the pattern. At each of our missions, he has presumably been on site or nearby to orchestrate the countermeasures."

"That's a lot to assume, Hudson. You know what they always say about assumptions. Something about making an ass out of you and me. Was this supposedly ingenious plan one of your making?"

Jace sat silently fuming. He had never wanted to deck someone so much in his life but striking a superior officer would mean prison time and losing his commission. So he tersely replied, "It was a collaborative effort, sir."

"Well, I guess it's better than nothing. So, Marshall, what do you think of the boys' little plan?"

"I think, given the extenuating circumstances surrounding Dr Martin's attack and the increased threats against Jace, this plan should be executed as soon as possible. The sooner we identify the traitor and his motives, the sooner we can all move on with our lives." Looking up at the team members, he asked for affirmation. "Are all of you on board with this assignment and support the intent?"

A resounding "Hooyah, Captain!" filled the room.

"Then you are dismissed. Be ready to execute in twenty-four hours."

All seven of them snapped to attention then filed out of the room one by one.

Chapter Eighteen

Jace headed back toward his house, anxious to see how Kat was settling in. They had twenty-four hours and he wasn't looking forward to telling her he had to leave. He made arrangements with Cory's wife Jenny to have Kat stay with her while he was gone, hoping she would understand his concern and not give him any grief on his overprotective nature.

When he pulled into the driveway and saw Kat open the front door, a sense of peace washed over him seeing her stand there welcoming him home. He had lived a solitary life for so long that he didn't realize such a simple gesture could feel so profound. The green of her silk blouse matched her eyes and she was barefoot.

When he got out of the car, he heard her say, "Nice car. You didn't tell me you drove a WRX STI."

"I know. I didn't want to brag that I had a better performance car than you."

Kat laughed out loud. "Oh, you wish! A stock SRT can damn near take an STI from roll, and, honey, mine is not stock. Besides, the machine is only half the equation. Driver's skill counts at least fifty percent and I think I proved my ability that day we drove to the wine country. I'll have you know—"

He walked up to the door and cut her diatribe short by sliding his hands into her hair and kissing her deeply. After several long, hot minutes, he broke away. "I like seeing you here, waiting for me to come home."

"Well, if I'll always get a greeting like that, I'll make sure to be here every time you get home." Kat blushed. "I mean... If we... That is..."

Jace put his fingers to her soft lips to stop her stumbling. "That's exactly what I want. Not necessarily at this house, but I definitely want to come home to you."

They walked into the living room. She had turned on the fireplace and had soft music playing out of the sound system. It looked like she had been reading some novel, and he turned it over to check out the title—*Desiring Danger*. Reading the summary on the back of the book, Jace looked over to Kat who was cutting up an apple on the island counter in the kitchen. He raised the book in his hand and raised an eyebrow.

Seeing his reaction, Kat smiled. "What? She's one of my favorite authors."

"You're reading a romance novel whose main character just happens to be a SEAL."

"Would you believe I bought the book before I ever met you and am just now getting around to reading it?"

Hearing the hopeful questioning tone, Jace responded, "No, try again."

"Okay, I bought it a few weeks ago. I don't know why, but I thought by reading about men similar to you I could somehow substitute us into the story. In some way it made me feel closer to you. It turns out to be a really good book, though. Full of intrigue and action... And really hot sex."

Jace heard that last part mumbled under her breath. He flipped through to where Kat's place was marked in the book. Skimming a couple of paragraphs, he was actually impressed. The in-depth narrative made him want to read the whole thing. He flipped a couple more pages and came across a very steamy sex scene. Sitting, he started to read and was simultaneously shocked and aroused.

Kat was right when she had said that first night they met that the mind is a powerful thing. Images of the two of them doing what he was reading about were inspirational. He shook his head to clear his mind, and remembering his plan to show her around the area, he put the book down and walked over to the kitchen counter.

"How would you like to take a drive and see some of the area? There's some great scenery, and it has turned out to be a really nice day."

"Sure, I'd love to. I did a little bit of research on the area after you left, but I'm sure the photos online didn't do it justice."

"I'm sorry you missed the leaves turning, but next year I'll take you inland to the mountains. I'm sure your photographer's heart will be in love. Some of the views have even taken my breath away."

Seeing her smile, he walked around the other side of the white countertop and crowded her back against the refrigerator.

"We will be together next year, and if I have my way, for many years after that. I know that with the inflexibility of my job, there may be some logistics to work out. I don't want you to feel that I'm pressuring you to leave the university right away."

She reached up and put her hand against his cheek. "I told you before, if I want to leave Wash U, I have enough contacts to find a position elsewhere. I'm not worried about my job. I just want to make sure that this—us—is what you want, and not some visceral reaction to the circumstances."

"I love you, Kat. I've been around long enough to recognize what I feel is real and not some transient emotion like infatuation."

She leaned up on her toes and kissed him, wrapping her hands around his neck and molding her body to his. Her soft breasts pushed against his chest.

She's not wearing a bra!

Her tongue skimmed across his lips. When he responded by opening them, she slipped inside and started stroking the roof of his mouth and rubbing her tongue against his. She combed her fingers through his hair.

Jace groaned. He had let her take the lead up to this point, but now it was his turn. He lifted her into his arms, and she wrapped her legs around his waist. He set her up on the counter and reached for her top. In his haste, a couple of buttons flew off and pinged somewhere on the kitchen floor. When he separated the halves of her shirt and saw evidence of his earlier discovery, he couldn't stop staring.

They'd been together enough that he knew every inch of her body, but its simple lushness always amazed him. Her nipples were hard and looked like plush mountains. The wide circles surrounding them were dusky brown. He bent his head and took one tip into his mouth. Latching on through soft suction, he tongued her. Using the flat of his tongue, he slid over the top of her nipple several times then flicked it with the tip. Taking her other breast in his hand, he cupped it in his palm. He lifted his head and kissed her again.

Her legs were still locked around his hips. He edged his hands under the edge of her short skirt and slid it up her thighs, and when he got to the center, he felt her dampness and heat through the silk of her panties. He guided her down onto the counter and pulled her hips to the edge. In one motion, he slid her underwear down and off her ankles. He noticed that they were black string bikinis with blue and green polka dots. She was never predictable, his Kat.

He wasted no time and slid his tongue through her silky, wet lips. Using his fingers to separate her, he laved long, leisurely licks around the entire area. Her hands came down on his head as she let out a mewling cry. Plunging his tongue deep inside her, he groaned as taste exploded across his senses. He had never enjoyed giving oral as much he did with her. Her taste was intoxicating, and the feel of her gripping his tongue as contractions pushed their way through her body was incredible.

He continued to lick and plunge in short little stabs and long thrusts, and after several minutes, he could tell she was close. He moved up to circle her clit with his tongue as he slid one long finger deep inside her. He pushed up with his finger and suckled on that little bundle of nerves.

A few more thrusts of his finger, and he added a second. He started to scissor them inside her hot channel and he felt the contractions start. Pulling them almost completely out then thrusting both back again while angling the tips so they rasped across the sensitive tissues at the top, he sent her over the edge, and she screamed out his name as her orgasm consumed her mind and body.

Pulling her into a sitting position, he wrapped her legs around his waist again and carried her over to the couch, where he set her down. He worked on shedding his pants and shirt while Kat unbuttoned her skirt. Once naked, he pulled Kat's skirt down as she lifted her hips.

Kneeling on the couch, he leaned over her and placed one hand on the cushion behind her head. Her legs came up on either side of his hips, and he guided himself to her entrance. No teasing this time—he entered her in one smooth stroke all the way to the hilt and began to move in slow, long drives.

The sensation of their skin against each other, no barrier, was incredible. He had always been obsessive about using protection. Kat was the first woman with whom he had not, and it certainly took an experience that had already been fantastic between the two of them beyond the heights of the stratosphere.

He felt every single ripple as she milked him, the tissues of her channel slightly swollen from their numerous encounters over the last couple of days. He wasn't afraid of hurting her, though, because she was so slippery it felt like gliding through hot satin. He kissed her deeply and pulled her into his body.

He adjusted her hips and his angle so he could achieve maximum depth, but it made little difference. He would never be able to get deep enough when it came to Kat. His entire body screamed with a need to completely devour her. If he could dematerialize and merge all of his molecules with hers, it might be enough. Not being able to do so, he made it so every inch of his body connected with her in some way.

Breaking apart from her lips, he leaned his forehead against hers and promised in a gruff voice, "I'll never get enough of you. Do you hear me, Kat? It'll never be enough. Open your eyes, look at me, hear me, and understand what I'm saying."

When she did, she stared up into his eyes. "I hear you... Never close enough. Our bodies may never blend as much as we want them to, Jace, but our hearts and our souls, those will always be completely united. That unity, that understanding is our miracle, the salvation we find in each other."

He took her lips in another endless, devouring kiss. He knew exactly what she was saying, and what he could not put eloquently enough into words he used his body to tell her. He sat up and pulled her legs over his shoulders so he could penetrate faster and harder, and with each thrust, he tilted his hips so to hit her G-spot. His fingers found their way to her clit again and he started to circle the bundle of nerves filled with blood and standing out from its hood.

Her legs tightened and her hips lifted into his thrusts. It didn't take long before they went over the edge together, Jace spilling himself deep inside her body as Kat milked his cock dry.

They had not been using protection the last several days, and by silent agreement, they understood that they wouldn't from now on. If they got pregnant, then they would welcome the child with open arms.

He could picture a little girl with Kat's soft, dark hair and his gray eyes, or a little boy with her thirst for knowledge and his sense of integrity and pride. He was enough of a traditionalist to hope that he could get a ring on her finger before they conceived, though.

After several minutes, he covered them with a light throw blanket from the back of the sofa, and once again he held her in his arms and fell asleep feeling complete.

* * * *

Kat moaned when she was awakened by Jace nuzzling her hair aside and placing a kiss behind her ear.

"Hey, sleepyhead," he whispered. "How about that drive? We want to get out there while it's still nice. The temperature is supposed to drop tonight."

Kat rolled onto her back and, lying half underneath him, she tried to blink the drowsiness out of her eyes. "Well, if someone would let me sleep at night, I wouldn't be taking naps in the middle of the day, now, would I?"

He gave her his killer, hundred-watt grin. "Now who would ever take advantage of you like that?"

She lifted her hand up to his face, felt the roughness of his cheek since he had not taken the time to shave that morning. "I can't imagine, but it's the best reason for lack of sleep I can think of."

Leaning down he kissed her lips softly. The tenderness of that kiss felt like a warm glow infusing her whole body.

She broke away with great reluctance. "We're going nowhere if you keep that up. Come on. Let's get dressed."

She looked around the room. "Where *are* all my clothes, anyway?"

Jace glanced over his shoulder. "I think your top and underwear are in the kitchen, but I may have popped a few buttons earlier. Sorry. I'll replace the shirt. You'll want to put jeans on if you have them, though, instead of that adorable skirt you were wearing."

"Don't be silly. I can sew the buttons back on. There's no reason to replace an entire top just because the buttons came off. Let me go upstairs and find some jeans and shoes."

He let her get up off the sofa and she felt his eyes on her as she walked naked across the room. She was no longer embarrassed or shy about her nudity around him. He let out a slight groan when she bent over to pick up her top and underwear. Then she threw him a little grin and wriggled her hips when she turned around.

A few minutes later, Kat came back downstairs dressed in a simple cotton sweater in bright pink and a pair of black jeans with heeled boots. Jace stood at the bottom of the stairs waiting for her.

She looked down at him and raised her eyebrow when she caught a look at the helmet. "I take it I'm going to meet the bike Peter tried to extort a ride from?"

"I thought this might be more fun, if you're up to it. If you'd prefer, we can take the car, though."

"Are you kidding? I'd love to go riding! I've never done it before, but have always been envious of the freedom I see in the riders I pass when driving in the country."

"Well then, let's roll." He tossed her the helmet and checked the fit for safety once she had put it on. Satisfied that it was tight enough on her head, he asked, "Did you bring a light jacket? The weather is warm enough, but when you're riding, the wind can make it feel much cooler."

She nodded. "I wasn't sure what the weather was going to be like so I brought a windbreaker and wool dress coat."

"You'll need the jacket today, but it's a good thing you brought the other one. You never know this time of year what the temperature will do."

She grabbed her jacket out of the closet. "Hope you don't mind, I put them both in here."

"Not at all. That is the general concept of the coat closet."

"Smartass."

They walked hand in hand to the attached garage, and he got her settled on the back of the bike. He climbed on and showed her how to hold onto him for support. Pressed up against Jace's back, Kat knew she was going to like riding. With a flip of a switch, the bike gunned to life, the throttle sounding like a rumbling roar of a caged animal. Jace pulled out of the garage and turned out of the driveway. The first time he made a turn Kat tightened her grip around his waist, but soon got used to the feel of the bike beneath them and let herself lean into each turn.

Jace wove his way through the base and it wasn't long

before Kat saw the bay off to her right. They toured the road along the shore for a while. Kat heard the bike engine get softer and felt the machine slow down. She peered around Jace's shoulder and saw that he'd pulled up to some kind of overlook.

They stopped and Jace shut off the motor. "Okay, brace your left foot on the peg and lift your right over the back of the bike. Use my shoulders for balance."

Kat did as instructed. It was similar to getting off a horse, but not nearly as tall. Jace got off the bike then hung their helmets on the handlebars. He took her hand and they walked to the edge of the promontory. They stood there for several minutes watching the ships. Having never seen a naval port before, Kat thought the sight was quite impressive.

As Kat took in the view, Jace put his hand on her back and pulled her against his side. She leaned her head down on his shoulder and put her arms around his waist. It was a very peaceful moment.

He turned her around so she was facing him with her back to the bay. "I need to tell you that I have to leave tomorrow. I can't tell you where I'm going, but I want you to know that the only reason I am is to hopefully finish this situation we've become involved in."

Kat saw him studying her. What did he expect her say? "That's okay. I'll be fine at your house."

He looked into her eyes. "You always surprise me, you know that? I was expecting disappointment or recriminations, but you just calmly tell me go ahead."

She was confused and slightly hurt. "I understood the risks and responsibilities involved in your job when we first met, and while I'll always fear for your safety, I trust you to make the right judgments for your own safety as well as that of your team. Have I ever given you the impression that I would act like a petulant child when you tell me you need to leave? If so, I'm truly sorry."

He shook his head. "No, sweetheart, you've never

given me that impression. I guess I just hear stories from other men and had a latent anticipation. I appreciate your support and understanding. You can certainly bet now that I've found you to come home to I'll be more careful of my choices in the field. I've made arrangements for you to stay with Jenny, Cory's wife, while we are gone."

He rushed on, "It's not that I don't trust you, but for my own peace of mind, I would appreciate it if just this once, under these circumstances, you would let me protect you this way."

She returned his gaze. "I don't want you to be afraid for me or be thinking about my safety when you need to concentrate on your own, so this time, under these circumstances, I'll do as you ask. Although I must say that I am slightly confused, because I assume living on a military base would be the safest place possible."

"Normally, you would be correct. However, we have reason to believe that the person involved in the situation may be linked to the military, and I just don't want to take any chances."

"Okay then, when is she expecting me, and where do they live?"

"Cory and Jenny actually live off base. We'll drive by so you can see. I told her you would be at their house tomorrow morning. Hopefully, I'll only be gone a few days. Now that I've gotten that off my chest, which I've been dreading all day, I might add, how about a little more scenic riding and a tour of the base facilities?"

They cruised, feeling the vibrations of the motor beneath them and the freedom of the open air surrounding them, for another hour. It was easy to see why he loved the area. The bay was beautiful, and the surrounding area was a great mixture of woods and small inlets.

The tour of the base was a real eye-opener. She hadn't realized just how big and utterly self-sufficient it was. As promised, on the way back to his house, they rode by where Cory and Jenny lived. She was looking forward to spending some time with Jenny, getting to know the woman better. They might even become friends.

If the chance of her and Jace lasting existed, then it'd be nice to have a girlfriend who was also a military partner. Kat had a feeling that despite how close she and Amy were, there would be some things that only those who share their lives with service members could understand.

Chapter Nineteen

Jace crept down the stairs of his town house. He'd navigated around his house in the dark often enough that he didn't need to risk turning on a light and waking Kat. He picked up his bag beside the front door and reached for the handle. A piece of paper taped to the flat panel caught his attention. He lifted it off and moved over toward the window. With the glow of the street light outside he was able to read the words left by Kat.

Stay safe. I love you.

He smiled. She must have gotten up in the middle of the night and prepared the note so he would see it when he left. He took one last look up the stairs. His heart longed for him to run up and give her another kiss to match the one he'd placed on her lips before crawling out of bed. But he knew there wasn't time, and he didn't know if he turned back that he'd have the strength to leave again. So he pulled open the door and stepped through. The first step out of the door was the hardest of his life.

Jace made it to the airfield a few minutes before 0600. The sky was dark and the C-40A a hulking shadow. He gazed at the moon for a moment. It was large, tinted orange, and low in the sky. To the east, he saw the colors of a new day begin to creep on the horizon. There was always something so peaceful to him about this hour of the morning. The blending of night to day made anything seem possible.

Someone elbowed him in the gut. With a grunt, he looked over. He figured it would be Peter. He opened his mouth to give the idiot a piece of his mind when he followed Pete's gaze and caught sight of Jefferson heading in their direction with Margolis walking between and two masters-at-arms. Jefferson looked actually jovial for once, which made Jace question what had happened the previous evening to put the smile on his face.

Maybe he got laid.

The team snapped to attention and saluted Jefferson as he approached. "Morning, boys. You ready to have some fun?"

"Hooyah, sir!" Jace shouted along with the rest of the squad.

"Okay. Get a move on. Wheels up in twenty."

They filed into the aircraft, took up their choice positions for the flight, and headed for the Navy's Forward Operating Location in Comalapa, El Salvador. Margolis was seated in the back of the plane, restrained. The two MAs would fly down to El Salvador as the prisoner's escorts, then after the sting operation, complete the arms dealer's extradition to the El Salvadorian government.

When they landed, Jace and the crew would take a vehicle to a village called Santa Marta on the Rio Lempe. It was the only river large enough to handle commercial traffic and fed directly into the Pacific Ocean. The operation was designed so that Margolis would pretend to off-load his weapons to a contact who would ship them downriver and out into international waters. Jace settled into his seat and closed his eyes. He had three and a half hours to catch up on the sleep he had missed last night from loving Kat well into the early morning hours.

* * * *

"God, it's fucking hot. Why would people choose to live somewhere where it's ninety degrees in December? That's just wrong," Peter griped, looking up at the sun.

Jace shouldered his pack and made sure Margolis was secure. In the background, Justin, Cory, Collin and Eric argued which location they'd been deployed to for an operation had the worst weather. Jace rolled his eyes. He walked over to join the rest of his team.

"You do realize that for a large percentage of the world's population it's summer right now, don't you?" Kurt teased.

Peter flipped Kurt off. "Whatever. Where's our ride?"

"I swear to God working with you jackasses is like herding cats. Now shut up and try to behave like professionals. Here comes Commander Goodson," Jace hissed. "By the way you're all wrong, the worst was that time we joined the SAS in a training exercise on Papua New Guinea."

"Oh, fuck, I think I'd actually blocked that one out of my memory," Peter said.

"Mother-fucking earthquake, exploding volcanos, man-eating coral, and rain forests from hell," Justin recited.

"Yeah and that was only the first three days," Cory said.

Jace nodded. The guys all made a bowing motion. The sound of boots on concrete behind him had Jace spinning around to see Commander Goodson only a few feet away. He saluted the man who was in charge of the strategic base.

Goodson returned the salute. "Welcome to El Salvador, gentlemen. Your vehicle is ready. I presume you have civvies to wear until you reach your destination. It would cause one hell of a shit storm to have a bunch of Americans in military uniform driving through El Salvador."

"Yes, sir."

Goodson smiled. "Didn't doubt it for a second. Good luck, men. God willing I'll see you all before your flight back to the States."

Jace and the team snapped a salute.

* * * *

Jace let out a sigh of relief when Santa Marta came into view. The three-hour drive had been relatively routine, but after the four-hour flight he was ready to stretch his legs for a while. Santa Marta was little more than a few hundred tin-roofed and mud-bricked homes. The community was so small that on most maps it wasn't even labeled. That made it an ideal staging area for Jace and his team. They set themselves up in an abandoned house to act as their base of operations.

Jace set his pack on the ground beneath the tin-roofed porch and leaned against the fallen tree trunk that held the structure up. There was a creaking sound and he looked up.

"Probably not the best idea there," Collin said.

Jace nodded. "Yeah, I'm thinking not. All right, everyone, I know this looks like a great little vacation house, but we have work to do. We all have our tasks so let's get to it."

Jace turned to Kurt. "How long before you have the communication link up and running?"

"Five minutes."

Jace nodded. "Get to it." He looked over at the two masters-at-arms. "I want the two of you to take Margolis for a walk. Make your faces known. Remember you're supposed to be working for him. He's an escaped prisoner looking to make a drug and weapons deal." Then he looked at Justin, Eric and Cory. "You three go set up for the fake interception." He turned to Collin and Peter. "Let's gear up."

From the hut, Kurt would monitor the team's progress and update them with any new information from command. Team one consisted of Justin, Eric and Cory, otherwise known as Webster, Odin and Ace. Team two consisted of Jace, Collin and Peter, or Ice, Waldo and Hickok. While team one was playing toy soldiers, team two would surreptitiously position itself to intercept the target.

"Uplink complete, Jace," Kurt reported.

"Good." He checked his watch. "I want Margolis in position in two hours. The meet with his buyer is scheduled for 1700 hours. Let's find us a rat."

Jace, Peter and Collin all changed into tactical gear then stealthily made their way over to their position. Throughout the day, Jace checked in with team one, making sure they were staying on task.

His, Peter and Collin's location was a stifling hotbox one hundred meters from the location of the exchange. They sat in that concrete oven with temperatures easily rising over a hundred degrees. Sweat glided between his shoulder blades. The humidity by the river made the air feel like they were breathing in a steam room. On top of all that, their little hut only measured about five feet by six feet. With three of them inside, each man had about a two-foot space to call his own.

One of the two masters-at-arms stood near Margolis, acting as the man's second. He was to arrange the meeting between Margolis and their target should the call come through. A CIA operative was in position to act as the buyer for the weapons. Jace had wanted the entire operation to appear legit, assuming their target was observing the activities.

He looked at his watch. It was already after 1700. Jace started to get a nagging feeling in his gut, which was never a good sign.

He got on the radio. "Gadget, this is Ice. No contact. Over."

Kurt's voice came over the airwaves. "Roger."

"Standby for further instructions." Jace looked over at Peter. "What do you think?"

Peter raised binoculars and scoped the action. The 'buyer' was doing his job and was starting the transaction according to schedule.

Just as they were starting to transfer the cargo from the trucks to the boats, they saw one of the masters-at-arms pick up a cell phone. Jace radioed in to Kurt and team one. "Tele-contact has been initiated. Over."

"Acknowledge and confirm. Will initialize trace sequence," Kurt responded.

After several minutes, the man put the phone down and walked over to Margolis. To an observer it appeared he was telling Margolis that he needed to take this particular call. Margolis took up the receiver.

Kurt had wired the phone for audio transmit and recording prior to deploying yesterday, so they hoped that even if the target didn't make an appearance, they would at least be able to get a recording for voice recognition.

When Margolis hung up the phone, Jace checked in with Kurt. "Gadget, is our man coming to the party?"

Kurt sounded frustrated. "That's a negative. The transmission was an obvious ploy. The voice was digitally disguised, and once Margolis picked up the phone, started giving a weather report for the coastal region. Over."

Jace looked over at Collin. "Well, damn." Then, back into the radio, "Was signal traced and recorded? Over."

"Affirmative. However, signal was coming from a secure satellite phone. The signal bounced across twelve countries. Digital enhancement had similar characteristics as previous. Will be able to confirm or negate when Dorothy goes back to Kansas. Over."

"Acknowledge. Will maintain position to confirm absence of target in the bushes. Proceed with interception as planned to ensure completion of operation. Over."

"Roger."

Jace, Collin, and Peter continued to sit in their hut. At exactly 1800 hours, team one stormed the location as planned and appeared to take down Margolis, the 'dealer', and his second. Jace, Peter, and Collin stayed in their position for another two hours to ensure everything was wrapped up. After six hours in their concrete oven, Jace was glad to get out even if they didn't get their target.

Collin and Peter exited the structure and secured the surrounding area. They gave the all-clear signal, and Jace stepped into the opening. He turned back quickly and started to bend down to grab his canteen when he felt a searing pain rip across the back of his shoulder.

* * * *

Kat climbed out of bed, noticing that the weatherman the

night before had been correct when he'd said a cold front was coming through. The room felt chilly against her bare skin. A nice, hot shower would chase away the fog of sleep that still held her captive. She'd heard Jace leave several hours ago, and had no idea how he planned on functioning with so little sleep.

Her shower didn't take long, and Kat dashed downstairs for a quick coffee and bagel. She carried them back to Jace's room so she could eat and pack her overnight bag at the same time. She'd slept a little later than she'd intended and now only had two hours before she was expected to report to Jenny and Cory's house.

Kat turned her head at the sound of something falling over. It was sort of muffled.

Maybe something fell over in a closet?

Better to be safe than sorry. She grabbed the stun gun Jace had given her out of her bag and slowly walked down the steps. When she reached the bottom, she set the bag down and pressed her back to the wall at the base of the stairs. She swept her gaze across the open space of the living room and saw no one, then peered around the corner down the hall toward the utility and bathroom. Both doors were open.

As she moved around the corner, she could view the kitchen area and saw that it was clear. She couldn't see behind the counter, but decided to clear the hallway first. Keeping her breathing steady and eyes alert for any movement, she crept down the hall and checked both rooms and the closet. Walking back toward the kitchen, she checked behind the counter.

Nobody's here. It's just an unfamiliar house.

She giggled at how she must have looked stalking around the house like she was in a *Mission: Impossible* movie. Walking over to the front windows, she peered out around the edge of the curtain and checked the area in front of the town house. She didn't see anyone.

Must be imagining things. Guess I'm still a little jumpy after the experience at home.

She picked up her overnight bag and the bag full of snacks, wine, and treats she and Jace had shopped for at the commissary the day before. Kat picked up Jace's car keys from the counter and made her way to the garage. She loaded her bags in the back seat then got behind the wheel. Starting the car, she tried to remember exactly which direction to turn to find the main gate for the base.

Halfway to the exit she saw a small black compact pull in behind her about three car lengths back. She kept an eye on the vehicle in her rear-view mirror, and seeing the car turn, she breathed a sigh of relief. She'd been paying so much attention to the black car that Kat had made a wrong turn, and by the time she found her way back to the correct road, it was nine forty-five.

She made the turn off base and noticed that the same little black car had pulled behind her again. She kept her eye on the road. It was nothing, another service member out running errands. The sound of an engine being gunned drew her eye back to the rear-view mirror. The black car had sped up and now rode her ass. The shape of the driver was decidedly male. Kat tapped on the breaks, but the car didn't back off. She accelerated above the speed limit.

She recognized the cross street she was approaching as the same one she and Jace had taken during their ride to the promontory. Her hand tightened on the gearshift as she kept her eye on the street. She'd have to time the turn exactly. She punched the clutch, downshifted and jerked the wheel to the left. Halfway through the turn, Kat hit the accelerator again and powered through the curve, racing back up through the gears to put some distance between her and the compact.

When she got close to the bay, the steering wheel started to violently shake then lost all steering ability.

"Oh, shit!"

The car was headed right for the sharp curve before the promontory. Kat tried to get the car under control. She downshifted to first gear to slow the car as much as possible then hit the brakes.

She had timed the deceleration just right so the car came to a rest at an angle on the side of the road. Hopefully it would be visible to anyone coming around the bend. Jumping out of the car, she took off into the forest on the opposite side of the bay. She heard the compact come to a screeching halt and figured whoever it was must have seen Jace's car on the side of the road. Adrenaline and fear caused her heart to race. If she let it, the fear would consume her. She listened for every heavy step of her pursuer. Her vision tunneled on the path of least resistance to her escape. She couldn't let him catch her.

She ran into the trunk of one of the trees, grabbing around the middle to steady her. She leaned her back against the tree. Her head pounded, still not healed from the bash to it four days before. Even though the doctors had said she only had a mild concussion, running full-out for ten minutes had caused enough pressure to build up that she was dizzy and slightly disorientated.

Get control of yourself. Slow your breathing. Panic and disorientation will only let him catch you.

She took the chance to glance around her hiding spot, but didn't see anyone. She didn't hear any footsteps, either. Maybe she lost her pursuer? She let out a sigh of relief, and turned back around.

He was there in front of her with a gun pointed right at her head. She froze, her eyes trained at the opening on the barrel of the gun. Her breath locked in her chest, and her knees threatened to crumble. Only her grip on the trunk of the tree prevented her fall.

"Did you really think you could outsmart me? Now, be a good girl and come with me quietly. I don't want to hurt you again if I don't have to, but know that I won't hesitate if you try any more smart moves."

Kat had never gotten a good look at the man in her room that night, but he appeared to have the same build. She didn't recognize his voice, but that wasn't saying much.

Her sense of self-preservation kicked in, and she took a step toward the man in the mask. Just when she was within arm's reach, she tried to take him by surprise by ramming her full body weight at his hips like a defensive tackle. Taking advantage of his momentary distraction, she took off through the forest again, zigzagging, hoping he wouldn't have a clear shot. Something sharp hit her right in the middle of her back, and for the second time that week, Kat's world went black.

****

Jace heard the commotion around him, but for a second felt like he was just a casual observer. Then he realized what had happened and got royally pissed off.
Damn. It feels like a hot iron was laid across my back.
He felt blood dripping down his back, and even in the heat of the day, the sensation gave him cold chills.
The shooter had known what he was doing. If Jace hadn't bent over, the shot would have entered the base of his skull, killing him instantly. As it was, it had managed to find the area that wasn't protected by his armor. Currently, the entire team had Jace surrounded, providing cover from any other attacks.
Cory pulled Jace further in and to the side of the small building. He poked and prodded at the wound. "I think you're going to live. You lucky son of a bitch, it just ran up your shoulder blade. I'll piece you back together when we reach a secure area. For now, this field dressing should keep you from bleeding like a stuck pig."
Jace gave a low groan as Cory wrapped his shoulder. "I hate this part of the job. Thanks for patching up my dumb ass. That was a real stupid move on my part, blindly walking out the door."
Cory thumped his good shoulder. "Hey, Collin and Peter had secured the exit. They said you bent over at the last second and if you hadn't, this—" he dug out the spent

bullet that had embedded in the wall—"would have found a very happy home in your brain. Besides, I have to patch you up. Kat would kill me if I let you bleed out. While she may appear sweet and innocent, I don't buy that routine for a second. That woman could be a real ball-buster if she wanted to."

Justin looked over his shoulder and called in the direction of the building. "If you ladies are done with your tea party, I would love to get the fuck out of here. Snipers make me twitchy."

Jace couldn't agree more. "Yeah, let's move. We need to get back to the hut and inform Command of status."

Kurt eyed Jace when he entered the ramshackle dwelling. Jace picked up the communications headset. "Come in, Command."

"This is Command." Marshall's voice came through the speaker.

"We have a situation, sir. Target did not make an appearance at the party, but some form of communication did occur." Jace really hated to report this next part, but he had to give full disclosure. "There was an incident when we were preparing to leave. A sniper took a shot at me—a sniper with a very good aim—and I have enough Irish luck that I'm talking to you now, sir."

"How bad are you hurt, son?"

"Just a scratch, but had circumstances altered, I'd be taking a dirt nap right now."

"Did you identify the shooter's location?"

"The only location that would provide the angle necessary for the shot would have come from an observation tower two hundred yards from our position. The area was investigated, but there was no evidence other than disturbance in the dust."

"Roger that. You get your team back home, and we'll continue this discussion then."

"Roger, sir. We'll see you then."

It was late. Jace's shoulder hurt like a bitch and all he really wanted to do was sleep, but he knew that wasn't an option, so he contacted the extraction team to set up a rendezvous. Margolis' custody had been transferred to the CIA and he was already on his way to the El Salvadorian officials. Disconnecting the uplink, Jace looked over at his team. "Okay, boys, pack it in. We're going home. Evacuation will take place at 0300 hours. That gives us a little more than two hours to make the fifty-kilometer trip back to Comapala. Not much leisure time here, so let's get our boots moving."

If all went as planned, they should be home by 0700.

Chapter Twenty

Kat's head felt like lead, and her brain was trapped in a fog. The first thing she noticed was that, although her clothing was intact, her shoes were gone.

Why would he take my shoes?

She opened her eyes and saw nothing. The darkness around her was complete, but judging by the feel of air around her, the space was cavernous. Stretching out her arms, she felt rock beneath her body. She had apparently been leaning against a wall, also of rock. In the silence, she heard water dripping.

Does the area around the bay have caves?

The temperature was cold enough to be a cave. Kat had been in enough caves while doing field work to recognize the atmosphere. From what Kat could remember in her studies of anthropological evidence in the state, most of the caves were in the counties of the western border.

How long does it take to get from Norfolk to the western half of the state? Seven to eight hours?

That meant she had been unconscious for a long time. She had no idea where she actually was, or how long she'd been there. Time had ceased to exist in her state. It was like when she'd had her appendix out. She'd woken up groggy and brain-fuddled, but at the time would have sworn that the nurse had just told her to count back from a hundred a minute ago.

The extensiveness of the surrounding area made it seem more menacing than a dark closet would have been. She felt very vulnerable. She couldn't see more than a couple of feet around her. The sound of something hard hitting

213

the stone floor of the cave echoed. Kat turned her head to the left, hoping she judged the direction of source correctly in the darkness. She pushed herself back against the wall, wincing as she discovered tenderness in her lower back. Then she remembered the sharp pain just before she passed out.

He must have shot me with some sort of tranquilizer gun.

That would explain the time lapse. The steps grew closer, and Kat did the best she could to disappear into the wall until she heard a chuckle in the darkness.

"It won't matter how hard you try to blend into that wall. I can still see you."

Kat thought he might be bluffing, so she silently edged to her right.

"I wouldn't go that way if I were you. About five feet to your right is a crevice into another chamber of this cave."

She slowly continued to edge over to see if he was right. Her foot fell into nothingness and she lost her balance. Falling against the stone floor, she landed on her splinted wrist. Pain shot up her arm like a lightning bolt.

"Told you."

Kat stared in the direction of her captor's voice. "What do you want?"

"How is your back? Those tranq guns can pack a punch, but they are better than the alternative… For now, anyway."

"It's fine. Now what do you want?"

"I have to tell you that I'm just the courier, so I can't give you the details you want. I've been instructed to hold you here by whatever means necessary until your true host makes an appearance."

"And when is he expected to arrive?"

"Sometime soon, but again, no details. You're welcome to explore around you, but I wouldn't venture too far if I were you. There's a lot of drop-offs and passages you'd never find your way out of. You just sit tight, and we'll get to you soon enough."

She heard him walk away. Scooting back to her left, away

from the edge, she continued to feel along the ground.

The man must have had some kind of night vision goggles or something. There's no way regular eyes, no matter how adjusted to the darkness, could have seen that clearly. She couldn't sit still and wait, but she also knew that the man was right. Without proper equipment or knowledge about the cave, too much exploration could kill her faster than his threatened bullet. Having a good amount of field experience, she had explored caves before and respected their power. There was a slight difference between exploring a cavern for anthropological evidence with a well-equipped science team and being dumped in one with no light, supplies, or sense of direction.

She felt her way around on all fours, making a grid in her head by counting off paces. Her eyes had adjusted to the darkness, but she still couldn't see much, not enough to safely leave her area. She did find a large boulder several paces to her left. She marked the location on her mental map, not knowing if having a natural shield would come in handy. After several minutes, Kat began to tire and worked her way back the way she'd come. Hugging the wall, she found the edge of the crevice from before and backtracked about five feet. Thinking this was close to the same spot she was in when she woke up, she lay down and closed her eyes to conserve her remaining energy.

* * * *

She was startled awake by a very loud bang. The sound echoed and reverberated around the chamber, giving her a better sense of its size. She had no idea what had caused it, but it had sounded almost like gunfire.

What idiot would fire a weapon in a cave?

There was too great a chance of the bullet ricocheting off the walls. A voice boomed out of the darkness.

"Are you ready, girl? I'm coming for you now. I dare you to hide from me. In fact, I'll make you a deal. If you are able to hide for more than two minutes, I'll reward you and make this a little easier on you."

The voice struck a chord of familiarity, but Kat couldn't place it. It was definitely not the same as the man earlier. Assuming he was also using goggles, the only place she thought might prevent him from seeing her was the crevice to her right, but she knew there was no way she would be able to hold onto the ledge with her wrist being the way it was. Instead, she took a chance and crawled on all fours to a small alcove she had found during her explorations. She knew it was ten paces straight ahead and three paces to the right. She reached her cubby just as she heard footsteps echo in the chamber.

She heard the voice call out into the darkness "Marco?" then more steps and again, "Marco?"

She refused to answer the childish taunt.

"Oh, come on, Kat, don't you want to play my little game?"

She felt like prey being stalked. Which way led to safety, and which way led to death? His voice echoing through the chamber sent chills up her spine.

She heard him getting closer to her hiding spot. She didn't move a muscle and tried not to breath, but sensed his nearness and knew the jig was up. Then she felt the blade of a large knife slide under her neck. The blade was cold against her skin. She felt the smooth, sharp edge poised to cut. One move, one swallow, and it would slice the tender skin beneath her chin.

"Gotcha!"

Kat was forcibly dragged by her injured wrist. She gave a slight cry but made no other sound.

"Sorry, sweetheart. That was fun, but you only lasted one minute. Now it's time to really play."

She tried to get to her feet and walk, but he was pulling so quickly that she couldn't maintain her balance. Her knees and feet were being scratched and cut by the sharp rocks. Still she refused to let loose any sound of distress.

They must have moved about fifty feet when he lifted her up and threw her against another solid rock wall. Her head bounced off the stone, causing her to see stars.

He pushed against her body to hold her up on the wall. Then the sound of metal clanging filled the air.

Are those chains?

She began to panic and fought against his hold. He quickly stopped that by sliding the point of the knife underneath her chin.

"Don't move, or I'll kill you right here. I already slit the throat of my delivery boy. Can't have any loose ends, you know. Now, if you behave, you might live long enough for that cock-sucking, bastard boyfriend of yours to rescue you. That is, if he isn't already dead from the bullet I put into him down south. He would be dead if he hadn't moved at the last second. My bullet was seconds away from splattering his brains all over the wall of that little hovel. Amusingly enough, they thought they could trick me into revealing myself with a sting operation."

Removing her splint, he slapped large cuffs around her wrists. They were placed high on the wall, forcing her arms to stretch high above her head, almost to the point of standing on her toes. Then he spread her legs almost painfully far apart and attached similar restraints to her ankles. The manacles were large and thick. It was obvious that they were drilled into the walls of the cave.

"Let's see what has Jace so enamored. You know, he's never taken to a girl like this before. Usually his affairs are no more than a quick fuck and a thank-you card as he ships off for his next mission."

Kat tried twisting, testing her bonds, but instantly stilled when he slashed down through her top and pants. With a few deft moves, he had removed every stitch of her clothing.

The cool air of the cavern hit her skin. Her arms and legs broke out in goosebumps. Her muscles clenched, trying to conserve body heat. She'd heard her captor take several steps back and stop.

"Well, you're a pretty little thing, but I don't see what all the fuss is about. I can see the defiance in your eyes, Kat. That's not going to help you. While I admire your courage, you cannot change the course of these events. They were put into place too many years ago."

The man came closer and slid his hands down her naked body. She refused to give any indication of how his touch made her skin crawl. He pinched her nipples between his thumbs and forefingers, twisting them hard. Her body squirmed to escape before her brain could command it not to. She clenched her teeth with pain, but held back the cries that rose in her chest.

Placing one hand around her neck, he squeezed just hard enough to almost cut off the air supply. Her pulse pounded and her ears rang. Kat's determination to withhold her reaction broke when, with the other hand, he stabbed his fingers into her vagina and thrust up high inside her, causing her to scream.

"Finally!" he cheered. His fingers continued to roughly invade Kat's body, despite the way she bucked against the restraints. "I love the sound of your cries. Sing for me, Kat. It's all sweet music to my ears. I knew I could break your stubbornness and defiance. Now you truly understand that it is I who control your destiny.

"Has Jace shown you the pleasures that can be found in erotic asphyxia? All I have to do is play your little traitorous body and squeeze just hard enough to reduce the amount of oxygen to your brain, and you will experience an orgasm unlike any before. You need to behave, though. Otherwise, I might squeeze too hard, then you'll never know pleasure again."

Kat spat in his face. "Get off me, you sick bastard!" Her shout was harsh from lack of air.

He yanked his hand out of her body and punched her hard in the ribs. Chained as she was, she couldn't bend over to protect the vulnerable midsection. Kat felt the bones compress in her body, and cried out when it felt as if she'd been stuck with a high-heeled shoe straight into her lungs.

"Was that a crack I heard? Broken ribs hurt like hell. Oh, well." He cackled.

"Is this the only way you can get it up? By hurting your partners, by controlling them through pain? That's really pathetic."

Kat received another hard punch, this time right in the stomach for her comment.

"You would do well not to piss me off, little girl. I think I'm going to leave you here for a while to ponder your transgressions. On the other hand, I think I'll show you just what it feels like to experience real pain before I go."

He took his knife and began cutting shallow slices all over her body. Not deep enough to puncture any veins or arteries, but they wouldn't begin to clot any time soon. He cut her on the neck just above the clavicle, on the wrists lengthwise down her forearms, and in the 'V' where her hips angled down.

"That should do for now. Oh, don't worry, those little cuts aren't going to kill you. We'll see if you're so feisty when hypothermia sets in. This cave stays about forty degrees year-round. I'll come back and check on you in a few hours. Right now, I'm going to see if your little boyfriend is on his way home yet."

As he walked away, she took deep breaths trying to calm her raging heart. She knew that the faster her heart beat, the more she would bleed. After she knew he was gone, Kat succumbed to the anger, fear and pain she'd refused to let him see, raising her head to scream as high and loud and long as she could.

* * * *

Things had most definitely not gone as planned. Jace winced as the stitches Cory had sewn into his back on the plane out of El Salvador pulled and a few new bruises he'd earned during their layover throbbed. But they'd finally landed in Norfolk ten minutes ago. As always, when he returned home, he let out a sigh of relief when his boots hit the cement of the flight line. He was home.

They'd had to make an unscheduled stop to help clear up a situation in Mexico where command had gotten word that some terrorists were staging an attack on the United States by bringing nuclear rockets across the border through some tunnels. Given what happened in Central America, they should have come right home, but Jace's team was the closest to the action so they'd been redeployed until the situation was resolved. Fortunately it had only taken one massive firefight, several incredibly loud explosions, and the deaths of several terrorists before that happened. All of Jace's squad returned in one piece. They were a bit dented and dinged, but salvageable.

Cory pulled out a cell phone from his pack and started dialing. That was Cory's MO. Before debriefing he would always call Jenny and let her know he was safe, no matter what time of day it was. Normally Jace smiled and went on with his business, but this time Kat was with Jenny and he stood next to Cory, anxious to hear his sweetheart's voice. He should probably give Cory a few seconds of privacy, though. He stepped away and turned to find Marshall standing in front of him. The look on his face was not a good one.

Marshall escorted Jace a few feet away from the other men. "I got a call from Jenny the other day. Kat never made it to her house. A few hours after they were supposed to meet, Jenny got worried about her, so she went over to your place and said she knocked on the door for fifteen minutes. Nobody ever answered. After driving around the base to see if maybe she saw your car in a parking lot, she called me. Not too long afterward, I received a call from the police. Your car had been found abandoned on the side of the road near the point. Their investigators discovered that the nuts on the steering arm had been removed, making the car impossible to drive. They also said that when they found the car, the driver's side door was wide open, and there were groceries in the back seat. Son, I'm sorry... There's no sign of her."

After what had happened in El Salvador, Jace knew without a doubt that the two were connected. Terror unlike anything he had ever experienced coursed through his body. His heart felt like it was being squeezed in a vise, and his lungs were sitting under a hundred pound anvil.

He looked over at Cory and saw the desolate look in his eyes. Jenny had just told him. This was no mistake. Kat had been taken.

Jesus, that was three days ago! Where is she...? What have they done to her by now?

His phone vibrated in his pocket. Jace yanked it out and looked at the caller ID. It was Kat's number. He opened the phone. "Kat? Is that you, baby?" The voice that came over the phone was a very familiar one.

"Sorry, Jace, Kat can't come to the phone right now. She's indisposed. If you ever want to see her again, you'll do exactly as I say. Take the car parked in your driveway and follow the map inside to the marked location. This is not where she is, so don't try to set up anything funny with your pals. I've got her stashed in a little cave, away from prying eyes. When you get there, get out of the car, put the keys in the driver seat, and lock the doors. Wait until I contact you on this phone again. Any questions?"

"How do I know you have her? How do I know she's still alive?"

Please God, let her be alive! I won't survive without her!

"You want proof of life? I made a little recording of Kat's and my last few moments together. I think you'll like it." Jace heard a click then he heard the man's voice. "Well, you're a pretty little thing, but I don't see what all the fuss is about." An eerie silence had Jace listening for any ambient sounds through the connection. Then the sound of Kat's scream pierced his heart through the phone. A hand landed on his shoulder and squeezed. Kat's voice came through the phone. "Get off me, you sick fuck…" More silence followed for a few seconds, then he said, "Don't worry, those little cuts aren't going to kill you. We'll see if you're so feisty when hypothermia sets in."

Jace couldn't take it any longer. He screamed into the phone, "I'll kill you! If you've hurt her, I'll make you wish you were never born!"

He just heard a menacing chuckle on the other end. "No, I think it's you who is going to suffer. You have four hours to get to the rendezvous."

Jace slammed the phone shut. All his team members had gathered around him during the phone call. He had put it on speaker so they could hear the exchange. Always the soldier, he wanted whatever help he could to gather all the intel possible. As they stood in the high moonlight on the airstrip, everyone was slightly stunned by what they had just heard.

Cory was the first to speak. "Well, let's go. We've got four hours. Captain Marshall, do you have a car nearby so we can get Jace to his house?"

"Yes, it's right over here. Was that who I thought it was?"

Jace looked up at him with haunted eyes. "Yes."

* * * *

Kat wasn't sure how long she had been hanging on the wall. Her cuts had bled for a while, but had now stopped. She knew she hadn't lost too much blood, but felt weak, anemic. During her reflection time, she thought about Jace and relived their times together. She remembered their first dance the night they met, the look in his eyes when he heard her sing at the church, the feel of his body against hers when they made love and the sound of his laughter. Those memories kept her warm and held the darkness threatening to consume her at bay.

A voice echoed out in the darkness. "I have a present for you, Kat. Your little boyfriend made it home alive. He sends his regards, by the way."

"I hope he told you to go fuck yourself!" she shouted.

Her voice was still harsh from the crushing of her throat and the hours spent in silence. A loud, gutsy laugh echoed off the walls of the cavern.

"I never would have expected such language from a respectable doctor like you. I told him we were getting along famously. He and I have a little date set in about an hour. We'll see if he follows instructions like a good little soldier. Until I get back, I'm going to let you have some music to listen to."

Suddenly the cave reverberated with the sounds of Jace's voice. "Oh, yes... Fuck me, Kat... Suck me... I'll kill you... You're dead... I'll make you wish you were never born!"

The loop continued. She could tell he'd spliced several conversations together to make his demented message. She recognized some of them from times they were together, and others must have been taken when the man talked to Jace earlier. It wasn't the words, but the sound of Jace's voice in both passion and rage that filled Kat's head now. The sounds never stopped. When the recording ended, it started all over again like a CD player on repeat for eternity.

Chapter Twenty-One

As Jace drove across the moonlit country roads, the cackling voice over the phone echoed in his head. Who would have thought that Jefferson was the traitor they had been searching for? What Jace couldn't wrap his head around was the motive. He knew that Jefferson had always been somewhat of an asshole, but delusional psychotic was not something he had seen coming.

He'd spent the last four hours thinking about his and Jefferson's interactions. He recalled the first time they had met, during BUD/S training. He knew Jefferson was about ten years older than him and had joined the Navy late. He had just beaten the age cut-off for eligibility.

The twenty-five-week BUD/S training was designed to physically and mentally challenge you to the highest levels of endurance. It took everything you had and more not only to survive, but to build yourself into a better soldier than you were upon entering the program. Jace remembered that they'd almost cut Jefferson from the program since the whole point of building a SEAL was to tear a man apart then build him back up, stronger, smarter, and more unified with his fellow soldiers. Jefferson never wanted unity. He spent whatever dredges of energy were left at the end of the day to play stupid head-fuck games with all the guys in the barracks. For that the Master Chief had threatened to ring the drop-out bell for Jefferson unless he got his fucking act together.

The guy was a real asshole. Over the last several years, he'd always seemed to get one lucky promotion after another. He was always in the right place at the right time, but in most of Jace's colleagues' opinions, never truly deserving of the accolades. Even other SEAL teams had heard of Jefferson and disapproved of his meteoric rise in the ranks.

Jace looked at the map in the front seat of the car. It marked a location slightly north of Salem, Virginia, north of the Blue Ridge Mountains.

Jesus! There are hundreds of caves in that part of the state. There is no possible way we can figure out by process of elimination where Kat is being held.

Marshall was working on finding out everything possible about Jefferson. Where he came from, where he held property, anything they could possibly use to figure out where he had taken her. Jace's objective was to get to the location on the map as quickly as possible. He looked at the clock on the dash. His four hours were almost up.

He said something about cuts. Was Kat slowly bleeding to death? Would he be able to reach her fast enough? Jefferson had said something about hypothermia... Oh, God. Had he taken her clothes? Was she stranded or locked up somewhere with no protection from the elements?

Please, God, tell me he didn't rape her!

The thought of his precious Kat being violated that way made him see red. His hands clenched on the steering wheel, and he pushed his foot harder on the accelerator.

I'm so sorry, baby! I wasn't there to protect you like I promised. I swear on that part of my soul that belongs to you, if we make it out of this, I'll make things up to you. I'll hold you in my arms so tight you'll beg me to let go. I'll pamper you in every way possible. Just don't leave me. Hold on for me, sweetheart. I swear I'll find you.

Jace's phone rang, interrupting his maddening thoughts. He looked down and saw Marshall's number. "Go ahead, sir."

"We've just reviewed Jefferson's personnel records. He grew up in Boston, Massachusetts. His parents are listed as deceased. His mom died two years ago, and father committed suicide twenty-five years ago. We did some further digging and found the news article from when he killed himself. Apparently, it was very public and messy. His company had been bought out a year before by some corporation out of Boston, and he couldn't cope."

Jace stiffened, a sudden thought causing dread to race through his body. "Did it say what the name of the company was?"

"Something called Patriot Enterprises."

Suddenly, Jace knew then what the connection was. "Mother fucking son of an ass whore!"

"I take it you know something?"

"I'm the owner of Patriot Enterprises. Well, on paper anyway. Twenty-five years ago, my father would have still been CEO. The company is a corporate restructuring firm. My dad basically bought businesses in trouble and either sold them or turned them around for a profit. If his intention was to sell, then he'd always make an effort to offer the former owners and employees a respectable way of continuing to support their families, but all that changed after my parents' death. My uncle, who'd been my dad's partner, took over since I was only ten at the time. He started a new regime where all that mattered was the bottom dollar. People, loyalty mean nothing to him. I was supposed to take over when I reached my majority, but had no desire to become another lemming to my uncle's despotism. I was admitted to the Naval Academy and never looked back. He's still pissed off at me. Every few months he calls to rant that I'm denying my heritage and shirking my family responsibilities."

Jace had never revealed this part of his history to anyone. He was sure Marshall would look at him differently now. He just hoped that the man would still respect him.

"Thank you for telling me. I'll keep that on a need-to-know basis. But this will help us to dig a little deeper now that we know there's a source outside the Navy that connects you to Jefferson. How close are you to the destination?"

"I'm nearly there. Another twenty minutes at the most."

"Okay, here's what I want you to do. Cory says you still have his cell phone. When you arrive at the meet, I want you to call and keep the line open to me. We'll monitor your exchange with Jefferson and listen for any clues as to where he's holding Kat. If he moves you, we can use the GPS chip to triangulate your location to help narrow down the possibilities."

"Yes, sir."

"The team is not too far behind you and can intercept her if we pick something up. We're assuming he'll want to stick close to where he's holding her. What I want you to do is try anything you can to get him talking about where she is. Remember what I said about keeping your head, Jace?"

"Yes, sir."

"In order for Kat to have a chance, we need you to be with us. Your head needs to be in the game. You need to act like a SEAL, not an outraged and terrified lover. Got that?"

"Yes, sir."

"Okay then, let's take the son of a bitch down."

Jace pulled the car over to the side of the road and looked around for any sign of Jefferson. Sitting inside the car for a moment, he checked the power supply on Cory's phone. They were counting on Jefferson disabling his, but not knowing about the backup unless he thoroughly searched him. Setting up the connection, he put the phone in the side pocket on his right pant leg.

The area was an isolated stretch of road—more of a gravel off-shoot, really—that cut between the mountains. Limestone cliffs common to the area rose on either side of the road. Looking around, he didn't see any sign of Jefferson, but could sense that the man was nearby. He didn't have long to wait. His phone rang almost the moment he stepped outside the car and locked the door as instructed. He pushed the button to connect the call.

"You're right on time. I'm impressed. Still dressed for the field, I see. Well, we need to remove a few items. Take off your vest. I want all weapons and ammo tossed to the ground, including that knife you like to carry in your belt. If you're using the comm link, remove it. I will check to see if it's in the pile. I want you to walk one hundred yards to your south and stand still. Turn in a circle three times with your arms out to the side."

Jace did as he ordered. When he stopped turning, he came face to face with Jefferson, and it took everything in his power not to immediately attack the man.

"How's the back?"

"It's fine. You always were a lousy shot." Probably not the best thing he could have said just then. He refocused. "Where's Kat?"

Jefferson snickered. "Like I'm going to tell you? Don't worry. She's close by, no more than an hour away. I just hope she can last another hour. Last time I saw her, she was looking a little white. Well, actually she looked red, black and blue, but you get my point."

Jace clenched his jaw. "What do you want? Why the elaborate cat-and-mouse game?"

"Isn't it obvious? I'm going to steal from you what you stole from me. You destroyed my family, so now I'm going to destroy yours once and for all. I've been trying to get rid of you for years, but you, being the resilient little bastard that you are, seem to always find a way out of the situation. So I've decided to take a slightly different approach. The sweet little Dr Martin is the first person you've cared about since your parents died, and so by destroying her, I'll get the added bonus of destroying you."

Jace listened to Jefferson's ranting and tried to keep a bored look on his face. "And just how exactly did I destroy your family?"

"Even the innocent must atone for the sins of their fathers. Your dad and uncle systematically destroyed my family. They tore apart my parents' company and sold it off piece by piece to whoever would give them the biggest profit. My father spiraled down into a depression so deep that he took his own life."

"Sounds like your father was not only a poor businessman but a coward." He wasn't sure if taunting Jefferson was the best idea, but it was guaranteed to keep the man talking. Hopefully he'd give up something the team could use.

Jefferson raised his gun to Jace's head and shouted, "Don't ever talk about my father! He was three times the man you will ever be! Let's go, superstar. We're going to take a little trip to join your girlfriend. I've decided I'll be generous and let you watch each other die. I'm not a completely unfeeling bastard, after all."

Jefferson threw a line of zip ties at him. "Put them on, hands in front where I can see them. Pull the tie closed with your teeth. Walk over and get in the back passenger side seat of that black compact."

Jace decided to take a calculated risk and said, "You know they're going to track us. They have your cell phone number and all issued phones have GPS tracking."

"You really think I would be stupid enough to not remember that? I disabled my GPS hours ago. Having said that, I think it's time to relieve you of your phone. We wouldn't want them to have too much of an advantage."

Jace had intended to get Jefferson riled up so he wouldn't be so focused and think of all the procedures for securing an adversary. He raised his hands and waved them in front of Jefferson. "Hello? Can't exactly dig through my pockets now, can I?"

Jefferson walked over. "Turn around, face the car and put your arms on the roof. Where is your phone?"

Jace rolled his eyes at the man. "You don't really think I'm going to turn my back to you, do you? Seriously, man. We had the same training. What SEAL in his right mind is going to turn his back on an armed and hostile target?"

Jefferson was looking very exasperated. "Fine! You are so goddamn annoying. It's going to be a real pleasure to kill you. Where is your phone? I know you have it on you, because you picked up when you were standing outside the car earlier, so don't try any stupid tricks."

Jace shrugged. "Fine. It's in my front left pants pocket. Oh, and asshole, don't get any funny ideas about copping a cheap feel. I'm spoken for."

For that smart little comment, Jace got smacked across the cheek with the gun. "Keep it up, jackass. You're just digging your own grave." Jefferson reached into the pocket and removed a small phone. He threw it onto the gravel roadway and stomped on it.

Jace looked at him. "Was that really necessary? Now I have to buy a new phone, reprogram all my numbers and download new ring tones."

Jefferson smirked. "Necessary? Probably not, but certainly enjoyable. Besides, you're not going to have to worry about replacing your phone when you're dead. Now that the pleasantries are dispensed with, get in the damn car."

Jace opened the rear door of the small vehicle and sat down in the seat. Just as Jefferson was about to close the door, he once again raised the gun and fired at Jace's neck. The dart hit him right in the vein, and he went down like a stone.

* * * *

Kat couldn't focus on anything anymore. Jace's voice blaring through the speaker had become a haunting soliloquy. Suddenly, the sound stopped and silence echoed throughout the cavern. The silence in itself was almost as deafening. She heard footsteps enter the chamber.

"Good evening, Kat. I've brought you another present."

She heard him set something down. It sounded heavy as it hit the rock floor. She squinted and saw a body lying on the floor. The body tilted to the side and even in the darkness she was able to recognize Jace's features.

He's here! But why isn't he moving or responding to anything? Oh, God. Has that psycho killed him already?

She turned her head toward where the man had set Jace

down. She decided to goad him a little see if she could get some kind of response. "Did you knock him out like you did to me? Had to take him unaware, huh? I figure you can't actually win in a fair fight."

He slapped her hard across the face and snarled, "What did I tell you about pissing me off, little girl? Oh, and he's not dead. At least, not yet."

She felt blood drip from her lip. *Well, at least I know there's still some in me,* she thought with some chagrin. Of course none of that mattered. What mattered was that Jace was still alive. There was still a chance they'd get out of here. "I'm not scared of you. If I die, then so be it. At least I won't go out sniveling to a weasel like you, a man who needs to tie women up and beat them to get his jollies." She heard a growl escape from her captor. *It must be working. I'm making him madder.* She hoped her plan to distract him with anger was the right course of action, because it could come back to literally haunt her. She could also sense that Jace was silently moving over by the wall.

She didn't look in his direction because she didn't want to give him away, so she decided to taunt her attacker some more. At least that kept his attention focused on her. "You think you're so tough. I bet you've never given a woman any real pleasure."

Jefferson reached back, pulled Kat's hair then leaned in and licked her throat. He crowded his body up against her own and snarled into her ear, "I thought you'd learned your lesson, little girl." He brought his hand up and grabbed her around the throat again.

This time Kat felt her larynx being crushed and let a choking sound out. She bucked against her restraints. Looking into his eyes, she sneered. "You'll never…win." Her voice cracked. "I'll never give in… To you." She heard the choking sounds escape from her mouth and felt dizzy from the lack of oxygen, but refused to let the blackness claim her.

"You think your superhero can stop me? He couldn't stop

me last time, and I've already made sure he can't stop me this time." At her confused look, he smiled. "Jace hasn't told you much about his past, has he?"

She couldn't speak under the pressure of his hand on her throat, so she just stared defiantly. He was close enough that she saw the demented fire in his eyes, and spittle was spraying from his lips onto her cheek.

"His uncle is the CEO of the largest commercial takeover corporation on the Eastern Seaboard. His father was the CEO before him. The business has been in the family for generations. Your hero is actually majority stock holder of one of the biggest corporations that destroys lives every single day." He started laughing. "He's an honest-to-God New England blueblood. His family has had the power to destroy others dating all the way back to the Revolutionary War."

His hand had released enough of the crushing pressure that she could take a much-needed breath.

The haze cleared from her eyes as she gasped out, "What does any of that have to do with you proving your lack of manhood?"

He ignored the insult and continued. "Jace's parents weren't killed by a drunk driver like everyone thought. I was seventeen at the time. It was always assumed that the driver of the car that hit them was drunk because he was never found. They assumed he had stumbled away from the wreck. The car wasn't registered to anyone, so there was nobody to track down. All I had to do was know where they were going to be on a given night and set my beautiful stage. It was orchestrated like magic."

Despite the release of his hand on her throat, Kat was growing weaker, but she had to keep pushing him. She imagined that Jace's eyes had turned to molten lead upon hearing the confession. The man was right. Jace hadn't told her much about his past or family, but she knew he loved his parents deeply and missed them. The loss of their parents was one of the things that had connected them from the very beginning. She was surprised Jace remained so still listening to the revelation. Kat would have attacked and clawed the man's eyes out, but she guessed the calm had been trained into Jace because he remained in his position, not giving away the fact that he was aware. If she could hold out long enough, she knew Jace would overcome this asshole.

"So, you got your revenge. You killed Jace's parents. He suffered their loss like you suffered your father's. Why come after him now?"

"Don't you get it? Jace's family is responsible for the destruction of my own plus thousands of others for the last two hundred years. When I killed his parents, my intent was to take away the very thing they had stolen from me — the security of home, of family.

"I knew he couldn't stand his uncle. Anyone who knows him thinks he's despicable. Making him live in that house for ten years was a joy to watch. I've been keeping tabs on him for years now. I even joined the Navy when he did. Last year, I was able to arrange it so I became the commander of his unit.

"It could have been finished, but then he started seeing you. For some reason, he fell in love, and once again had that security, that family that I took away from him all those years ago."

Kat felt cold, her head was pounding and her teeth were chattering. She'd stopped being able to feel her arms and legs hours before.

Jefferson continued his ranting. "Before I end your miserable existence, I want you to see something." He took a gun out of his pocket, and aiming it in Jace's direction, fired. Kat heard the impact of the bullet.

She gathered what was left of her strength and screamed, "No!" What came out was really no more than an aching whisper.

"Your voice is getting weaker. Are you tired? All you have to do is give in and accept your fate. There really is no use in fighting it. Jace is finally dead, and now so are you."

He tossed his gun and reached in his pocket again, this time pulling out a very large knife. She watched and was helpless to stop as he drew his arm back, then thrust the knife into her side. Even though it felt like ice was running in Kat's veins, she felt the searing heat of the blade slicing into her flesh. Her vision started going dark, and his voice seemed to move farther away.

"I just sliced into your spleen. Did you know that the spleen receives five percent of all output from your heart? You can relax. I guarantee you that with no treatment currently available you have a very short time to live. I'd say we have about thirty minutes to enjoy some of the favors you've been offering Jace so recently."

He bit down on one of her nipples. She vaguely felt his teeth sink into her skin. He used one hand to stab his fingers up into her again, brutally slamming them in and out, separating them to pull and tear at the delicate tissues. She heard the rasp of his zipper being pulled down and the whisper of skin on skin as he pumped himself, letting out harsh grunts. She knew he was going to rape her, and yet couldn't summon the strength to fight any longer. Jace was gone and her body was tired. She could feel her life force slowly slipping away. She knew she should fight, she knew that rape was the ultimate violation. Jace would not want her to go out meekly submitting to this torture.

She felt him grab her hips and tilt her forward, the manacles cutting into her wrists as he pulled her down, poised to thrust inside. She gathered the last of her strength. She tightened her muscles and opened her mouth to scream and twist to fight him as much as possible. A clicking sound came from her right.

"I told you before you're a lousy shot," Jace said.

The gun exploded, and the man's head immediately followed. With that, she finally let the darkness claim her.

Jace ran forward and lifted Kat's weight off her wrists. He could see she had passed out. Looking at her side, he caught sight of the deep laceration on the left. He knew that Jefferson wasn't lying when he said he had targeted her spleen. The man was a master with the knife.

He tore off his shirt so he could apply pressure to the wound and frantically searched for a pulse, but couldn't find one. Her head was hanging down and her eyes were closed "Baby? Oh, God... Sweetheart... Please look at me. Open your eyes, Kat! Wake up!"

Jace's eyes swam with tears. She wasn't responding. He was too late. He found the key in Jefferson's pocket and opened the restraints around her wrists and ankles. She was a complete dead weight against him as she fell into his arms. She felt like a block of ice. He tilted his head close to her mouth and felt a slight puff of air against his cheek.

Oh, thank God!

He continued to apply pressure to her side as he grabbed her up. Just then, he heard a sound behind him.

"Who's there? Identify yourself!"

"It's Cory and Collin. Is the area secure?"

"Yes! Goddammit, get down here! I need a medic immediately. I'm losing her! Please help me!" he shouted into the opening of the cavern.

Cory and Collin both came running into the chamber with their weapons in hand and night vision goggles strapped on.

Jace looked at Cory, terrified beyond anything he thought he was capable of feeling. "Help her... I can't lose her."

"Okay, buddy, let's get out of here. We have a rescue flight waiting outside the cave. You want me to carry her?"

Jace gathered Kat closer to his chest.

Cory saw the move and grabbed a thermal blanket out of his kit "Okay, let's put this on top of her. She must be close if not already experiencing hypothermia. At the very least, she's gone into shock." Cory did his best to wrap the blanket around Kat.

"I'll pick up the garbage and lead the way out," Collin said.

Chapter Twenty-Two

As they climbed out of the cave, Jace held Kat's body close to his own in a valiant attempt to transfer some of his body heat to her.

God, she feels so cold.

When they exited the mouth and moonlight hit her ghostly pale skin he noticed that her lips had turned a scary shade of blue. The blood from her side continued to leak onto his chest. He could almost feel how, with every amount that left her body, it took a part of Kat's soul with it.

He saw and ran over to the Navy Seahawk SH-60 that sat on the ground, rotors turning at full speed, waiting for them. Two corpsmen were inside and they pulled Kat from his arms as he jumped into the chopper. One of the medics looked over at Jace. "Status!"

"Deep-penetrating wound of left abdomen, most likely transecting spleen. Assailant was master knifeman and knew how and where to hit. Prolonged exposure and other physical trauma likely," Jace snapped out.

The medic was quickly checking Kat's vitals as they lifted off. "Her temperature is only ninety-one degrees. We need to increase her core temperature." He looked over at the other medic. "Start Res-Q-Air!" He worked to arrest the bleeding from her side.

They arrived at the hospital in Roanoke within twenty minutes. As they raced into the trauma center, Jace was held back by a nurse. "Sir, you have to let them work, if you want them to save her." She looked him over. "Sir, how badly are you hurt?"

Jace kept watching through the window in the trauma

room. The nurse raised her voice louder. "Sir! How badly are you hurt?" Jace looked down at himself, and seeing the blood all over his chest, he looked up at the nurse and weakly said, "It's all hers."

He heard the corpsmen yell out status to the doctors. "Thirty-year-old female, BP eighty-six over sixty, hypothermic with penetrating left abdominal wound. Res-Q-Air applied in transit."

Although it looked like a three-ring circus in the room, Jace recognized the methodical orchestration of the nurses and doctors. It reminded him of some of the missions he'd participated in.

"We need two units typed and matched, I want warm IV running wide open. We need an abdominal CT right away to assess internal bleeding," one doctor ordered.

The blood arrived and was hung on a metal pole next to Kat's head. Jace thought she was stabilizing when suddenly one of the nurses yelled out "BP is crashing, patient is in V fib!"

Jace raced forward and put his hand on the window. *Hold on, baby! Don't let go! I'm right here! I'm not leaving you, so stay with me!*

The doctor ran to the other side of the gurney. "Paddles!"

It was as if he was watching a slow-motion movie. He saw a nurse hand the doctor the paddles and someone called, "Charge to two hundred! Clear!" He saw Kat jerk as the electric shock ripped through her body. Everyone waited for the briefest of seconds, and the nurse yelled, "Still V fib!" Looking at the monitor, the doctor ordered, "Increase to three hundred! Clear!"

He watched as they once again shocked her chest. His mind refused to accept that technically she was dead. For the first time in many years, really since his parents died, he closed his eyes and prayed. Reciting every prayer he ever learned in Catholic school, he begged and bartered for a miracle.

"We have sinus. Let's move upstairs, folks, no time for

CT. We're going to have to open her up and see where she keeps leaking from."

As they wheeled her into the elevator, Jace vaguely heard shouts as the team came running through the trauma center doors. Cory reached Jace first and grabbed him by the shoulders to turn him around.

"Jace! Jace! What's the status here? Commander, what is the status?" he demanded.

Jace saw Cory make the hand signals for Collin to go over to the nurses' station then Jace was dragged over to an open gurney and pushed down.

"We need to get you cleaned up, buddy. Have you been checked out?"

Jace numbly shook his head.

"Okay, let me see what I can do."

Cory gestured for a nearby nurse to come over. "Can I get some extra scrubs or something? He's covered in blood, and we need to get him checked out."

The nurse looked Jace up and down. "He reported all the blood was hers, and wasn't complaining of any injury. But I'll get you something clean to have him wear."

"Thank you. I'm a trained medic. Mind if I check him over, just in case?"

The little blonde shook her head "Go ahead. Let me know if he needs to be seen, though, okay?"

Collin came back and pulled Cory a few feet away. Jace read his friend's lips, but couldn't really process the sound of his voice.

"She went into V fib, man. They had to shock her twice before they could get her to surgery upstairs. The nurse said she was stabilizing then her vitals dropped like a stone."

"Shit... He saw that, too. I know he did. Look at the window to the trauma room. There's a bloody handprint. He stood there and literally watched her die." Cory cursed again. "Okay. We need to get him cleaned up and go upstairs. I'm sure it'll be a while before they have any news, but at least it'll give us something to focus on. See if you can dig him up some coffee or something, so we can snap him out of this trance."

Collin nodded. "You got it."

Cory walked back over to Jace. "Hey, man, how are you doing?"

His brain snapped to attention. What the fuck was he doing sitting here like some stoned-out victim when Kat was upstairs fighting for her life? He shook his head and started to jump off the gurney with the intention of running after Kat. Cory grabbed his arm.

"Hold up, buddy. We need to clean you up first. There's no way they're going to let you upstairs looking the way you are."

Jace looked down at his bare chest. "Yeah, you're right. Sorry. Do they have some towels or something?"

Cory handed him a damp towel. "They're digging up some scrubs for you to wear. Are you hit anywhere?"

Jace looked himself over. "Nah, he got me with the dart in the car. Stings like a bitch, but nothing to worry about. When Jefferson fired the Sig at me, I had moved, and he really didn't aim in the dark. I jerked so that it looked like he hit me and I guess he was distracted enough to buy it."

The nurse came over with the scrubs and Jace took them with thanks.

"The surgical waiting room is on the third floor. You said Jefferson claimed to have cut into her spleen, but it's very possible he also hit something else. That could be why she crashed so suddenly," Cory said.

Just then, Collin came back with three tall cups of steaming hot coffee. "I figured we could all use a little pick-me-up. It's going on 0400, and I know I sure as shit have barely slept since we left for El Salvador. Peter and the rest of the gang are already headed upstairs."

Jace accepted the coffee with thanks. "You guys don't need to wait. Go home to your families. I'll let you know when I get an update."

"You are family, Jace. We're staying."

* * * *

The hours passed slower than molasses. Jace alternately paced between the plastic chairs lining the wall and the windows on the opposite side of the room. The scent of antiseptic mixed with the coffee he kept drowning himself in. The sounds of the hospital were like any other. Monitors beeped, pages were called over the intercom system, and occasionally he heard the sound of running feet.

Dawn was starting to creep over the horizon when he saw the surgeon come through the set of double doors Jace had been watching since he snapped out of his fog and came upstairs with the guys. The doctor was still dressed in scrubs and a surgical cap. As he walked toward them, he removed his cap. He looked tired, but not dejected. Hope bloomed in Jace's chest.

As the doctor reached the waiting area, he looked around. "Jace Hudson?"

"I'm Jace."

The doctor held out his hand. "I'm Dr Farrell. Would you like to follow me, and I'll give you an update on Ms Martin?"

He looked around at his team members. "These are my men, Doctor. Whatever you have to tell me, you can say in front of them."

"Okay then, why don't we sit down? First of all, let me tell you that Ms Martin did make it out of surgery. The wound to her side caused a significant laceration of her spleen. The laceration was causing that blood to leak into her abdominal cavity at a rapid rate. When we put the blood in downstairs, it came right back out, which is why she crashed so quickly.

"We were able to save her spleen using a procedure called splenorrhaphy. Basically, we sutured the laceration closed. She was extremely fortunate, because the cut was centimeters away from her splenic artery. Had that been cut, she would have bled out in a matter of minutes. She did require a blood transfusion to restore her hematocrit levels.

"She has two cracked ribs that appear to have been caused by physical trauma other than the stabbing. The abrasions on her wrists and ankles are superficial, but will take time to heal. It's obvious that significant pressure had been applied to her throat, but according to the otolaryngologist, no apparent permanent damage was detected. Our orthopedic surgeon reduced the fracture in her radius and cast it. We'll monitor her closely for any other injuries that were masked by the trauma.

"Her core temperature has risen to near normal levels, so there should be no adverse effects from the hypothermia. We'll continue to use warmed oxygen and IV fluids to assist in the recovery process. She's been taken to surgical ICU for recovery. As soon as she's settled, you can go see her, but only for a short while. What she needs most right now is rest. I'll expect her to be out for another several hours."

Jace listened to what the doctor was saying and he hated to ask but knew the question couldn't be avoided. "Doctor, I saw first-hand that Kat was sexually assaulted, but at the time full penetration had not been achieved. Is there a way you can tell if he had raped her before I got there?"

"The police will run a sexual assault kit and be able to give you that information. They will forward that information to the NCIS team. I assume a military investigation will also be taking place. I understand the assailant was an officer."

Jace then stood up and held out his hand. "Yes, he was. However, there will be no trial for his actions. Thank you, Doctor. I'll never be able to repay you for saving her."

"It was my pleasure. She's a fighter. We almost lost her downstairs, but she refused to give up." He looked meaningfully at Jace. "I guess she was holding onto something worth living for. Do you know if she has any family we can contact?"

"I know she has two younger brothers, but they live on the West Coast. I'll see if I can get you their contact information. Her mother and father are both gone."

Dr Farrell held out his hand. "Thank you." He looked at

the rest of the team. "Thank each of you for your service."

He acknowledged the doctor's words. Shortly after the doctor left, a dark-haired nurse wearing bright-pink scrubs and squeaky running shoes came around the corner.

"Lieutenant Commander Hudson? If you want to follow me, I'll take you to Ms Martin's room."

Jace looked over at his team. "Thank you for staying, guys. I'll come back out and let you know how she's doing, then I want you all to go home." For the first time in what seemed like days, he smiled. "And yes, that's an order."

He followed the nurse down through two hallways until he saw Kat's slight form lying in the bed behind a glass wall.

The nurse advised, "You have five minutes."

"Thank you." He walked through the doorway.

What he saw made his steps falter. She looked so small and vulnerable, hooked up to all the tubes and machines beeping around her bed. He walked over to the side of the bed and reached down for her hand. It was still chilled, but didn't feel like ice as it had before. In the harsh light of the fluorescent lights, he got his first real look at the bruising around her neck.

Seeing the individual marks from Jefferson's fingers, rage heated his blood like no coffee ever could. The knowledge that Jefferson had put his hands on her in both anger and violation ate at him, making him want to kill the man all over again.

Her right hand was swathed in fiberglass. He looked at the wrist attached to the hand in his own and noticed it was wrapped in bandages presumably for the abrasions Dr Farrell spoke of from the shackles that had held his Kat prisoner. Leaning down, he very gently kissed her forehead, and unable to stop himself, he also gave the slightest trace of a kiss on her lips.

"Thank you for fighting. Thank you for not giving up. I love you. I want you to rest, and I'll be here waiting for you to wake up. I'm going to call your brothers so they know what happened and that you're okay. Hopefully, they'll forgive me for not protecting you." He gave a slight chuckle. "Nothing like baptism by fire with your family."

The nurse came back in. "I'm sorry, sir, but you need to leave now. If you'd like to stay close, we can set you up in a private family waiting room. Dr Farrell said given the special circumstances, even though you're not technically related, it would be fine."

Jace nodded. Leaning over once more, he kissed Kat softly on the lips. The heart monitor beeped as Kat's heart rate jumped a few points.

The nurse smiled. "Guess she recognizes you. You can visit for a few minutes every hour, okay?"

Jace smiled at the young nurse. "Thank you for taking good care of her."

He went back and reported Kat's progress to the other team members. He looked over at Collin. "What's the status with Jefferson and the location she was being held at?"

"I carried his body out of the cave. He's being transferred to the NCIS morgue at the Norfolk field office. Nobody is questioning the necessity of the shooting. Apparently, he owned the land the cave was located on. He had used the area in the past for sexual rendezvous. The manacles in the wall were designed for that purpose. Obviously, an investigation will be opened into his actions and operations of the past. For all intents and purposes, with regards to our responsibilities, it's finished."

Jace absorbed the information.

Somehow it doesn't feel finished. Kat's recovery is just beginning.

With the long road ahead he would make sure to be there beside her, providing whatever support she needed or wanted from him. "What about his wife? Has she been notified?"

"Captain Marshall said they found out that she left Jefferson two months ago, and has been staying with her mother in Richmond."

Jace couldn't imagine how the woman must feel to learn that not only was she suddenly a widow, but that her husband had been a psychopath. He hoped the Navy would provide counseling services and continue to provide her with benefits. He didn't know how Jefferson's defection would be played off. However, he had a feeling the brass wouldn't want a lot of attention brought on the matter. He was of the mind that she shouldn't pay the price for her husband's actions, but knew the situation was out of his hands. He'd call Marshall later, and find out what the plan was.

Jace looked into the eyes of each team member. "Thank you... All of you. Now get out of here." He turned to head back down the hall, but stopped. Coming about face he saw his men quietly talking in the corner. "Wait... Kurt, do you think you could track down the contact information of Kat's brothers? I have their names and locations, but their numbers were in the phone Jefferson confiscated, and I don't have access to any other address book."

Kurt nodded. "Sure. If they have a computer on site that I can use, I can pull up the information right now."

"Okay, let's see what we can find. I'm going to be staying here. They're letting me stay in a private family waiting area."

They headed for the nurses' station to find out if there was a public computer terminal on the hospital grounds. The nurse was nice enough to let them use the one at the desk. "It's not technically allowed, but given the circumstances, I think it's okay. I just have to be sure to log out of the hospital administration manager."

After a few clicks of the mouse, she gestured to Kurt. "It's all yours."

Kurt was able to log into the federal database and found Kat's brothers in no time. Jace wrote down their contact information and planned on calling them as soon as he was in a private area.

The nurse came back over and noticed what they were

doing. "So you guys are like Rangers or something?"

Kurt looked up her and flashed a Hollywood smile. "Rangers! Please. Those landlubbers are Neanderthals. We're Navy SEALS. That young woman you folks saved was critical in bringing down a terrorist who had systematically been sabotaging military operations for the last several months. Not to mention she's the love of this man's life, future wife and mother to what I'm sure will be several children."

The nurse looked from them to the patient's room with new appreciation. "Wow. That is not only incredibly heroic, but so sweet and romantic too." She looked over at Jace. "You're a very lucky man, Lieutenant Commander Hudson."

He glanced over at the window into Kat's room. "Yes, I am."

The nurse escorted him to the private waiting area. His brain was beginning to shut down, now that the coffee and adrenaline were leaving his system. He knew he needed to get some sleep, but wanted to make sure Kat's brothers were called first. They were both on West Coast time, which would be almost 0600 now. He would probably be able to catch them before they headed into work. He reached into his pocket for Cory's phone

I'll pay him back for the minutes.

He called Jack in Seattle first. After about the third ring, the phone was picked up and a groggy voice answered, "Hello?"

"Is this Jack Martin? Brother to Dr Kat Martin of St. Louis, Missouri?"

The voice on the other end of the line answered warily, "Yes, who is this?"

"My name is Lieutenant Commander Jace Hudson of the United States Navy. I'm calling to let you know that your sister has been involved in an incident and is currently in critical condition at Hope Mountain Hospital in Roanoke, Virginia."

The voice was suddenly very much awake. "What happened, and what the hell is she doing in Virginia?"

Jace explained the series of events leading up to that morning. He didn't tell her brother all the details of the attack or previous terror she had been subjected to. He figured if she wanted her family to know, she could tell them when she came to.

"And who are you to my sister exactly?"

"I'm the man who's going to marry her as soon as possible. She doesn't know this yet, but I don't think it will be hard to talk her around. I also need to tell you that the reason she was exposed to this attacker was my fault. I can't divulge all the details due to national security reasons, but I can tell you that the attacker was directly after me and she was used as a pawn. I want to apologize for not protecting her like I should."

The phone line echoed with silence after his confession. Would Kat's brother accept his apology?

"Well, it seems to me that you were also the one who saved her life, so regardless of how the incident occurred, I want to thank you. I'll contact Christian and let him know the situation. We'll both make arrangements to come there as soon as possible."

Jace let out a long breath. "I'll be happy to reimburse you for the travel expenses."

"That's not necessary. How can I reach you?"

"If you call this number when you land, I can direct you to the hospital."

Jace said his goodbyes then leaned back in the chair.

That didn't go so badly.

He yawned deeply, causing his jaw to crack. What he really needed to do now was catch a brief nap before he was allowed to see Kat again. He pushed the chair into a reclining position and closed his eyes. Fortunately, owing to his training, he could recharge his batteries with very little sleep in about any position. He also figured her brothers would be arriving by that evening, and he wanted all his mental circuits firing when he met them face to face.

* * * *

The sound of a knock woke him up. Jace's eyes popped open to see the nurse from earlier standing in the doorway.

"Commander Hudson? I'm sorry to wake you, but Ms Martin is coming round and asking for you."

He nearly jumped out of the chair and jogged down the hallway. He really didn't care if he appeared like a moron, running through the hospital. As he approached Kat's room, he slowed down.

Looking through the doorway, he saw her reclining in the bed. The back had been raised slightly higher, but they didn't want her sitting completely upright yet. As he walked to the side of the bed, he once again lifted her left hand in his.

Her eyes fluttered open, and Jace had never seen a more beautiful sight. "Hi, sweetheart... Welcome back."

He lifted her hand and pressed a kiss into her palm. "The doctor said it may be difficult to talk at first, so don't push it, okay?"

Kat nodded her head.

"I've talked to Jack. He and Christian should be here sometime tonight."

Kat softly asked, "Are you okay?"

He smiled, leaned down and placed his forehead against hers. "You're lying here in this bed, having recently been sewn back together, and you're asking me if *I'm* okay?"

"Thought you were dead... Saw him shoot."

Jace shook his head. "He never hit me. I just made it look like he did so I could catch him off guard." His relief at seeing Kat aware was so great that his knees gave out and he dropped down into the chair next to the bed.

Holding her hand in his, he blinked back tears. "For a short while, I actually lost you, and it nearly destroyed me. I love you."

Kat placed her hand against Jace's damp cheek. "I love you too. There is nothing for you to feel responsible about. If it hadn't been for you, I would have died, and I'm not just talking about in the cave. At one point, for a brief moment, I felt very free. The pain had faded away, and I was so warm, it felt like I was sunbathing on a tropical beach. Then I heard you calling to me. I heard you begging me to hold on... To come back."

"Baby, don't talk right now. I don't want you—"

Kat put her fingers against Jace's lips. "I understood then that I had to make a choice. I could let go and exist in peaceful surrender, or I could come back and fight. I thought about everything I still wanted to do and experience in life. You know the first thing that came to mind? I pictured you and me. I pictured the two of us walking along beaches and hiking in the mountains. I pictured children and a small house that we could make into a home for our family. That's what made me choose to come back. You brought me back."

Jace stood up and, leaning over, kissed her. The kiss was more than an acceptance of her declaration. It was a promise, a promise to fulfill each one of those dreams Kat mentioned. It was then that they heard a voice from the doorway.

"Well, you don't look too worse for the wear."

Jace looked over and saw two men casually leaning against the doorjamb. Their features were close enough to Kat's that the conclusion that the men were Jack and Christian was an easy one.

"How long have you been standing there?" Jace asked.

Christian met Jace's gaze. "Long enough."

The two men came into the room and Jace got his first real look at his future brothers-in-law. He knew from Kat's descriptions that although he was the youngest, Christian was the taller of the two brothers, almost matching Jace's height. If you lined up the siblings, they made a ladder by age. Both men had appearances that could have blended easily onto the covers of either a *GQ* magazine or an outdoor adventure guide. Kat had said that both were married, but neither had any children yet. In fact, as Jace looked outside the door, he caught a glimpse of two women holding hands and with tears in their eyes.

Jack and Christian walked up to the other side of Kat's bed. Christian smiled, shooting a glance in Jace's direction. "So, what have you been up to lately, sis? We leave you alone for a few short months…"

"Oh, you know, the usual—high-speed car chases, kidnappings…" She looked in Jace's direction and squeezed his hand. "Falling in love. How are Emelyn and Krista?"

Jack looked fondly on his sister. "They're fine. In fact, they're waiting outside."

She glanced over their shoulders, and seeing the other two women, waved her hand for them to come in. "Hi. Well, now that the whole family is here, I'd like to formally introduce you to Lieutenant Commander Jace Hudson of the US Navy, the man who saved my life and stole my heart."

Epilogue

The breeze was cool on Kat's skin. The smells of wood burning in the fireplace and snow in the air filled her senses as music from the party played in the background. She was having a marvelous time, but wanted a few minutes of peace and quiet. Standing on the back deck of the lodge nestled in the Blue Ridge Mountains, she quietly reflected on the past couple of months.

After a week-long stay in the hospital, she'd been released into Jace's care. A couple of weeks later, she was getting around better, growing stronger day by day. Still, it had taken her a good five weeks before she'd begun to feel like herself again physically. Psychologically, she was also getting stronger.

She had seen a trauma counselor a few times, but felt better just talking with Jace and working on her fears through relaxation and meditation. She still woke up with nightmares on occasion. So many nights, Jace would wake her from a dream or she would jolt awake with a cry, thinking she was back in the cave. He was so sweet, buying and installing a nightlight in their room so she wouldn't feel trapped in the dark if she woke up. In the silent, dark hours, Jace would hold her and stroke her back, gently calming her and assuring her she was safe and loved.

Kat watched as snowflakes began to float down around her and remembered another time she had seen the delicate flakes float to the ground.

* * * *

It was Christmas Eve, she and Jace were sitting in front of the fireplace in his town house relaxing against each other watching snow fall outside the window and listening to their favorite music.

At the stroke of midnight, Jace leaned down and whispered into her ear, "Now that it's officially Christmas morning, I think you deserve a present. Go look up on the mantel of the fireplace."

She stood, walked toward the dancing light and saw a small white box with a red velvet bow tied around it. Taking down the small box, she untied the bow and lifted the lid. Inside was plush blue satin bedding that nestled a stunning platinum engagement ring. The band was wide and looked like it was made of the most delicate wire, the shapes twisting and locking around each other like ancient Celtic designs. The center stone was a two-karat, radiant solitaire with rich, royal-blue sapphire baguettes on either side.

Kat stood there completely stunned. "Jace... How did you...? I don't need..."

He got up from the sofa and stood behind her in front of the fireplace. He turned her around so the fire was to their side. The dancing flames cast shadows and the sparks were reflected in his eyes.

He lowered them both to their knees. "You are the most beautiful and courageous woman I have ever known. The light reflecting in these stones reminded me of the light and strength I sense in you. I love you, Dr Kathleen Martin. I want to spend my life with you. Will you marry me?"

As Jace slipped the ring on her finger, tears slid down her face.

* * * *

Jace came to stand next to Kat. "You're starting to blend in with the snow in that white dress." Jace wrapped his body around hers as he held her from behind. "I don't want you to catch a chill. You should go back inside."

She leaned back against him and continued to watch the soft flakes fall. "I just wanted a few minutes of peace. It's really beautiful tonight, isn't it?"

Jace turned her around to face him, and she saw the desire and passion light his eyes. "Beauty was watching you walk toward me earlier in the candlelight. The crystals of your gown sparkling in the light, and that dress flowing around you made it look as if you floated rather than walked down the aisle."

He combed his fingers through her loose hair. When they'd reached the lodge she had taken the jeweled comb out, and her hair now fell gently around her shoulders in soft waves. The flakes started to increase, but Kat was oblivious as she gazed into the eyes of her husband.

"How about it, Mrs Hudson? Are you ready to ditch this shindig and go celebrate Valentine's Day in a proper way?"

She wrapped her arms around his neck. Lifting her face to his, she whispered, "Absolutely, Commander."

They hadn't made love since before the attack. At first, Kat was trying to physically recover, then they decided to wait until after the wedding. As the weeks passed and he continued to hold her at night, she found himself eagerly anticipating the time when they could be together again.

He leaned down and kissed her gently. As his lips skimmed across hers, Kat closed her eyes and threaded her fingers through his hair. Seeking more, she pushed up to meet his mouth, demanding he deepen the kiss. He slid his tongue between her lips and tasted the champagne they had toasted with earlier. He pulled her closer against his body, wrapping his arms around her back, and Kat felt the blood rush from her head as he slanted his lips against hers.

God, this feels good! It's been so long since we held each other like this.

She felt like fireworks were popping all along her body and trembled, but not from the cold. He continued to kiss her, devouring her like she was his last meal. Suddenly, they heard someone bang on the window behind them. Looking over Jace's shoulder, Kat saw Peter with a shit-eating grin on his face.

"Hey, you two, you're going to melt all the snow! Get your asses back in here."

Jace took her hand and led her back inside the reception. Their desires would have to be put onto simmer just a little longer. He twirled her onto the dance floor as a slow heady beat vibrated from the speakers. She realized it was the same song they had danced to the night they met.

"It looks like we've come full circle," her husband said.

She molded her body against his. "That's the thing about circles. There's no beginning and no end, so we've got a whole lot of turning left to do."

They danced into the early hours of the morning and when they finally left the party, they traveled by horse-drawn sleigh to a secluded cabin deep on the property of the lodge where Jace carried her over the threshold. As they entered the vaulted great room, a fire was already roaring in the stone fireplace. Rose petals were strewn across the floor, and there must have been fifty candles flickering in the darkness.

Kat caught her breath and stared at the room in wonder. "Oh, Jace. It's so beautiful. How did you manage this?"

He shrugged. "I wanted tonight to be special, so I arranged the setup a few days ago, and a few minutes before we left, I called and had someone light everything."

She walked over to him and enfolded him in her arms. "I love you so much. Can we make love by the fire just like our first time?"

"We can make love wherever you want, and hopefully very often, over the next several days. The fire looks like a good place to start."

He leaned down and kissed her, slowly walking them toward the hearth. Along the way, he grabbed the throw pillows off the sofa. There was already a synthetic fur rug in front of the fire that looked soft as down. He reached behind her and slid the zipper of her wedding dress down. The silk whispered over her skin as it pooled at her feet. When she stepped out of the material, she heard Jace catch his breath.

She had on a strapless bra of the sheerest material and ivory garters with silk stockings caressed her legs. Since her injury, Kat had been doing a lot of physical therapy, and her muscles showed the tone and strength of her new body. It was still soft and curvy, but she'd taken up martial arts in an effort to never be in another situation where her lack of training increased her vulnerability.

Jace kicked off his shoes and socks, undid the gold buttons of his uniform and removed the jacket.

Stepping forward, she put her hands to his waistband. Jace's stomach muscles contracted at the touch. She undid fastenings and let the material drop from his hips.

He reached for her and she saw that his hands shook. He pulled her tight and kissed her deeply, reverently, passionately. They removed the rest of their clothing in slow succession, savoring each inch of skin as it was revealed. When their bodies finally touched with no barriers, they each let out a moan that echoed through the room.

His voice was gruff with passion when he lowered them to the floor. "God, I've missed having you like this. I've missed touching you, missed watching your body come alive. Your skin flushes and your eyes turn a deep forest green. I love hearing your breath catch when I suckle your breasts and feeling your body as it tightens around my cock."

Kat raised her body underneath his. "Ohh... Please don't make me wait any longer."

"Patience, sweetheart. We've waited this long. Another hour of anticipation will just heighten the pleasure."

She looked at him like he was nuts. "An hour?"

"Oh, yes. I plan on savoring you for a nice, long time before we consummate our union, my beautiful wife."

He slowly worked his way down her body, kissing every

limb in multiple spots. He spent time nuzzling the inside of her elbow and wrists, trailing his fingers down her legs and behind her knees. Kat was floating on a haze of pleasure. Her nipples had puckered, and she moaned when Jace took them between his lips then blew on the heated peaks. He spent long minutes gently pulling them into his mouth.

Kat loved it when he used the flat of his tongue to rasp over the sensitive tips. She felt him use his teeth to nip and swirl his tongue to ease the sting. He continued to kiss down the length of her body. When he reached the scar on her abdomen from where they had to cut her open, he paused, then placed kisses all along the healed line.

He continued his path and finally reached the apex of her legs.

"Sweet heaven," he said softly.

He slid his fingers through her wet lips, and she shuddered. She had almost forgotten what this felt like. The heat as it rose through her body, the ache that built until she felt like she'd explode if she didn't get some kind of release, but at the same time she didn't want the incredible journey to end.

As his fingers stroked her, she began to writhe on the floor. When they tapped against her clit, she just about leaped into the air. Finally, she felt two of his fingers enter her, and the sensation was at once stinging and exquisite. The pleasure of having a part of him inside her again was so great she let out a cry. As the wave began to build, she reached out, needing to have some kind of connection to him other than just his hand.

Sensing her need, Jace rose above her and aligned his body with hers. He wanted Kat to feel him alongside her. He kissed her deeply, continuing to thrust his fingers in her silky, wet heat. The feel of her against him was making his blood pound, his balls tighten, and his eyes back into his head.

He felt the tremors course through her body as she reached

her first peak and watched in reverence as she came alive beneath him. Her right arm snaked underneath his left to grasp his back, and her left arm wrapped around his neck. As the waves crashed through her, his body became her lifeline.

Finally, he couldn't wait any longer. He removed his hand and fit himself between her legs. She cradled his body perfectly as he aligned their hips.

"Open your eyes for me, Kat. Remember the first time we made love and you watched me take you?"

Her eyes opened with a dreamy haze of satisfaction, and she nodded.

"This time I want you to look into my eyes and feel how I connect not only our bodies but our souls…" He nudged himself into her opening. "I am your husband…" Another inch slid in. "You are my wife." Another couple of inches. "Together, our fates are forever sealed." As he said the last, he slid completely home.

Never had their lovemaking been so perfect, never had it meant so much, and when he finally reached that elusive peak with Kat, their minds merged on a level that can only be understood between two people whose bodies, hearts and souls truly become one.

The Perfect Union

Excerpt

Prologue

November 2006

Calleigh Wells was so glad the sun came out from behind the clouds as she walked down the street. Boston had been in a dreadfully rainy pattern over the past week. It had been cold but not enough to turn to snow. She lifted her head to the sky to soak up the burgeoning rays. Now, the temperature was low, but at least, the sun was shining.

She opened the door to *Bean Town*, her favourite coffee place, and stepped inside. The warm air from the heat flowed over her cheeks that tingled from the crisp air. There were four people ahead of her in line as she tried to decide if she wanted her standby hazelnut latte or if she wanted to be adventurous and try the caramel macchiato.

She felt a vibration against her side and opened her purse

to see an incoming call on her iPhone. She didn't recognise the number, but it was a long distance area code.

"Hello?"

"Is this Mrs. Wells?"

"May I ask who's calling?" She moved forward a step, glancing to the board and decided to be adventurous on another day. The hazelnut sounded good right then.

"This is Sergeant Cooper. I'm trying to locate Calleigh Wells, wife of Sergeant Kevin Wells."

"Oh God. No." Her heart stuttered, and she couldn't breathe. There was only one reason someone from the Armed Forces would be calling her.

"Mrs. Wells, I regret to inform you that your husband had been injured in the line of duty. He is being transferred to Ramstein Air Force base in Germany."

She blindly reached out to keep herself from falling down. When she looked up, she had hold of the man's shirt in front of her. He turned around with a questioning look, but it immediately changed to concern.

"What happened? Is Kevin okay? What—"

"I'm not at liberty to discuss the event. If you wish, I'll put you in contact with his unit liaison. They will be able to make arrangements for you to fly to Germany. Do you have a pen and paper handy?"

"No…wait…please." She looked at the two men standing side by side in front of her. "Do you have a pen and paper I can borrow?"

The man with black hair held out a pen while the man with auburn hair grabbed a napkin off the counter beside them. Taking the items, she put the phone back up to her ear. "Okay, I'm ready." She wrote down the information and ended the call.

She couldn't seem to move. Her feet were cemented to the floor. She looked around aimlessly, but nothing was in focus. The colours blurred, and her vision swam. She felt herself being guided over to the side and found herself sitting in one of the chairs scattered around the room.

The dark haired man knelt down in front of her. "Are you okay?" He looked up at his auburn-haired friend who had pulled the chair out and was resting his hands on her shoulders. Taking her cold hands between his, the first man rubbed. "Miss? Do we need to get you help?"

His deep voice cut through the haze in her mind. She looked down into a pair of bright sapphire blue eyes. "I need to go home."

"Okay. Did you drive here?"

She shook her head no. She tried to dial the number to her house, but her hands shook too badly. She held out her phone to the man in front of her. "Can you call? I can't get it to work. My mom can come get me. She has my babies."

He took the phone from her shaking hands, and handed it to his friend. "Tell you what? Why don't we make things easier on your mom? Conor and I will take you home. I'm Rick." He stopped the woman's head from shaking back and forth by putting a hand to her cheek. "We are completely safe. I promise you. You can talk to your mom the entire way there if you want." He helped her to stand and turned her around so she could see Conor behind her.

"Miss. I think I got the number ye wanted," Conor said, holding out the phone.

She took the phone from the tall man. Her vision was still blurring and all she could decipher were images of red hair and blue-green eyes. She noticed that he had some kind of soft lyrical accent. "Thank you."

Putting the phone up to her ear she heard her mom's voice.

"Mom?" she interrupted. "They called. Kevin's hurt." Tears started slipping down her cheeks. "I'm at *Bean Town*... No, I walked... These two men said they'll drive me home." She listened for another minute then held out the phone to the man with the black hair and blue eyes. "She wants to talk to you."

Rick took the phone from her hand. "Hello? Yes, ma'am. My name is Richard Connor. My friend and I were here at the shop when your daughter got the call. We'll be happy to bring her home. She's in no condition to be out on the streets by herself right now. I assure you we mean her no harm. Can you give me an address?" He listened then continued, "Okay we should have her there in about twenty-five minutes." He ended the call and gave back the phone.

Conor walked around to stand next to Rick. "Can ye tell us yer name, miss?"

"It's Calleigh. Calleigh Wells."

"Calleigh, I'm Rick Connor and this is Conor McGuire. Let's get you home to your family." He escorted her to the door Conor held open for them.

They walked half a block down and stopped in front of a dark sedan of some kind. The auburn-haired man opened the front passenger and assisted her into the seat. She sat in silence as the door was secured, habitually reaching for the seatbelt. She thought they seemed nice, and she was desperate enough to trust two strangers.

Rick looked over the top of the car at his best friend. "What in the hell just happened?"

Conor shrugged. "It doesn't sound good. I think somethin' might have happened te her husband or brah'der or somebody. Feck man, she said she had babies at home. I hope to hell 'tis not her husband."

"Yeah, me, too. Let's get out of here. The mother said she lives in Mission Hill."

The two men climbed into the car. She sat silently for several minutes before realising it was pretty rude not to talk to her two rescuers. She could worry in a little bit. The sergeant on the phone said injured not dead. Kevin wasn't dead. It would all be okay. She figured her mom must have given the men directions to the house because they seemed to know where to go.

What are their names again? Rich? Rick? And the other one is Connor? Wait I heard the name Connor twice I'm sure of it. So who's who?

She turned to face the man driving, the one with black hair. "Excuse me, but maybe I didn't hear you right. You're both named Connor?" She swivelled around as the auburn haired one in the backseat laughed.

"That is going to plague us 'til our deaths, man. His last name is Connor. With two 'n's, my first name is Conor with one. It's how we met. We were on the soccer team at B.C. First day of practice, coach called out 'Connor', and we both answered at the same time. We've been friends ever since."

"I went to B.C. too. Class of 2003."

"We graduated in 2000," Rick said. "So you said you have children at home?"

She smiled at the thought of her precious little babies. "Yes, I have twin boys. They're two months old." She figured she owed these two some explanation of her erratic behaviour. "Their father, my husband, is in Iraq. Army Reserves. The phone call was from a sergeant informing me that my husband's been injured, but that was all he could tell me. I sure he's fine…right? I mean if it was serious they would tell me or send someone or something wouldn't they?"

Rick watched the beautiful woman next to him. She was looking at him like he had all the answers, and damn, if he wished he didn't. Her honey-blonde hair was pulled back in a ponytail and fringe fell over her forehead to end right above her eyebrows. She had bright brown eyes that looked like gemstones under black sooty lashes. She was a tiny thing, too, probably just over five feet. The pain and uncertainty in her eyes made all his protective instincts kick in.

"I don't know what military protocol is, but it stands to reason that if things were dire they would do something other than call you on a cell phone."

He looked at Conor in the rear-view mirror to see if he knew but saw the man shrug. Conor's dad had been Air Force, stationed in England, before retiring. He wanted to keep Calleigh's hopes alive and distract her mind for right now. "What are your little boys' names?"

"Michael and Brandon. I guess the good thing is that if Kevin is coming home he'll be able to meet the boys. He was deployed eight months ago, so he's only seen them in pictures and over the internet." She smiled "They look so much like him. Both have his green eyes and his mouth, but so far they have my blonde hair."

"They sound like *dathuil ógánach*. I love little kids. Always wanted brothers an' sisters, but not te be."

"Conor, those words, they were beautiful sounding, but I don't understand. What did you say?"

"I said they sound like handsome youth. 'Tis Irish Gaelic. I grew up in Ireland."

"I noticed your accent earlier but couldn't quite place it."

Rick laughed. "That's because Con's a real mutt. Born in Ireland and lived with his Mom then spent summers in England with his Dad. He transferred to the States when he started college, so he's picked up a little American in the past few years. Most people only understand half of what he's talking about. If you get lost, just smile and nod. I do it all the time."

Conor kicked the back of his seat. He laid on the Irish brogue nice and thick, "Ye bloody arse. Stop acting de maggot. Total ballsch ye donna understan' me."

Rick looked over at Calleigh and saw her first genuine smile. It lit up her entire face. He rolled his eyes. "See told you."

Seconds later, they pulled up in front of a quintessential Boston brick rowhouse. The stone base had wrought iron rails leading up the steps, and flower boxes graced the bow windows.

"Wow. Very Nice."

"Yeah, we rent the first and second floors. I have a neighbour in the basement apartment. We got a deal on the place because the owners are army friends of Kevin, stationed overseas." She turned so she could see both men.

"Please come in. I'll introduce you to my mom, and you can meet the boys if they're awake."

Rick opened the door and walked around to get Calleigh's, but Conor beat him to it. He looked up, and a woman in her early fifties was standing on the front steps. He guessed she was Calleigh's mom, since they looked like carbon copies of each other. He tensed when he took a closer look at the woman's face. There were tear tracks down her face. When they walked up the steps, the older woman pulled Calleigh into her arms and held tight.

They all walked inside, but Calleigh stopped dead when a man in uniform stood from the sofa and turned to face her. His face was grim as he held his hat under his arm.

"I'm very sorry, Mrs. Wells. I regret to inform you that your husband Sergeant Kevin Wells—"

"I already received the call of his injury, Captain. What do I do now?"

"Ma'am, there was a miscommunication. Your husband was not injured. He was killed in action."

Rick and Conor both caught Calleigh as she fell into a heap. Sobs echoed through the room. Her cries of denial ripped into Rick's soul. His arm wrapped around her, holding her head to his chest. Conor's wrapped around her waist as the heaving shudders racked her small body. They'd only known her for a short hour, but she'd already wormed her way into his heart. Her clear love of her husband and little boys was a testament to her character. He vowed then and there to protect this woman and her children from that day forward. Looking into Conor's eyes, he knew the man felt the same.

Chapter One

September 2009

Conor walked into Rick's office and saw that he was on the phone. He settled himself into one of the padded leather chairs, turning the small box in his hand over and over. Inside was their present to Calleigh. Tonight, they would celebrate her twenty-seventh birthday. More importantly though, tonight they would begin their quest to make her theirs. It had been three years since the death of her husband. For the first two, they had lived up to their silent vows of that horrible day. They'd become good friends to Calleigh and her family.

Helping her through the grief had been difficult, but they'd made a little family of their own with small traditions that helped move the days forward. His favourite was movie night. Every week, one of them would choose a movie, and after the boys were put to bed, they would pile on the living room sofa and watch with all the lights out and a huge bowl of buttery popcorn in their laps. Usually, Calleigh ended up with her head in one of their laps, sound asleep. He loved to stroke her silky hair or give her foot massages to soothe her after spending all day at her job at the hospital.

Last week, they celebrated Mikey and Bran's third birthday. The boys had gotten to choose the movie, and *Finding Nemo* had swum into the living room in full colour. They had been so excited when he and Rick had carried out a giant cake with all the characters from the movie printed on it.

His head jerked up as Rick hung up the phone and he

watched him walk over to sit in the chair opposite him.

"Did you get it?" Rick asked.

He held up the small box. Opening the lid, he showed him the necklace they had designed for Calleigh. It was a three-stoned pendant, a bastnäsite with blue sapphire and aquamarine gems on either side.

Rick picked up the box and turned it from side to side, watching the light reflect off the coloured gemstones. "Think she'll see the significance?"

"If she doesn't, I'll be happy te point it out te her." Conor smiled.

He looked at Rick and could tell the man was nervous about the taking this next step. Conor had initially questioned the decision but could no longer deny his feelings for Calleigh. Over the past year, the dependable friendship had turned into something much deeper. He wanted the woman, like no other. Every time he and Rick brought someone home, he saw the resemblance to the sexy siren who filled their thoughts and made their bodies burn.

Whether they shared a woman or he picked up one on his own, she always had blonde hair and brown eyes but they never sparkled like Calleigh. At the end of the evening, he generally felt hollow, physically satisfied for the moment but never complete.

"I know yer nervous about changing things between us, but I canny fight it any longer. She's been casually talking about getting back out there more and more. I willna do this without ye, but I love her. Ye love her. We both adore those little boys, like they're our own. It's time we stop bringing home substitutes. It's time we made her ours."

"I know, I know. I want her as bad as you do." Rick ran his hand through his hair. "Fuck, every time in the last year we've had some nameless pickup between us, I've pictured her in our bed. I've even had to hold back crying out her name when I came a time or two."

Conor knew exactly what his best friend was talking about. He'd almost done the same, and more than once when their eyes had locked in that crucial moment, he'd known they'd both been thinking the same thing. He looked over at Rick's desk as his phone rang again. Jumping up, the man went to answer the summons.

"Rick Connor... Hey, Calleigh. Happy birthday, angel." He spun around in his chair catching Conor's eye. "Of course, we'll be there for dinner tonight. Six o'clock right?" He laughed. "The boys did what? I can just imagine... Sure we can talk about it... Okay, see you then." He hung up the phone. "Calleigh said the boys, with grandma's help, made her a huge birthday sign with their handprints painted on it. Unfortunately, the paint didn't get put away, and they decided it needed just a few more decorations. Only it happened to be lying on the sofa at the time."

Conor was laughing so hard he had to clutch his stomach. "Go on otta that!"

"I'm not kidding. You know you have to watch them twenty-four-seven." Rick was laughing, too. After several minutes, he stood and walked over to look out the window of his office. "She said something about wanting our advice at the very end. It sounded serious."

That instantly sobered Conor's mirth. "Feck. I hope nathin' is wrong with the boys."

"No. I don't think so. It sounded more like a personal problem. I hope to hell nobody is haranguing her. If they are, I'll put a stop to that real damn quick." He looked over his shoulder and saw Conor stand then come over next to him. He held out the box in his hand with the lid still open then put his hand on Rick's shoulder.

"I willna let anything happen to *Ár Ghrá*."

More books from Trina Lane

Book two in the Perfect Love series

What will it take to find his perfect partner?

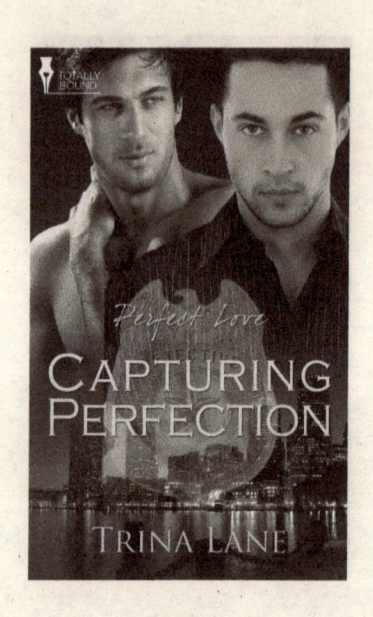

Book three in the Perfect Love series

Two men united by a bond neither time nor trauma could break now seek to capture the love that beats within their hearts.

Book one in the Pahntom River series

One man is determined to claim her, the other is destined to love her.

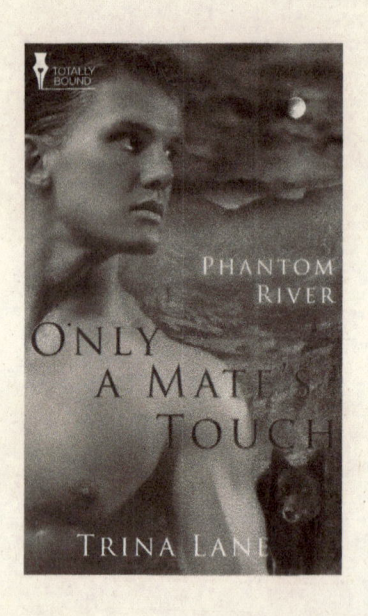

Book two in the Pahntom River series

Only two who are truly destined for one another will find their souls and become complete.

About the Author

Trina Lane

If you look up the word conundrum in the dictionary, there should be a photo of Trina Lane. Her personality is so multifaceted that her friends have spent countless hours scratching their heads in wonder. A scientist with a passion for history, music and photography she loves to travel and experience new places but is terminally shy around people she doesn't know.

Trina has been devouring romance novels since her tender teenage years, although only began writing in 2007. When her debut novel was met with resounding success, she said "Hey I can do that again". The rest as they say is history.

Her choices in reading and writing material are as diverse as her iTunes library, which contains music from Mozart to Metallica. Her one concession is all stories must have a happily ever after ending-did we mention she's incurably romantic?

She lives in Missouri with her loving and indulgent husband, and orange tabby cat—affectionately referred to as 'Houdini' for his stealthy escape attempts.

Trina Lane loves to hear from readers. You can find contact information, website details and an author profile page at https://www.totallybound.com/

TOTALLY BOUND

Home of Erotic Romance